WI

The Glass House

"An exciting Regency mystery that also captures the ambience of the era." —*Midwest Book Review*

"Ashley Gardner brings Regency London alive . . . Captain Gabirel Lacey is an admirable and believable sleuth. —iloveamysterynewsletter.com

A Regimental Murder

"Ashley Gardner is a name worth following as this author shows deep talent for vividly re-creating the era and people of the Regency period inside a powerful mystery." —*BookBrowser*

"Gardner has inhabited [Lacey's] world with recurring secondary characters rich in personalities, who continue to evolve. The icing on the cake is the intriguing, masterfully told mystery." —*The Best Reviews*

The Hanover Square Affair

"With her vivid description of the era, Gardner brings her novel to life." —*Romantic Times* (4 1/2 stars, Top Pick)

"Ashley Gardner's debut novel compares favorably with writers who have made the bestseller list." —*BookBrowser*

Regency England Mysteries by Ashley Gardner

THE HANOVER SQUARE AFFAIR
A REGIMENTAL MURDER
THE GLASS HOUSE
THE SUDBURY SCHOOL MURDERS

THE
Sudbury School
Murders

ASHLEY GARDNER

BERKLEY PRIME CRIME, NEW YORK

THE BERKLEY PUBLISHING GROUP
Published by the Penguin Group
Penguin Group (USA) Inc.
375 Hudson Street, New York, New York 10014, USA
Penguin Group (Canada), 10 Alcorn Avenue, Toronto, Ontario M4V 3B2, Canada
(a division of Pearson Penguin Canada Inc.)
Penguin Books Ltd., 80 Strand, London WC2R 0RL, England
Penguin Group Ireland, 25 St. Stephen's Green, Dublin 2, Ireland (a division of Penguin Books Ltd.)
Penguin Group (Australia), 250 Camberwell Road, Camberwell, Victoria 3124, Australia
(a division of Pearson Australia Group Pty. Ltd.)
Penguin Books India Pvt. Ltd., 11 Community Centre, Panchsheel Park, New Dehli—110 017, India
Penguin Group (NZ), Cnr. Airborne and Rosedale Roads, Albany, Auckland 1310, New Zealand
(a division of Pearson New Zealand Ltd.)
Penguin Books (South Africa) (Pty.) Ltd., 24 Sturdee Avenue, Rosebank, Johannesburg 2196, South
Africa

Penguin Books Ltd., Registered Offices: 80 Strand, London WC2R 0RL, England

This is a work of fiction. Names, characters, places, and incidents either are the product of the author's imagination or are used fictitiously, and any resemblance to actual persons, living or dead, business establishments, events, or locales is entirely coincidental.

THE SUDBURY SCHOOL MURDERS

A Berkley Prime Crime Book / published by arrangement with the author

PRINTING HISTORY
Berkley Prime Crime edition / June 2005

Copyright © 2005 by Jennifer Ashley.
Cover design by Marc Cohen.
Interior text design by Kristin del Rosario.

ISBN: 0-425-20361-1

BERKLEY® PRIME CRIME
Berkley Prime Crime Books are published by The Berkley Publishing Group,
a division of Penguin Group (USA) Inc.,
375 Hudson Street, New York, New York 10014.
BERKLEY PRIME CRIME is a registered trademark of Penguin Group (USA) Inc.
The Berkley Prime Crime design is a trademark belonging to Penguin Group (USA) Inc.

PRINTED IN THE UNITED STATES OF AMERICA

10 9 8 7 6 5 4 3 2 1

PROLOGUE

IN March of 1817, I journeyed from London up the Thames and into Berkshire, where the countryside opened around me like the promise of heaven. The stink of London and the river dropped away, and the vistas of green fields, swaths of wood, and soft spring skies revived my tired vision.

I was traveling to Sudbury, which lay on the banks of the Kennet and Avon Canal near Hungerford, to take up a post as private secretary to Everard Rutledge, headmaster of the Sudbury School.

I rode in the luxurious coach of Lucius Grenville, a wealthy and influential man about town with vast riches and tastes imitated throughout the polite world. Grenville had arranged the post and lent me the coach, though he had not accompanied me. Instead, his footman, Bartholomew, who in recent months had become my manservant, journeyed with me. The young man had insisted on it, believing he'd find more adventure with me in the quiet countryside than in bustling London.

Why Grenville felt enough friendship to me to help me, a penniless dragoon captain on half-pay, only he could say. I'd met Grenville the year before at a soiree at his house, during which the staff hired for the night had attempted to rob him blind. I had thwarted the robbery, and our friendship had commenced. Between that incident and today, I had found myself involved in no less than three investigations into the deaths of Londoners: the first, a wealthy MP in Hanover Square; the second, a regimental colonel from the Peninsular Wars; the third, a young woman of dubious repute found in the river, whose connections had made her very interesting.

Grenville had assisted me in solving these crimes, insisting that he did so for a selfish reason—to relieve his ennui. For that, he claimed he was grateful, and he used his connections to find me this post.

I did look forward to a new interlude in my life, but I also left London with some reluctance. My circle of acquaintance had grown in the past year, and I had begun to fill an empty life. I was leaving behind my friends, Grenville, Louisa Brandon, wife of my former colonel, and Lady Breckenridge, a young widow for whom I had begun a growing regard. Lady Breckenridge and I had begun our friendship shakily, but before I'd departed London, I had asked her to write to me. She had smiled and agreed. Not only that, she had supplied me with a walking stick to replace one I had lost.

I had not quite sorted through what I wanted from Lady Breckenridge, nor did I believe she had quite made up her mind what she wanted from me. For now, we were friends, or so I hoped. As I traveled, I wondered whether she'd keep her promise to write. Lady Breckenridge was the widow of a peer and the daughter of another peer, and she might well decide to not bother herself with a nobody like me.

I also wondered whether Louisa Brandon would write. She'd made plain to me only weeks before that my enmity with her husband hurt her deeply, and she blamed me for much of it. Her anger had cut at me, and I did not believe she had yet forgiven me. To leave that unresolved, to remember the relief in her eyes when I'd told her one afternoon in Hyde Park that I was departing London, distressed me beyond measure.

But I had little choice. I needed the post. I had no income other than my half-pay duly doled out to me by the army once a quarter. And perhaps, I thought, my sojourn in the country and the relatively quiet life of a personal secretary to a prominent man would soothe me and my illness of melancholia.

But if I had known then what lay in wait for me in Sudbury, I would have turned the chaise around and returned to London as fast as the horses could run.

CHAPTER 1

"AND I want it stopped," Everard Rutledge growled.

One week after my arrival at the Sudbury School, Rutledge faced me over his desk in his private study. The headmaster had a large, flat face, a bulbous nose, and short graying hair that looked as though perpetually whipped by high wind. His coat hung untidily on his large frame, his ivory waistcoat was rumpled, his yellowing cravat twisted. The effect was as though a bull had climbed into an expensive suit and then gone about its business.

He had just told me a story of vicious pranks that had been perpetrated in the school—a chandelier in the dining hall coming down, a fire in the maids' attic, threatening letters written in blood, and three boys falling ill due to poisoned port.

"Not nice," I remarked. "Worse than the usual pranks boys play on each other."

"Exactly," Rutledge barked. "What do you intend to do about it, eh?"

I looked at him in surprise. I had not thought discovering pranksters would be in the sphere of the secretary's duties, but Rutledge glared at me as though waiting for me to produce the name of the culprit then and there.

"What would you have me do?" I asked him.

"Well, damn it, man, is this not why you are here? Grenville told me you were a master at poking your nose into things that did not concern you."

"I do hope Grenville did not put it quite like that," I said mildly.

Rutledge scowled. "He neglected to tell me how impertinent you are. I cannot imagine you made a very good soldier."

"My commander would agree with you," I said. Colonel Brandon, once my closest friend, had often lectured me about my tendency to disobey orders and tell my superiors what I thought of them.

"But please continue about the problem," I said, my curiosity piqued in spite of myself. "If you wish me to discover which boys are responsible, I will need as much information as I can obtain."

"You will do it, then?"

I wished I had been asked, rather than simply expected. Lucius Grenville had much to answer for. "I admit interest," I said. "That these tricks have been perpetrated for three months without anyone being the wiser is intriguing. Someone has been uncommonly clever."

"Uncommonly indecent," Rutledge snarled. "When I put my hands on him—"

I knew the rest. Rutledge, I had learned in the week since my arrival, believed in strict and severe discipline. This was not unusual for a school's headmaster, but Rutledge seemed to enjoy meting out punishment more than did most sergeants in the King's army.

Rutledge's harsh methods so far had produced no result. I could see that the students here feared Rutledge but did not respect him.

He leaned across his desk. "I do not think you grasp the seriousness of the situation, Lacey. The sons of the wealthiest men in England attend the Sudbury School. Their money could buy you, and even Grenville, a dozen times over. I do not wish for fathers to become unhappy at their sons' complaints. Do you understand?"

"I understand well enough."

The Sudbury School did not house the sons of lords and statesmen; rather, their fathers were nabobs and merchants and men prominent in the City. They were the merchant class, the middle class, the sons of men who had started with nothing and gained fortune with the sweat of their brows. Boys finished Sudbury School, went to the City to add to their father's fortunes, and in turn sent their own sons here.

Rutledge did not care a fig about money, personally. The unkempt manner of his clothes, his obliviousness to the comfort of his study, his evenhandedness in dealing out punishment to the boys, told me this. Rutledge would be as much at home in Carleton House as in a hovel—in other words, he'd never notice.

What Rutledge cared about was the Sudbury School. His form of honor, if you will. Rutledge was gentleman born, had attended Eton with Grenville. But he'd stuck his claws into this school for bankers' sons, and by God he intended it to be a success. Its reputation was his reputation.

Rutledge went on, "I know that you yourself were the victim of a prank, Captain, though you chose not to report it. Sutcliff, my prefect, had to tell me. What were you thinking, man?"

Bartholomew, a few nights ago, had thrown back my bedding to reveal a grass snake, half-suffocated on the featherbed. I had lifted it between my fingers and laid it gently in the branches of the tree outside my window.

I said, "I was thinking it was harmless and did not need to be brought to your attention."

"Harmless?" Rutledge almost shouted. "And why, pray, did you believe it harmless?"

I half-smiled. "I assumed a few boys were simply testing out the new man. To see whether I fussed or laughed."

Rutledge's expression told me that levity had been the incorrect response. "You should have reported it to me at once, and the boys found and punished. You encourage their behavior."

I held my temper with effort. "I doubt it connects to the more serious pranks."

"How can you know that?"

"Poison in port and fires in servants rooms are considerably more dangerous than one bewildered grass snake."

Rutledge's annoyed expression told me he did not agree. "So the question remains, Captain . . . what do you intend to do about it?"

His belligerence was ruining a fine spring day. I had hoped to escape for a walk after my duties, but Rutledge had ordered me to stay. Then he'd laid aside his papers, rested his fists on his desk, and told me all about the pranks.

"I will question the boys," I told him. "They likely know who is involved but are reluctant to speak. Even if they do not know, they might be able to point to something. I will speak to the prefects of both houses, as well. They are much closer to the boys than you or even the tutors can be."

Rutledge peered at me in disappointment. "I expected more from you, the way Grenville boasted. The students have already been questioned. I had them all thrashed, but to no avail. You will get nowhere with that line of thinking."

"The students might be more willing to speak to a sympathetic stranger than their headmaster or even a prefect," I pointed out. "Servants, too, see things, hear things. I shall have my man talk with them."

Rutledge dismissed this with a wave of his hand. "Useless. They will not tell you, even if they do know."

I grew annoyed. "Did you expect me to pull the solution out of the air? I must begin somewhere."

"Yes, yes, very well. But I expect you to tell me everything. Everything, Lacey."

I did not promise. I'd tell him what he needed to know, nothing more. I had learned in my life that problems were often more complex than they seemed, and most people did not want to know the entire truth. Rutledge was a man who saw everything in black and white. Subtle complexities would be beyond him.

He dismissed me then, curtly. Without regret, I left the warm and comfortable room for the cold hall.

The case intrigued me, but Rutledge had not endeared himself to me. I was also put out with Grenville and intended to write to him so, first for not telling me that my employment here was simply a means for solving a puzzle, and second for not warning me that Rutledge was such a boor.

A walk in the brisk March air, I thought, would do me good.

It was late afternoon, and boys and tutors spilled through the double doors to change their clothes for chapel or dinner or more studies. There were thirty boys in this house, which was called the Head Master's house. I had not yet met all the students, but I had started to recognize a few. Ramsay was a towheaded boy of about thirteen who always looked apprehensive. Timson, the same age, had a roguish look, and it pained me to realize that he reminded me of myself at that age. Frederick Sutcliff, the prefect, was tall, lanky, older than the other students, and generally despised. He was full of himself and not above a little harsh discipline that he did not report to Rutledge. His father was also one of the wealthiest men in England.

The Classics tutor, Simon Fletcher, gave me a nod. He did not live in this house, but in the one opposite, called Fairleigh. Fletcher liked a quiet pint in the village tavern, and I'd met him there on more than one evening. The mathematics tutor, Tunbridge, was lecturing his star pupil as usual, a spindly youth of sixteen with a heavy brow.

The lads stared at me as I made my way down the

stairs and out of the house. They always stared because I was a tall, broad-shouldered man obviously wounded in the war, and also because they'd heard I'd refused to toady to Rutledge. This had raised me to a certain admired status.

Some of the boys nodded and said a polite, "Captain." Most of the others simply watched.

Cool damp air awaited me outside in the quad, and I breathed it in relief. Rutledge's study was comfortable enough, but his moods fouled the air.

The setting of the Sudbury School was fairly peaceful. The houses had been built in the time of Henry VIII. They had dark, narrow staircases and galleries that creaked, small windows, and crumbling plaster. But the estate had been owned by a family of vast fortune, who were able to fortify the houses and modernize them as time went on without marring their beauty.

The Head Master's house comprised the north and east sides of the quad, and Fairleigh, named for one of the founders of the school, the west side. The south building housed a large hall and two smaller ones for lectures, tiny classrooms, a common dining hall for the boys, and a more formal dining room, in which Rutledge hosted visitors to the school.

I left the quad through the gate and began walking to the stables. The Berkshire countryside certainly smelled cleaner than London's grime-filled streets. Here was the fragrance of new grass, wet earth, and the faint musty odor that came from the quiet canal that flowed past the school.

Rutledge at least did not mind me taking a horse every morning and riding about the green swards or along the towpath beside the canal. Rutledge was mad for sport and approved of men who liked to ride. I was still a cavalryman at heart and was glad to have the opportunity to ride regularly again.

I reflected as I walked that I had come to Berkshire to find peace, and so far, it had eluded me. But perhaps peace was not in a place but within one's self. In that case, I might never find it. There was little at peace inside Gabriel Lacey.

In the stable yard, I met Sebastian, a young Romany who had been taken on by the head groom to assist him. He was cleaning tack and not looking happy about it. Sebastian was excellent with horses, and he and I had become friends of a sort. I had been surprised at first to discover that Rutledge allowed a Romany to work in his stables, but Sebastian told me Rutledge had not known about it until after the fact. Sebastian had proved handy enough—and came cheap—and Rutledge had decided to look the other way.

"Good afternoon," I said genially to Sebastian.

He gave me a nod. The other stable hands ignored me. Two leaned on rakes and chatted, one sat on a crate smoking a pipe while he mended a bridle.

Sebastian was usually effusive, but today, he frowned at the saddle he polished. "Did you want a horse, Captain?" he asked in his melodious voice.

"No. I'm out for a short stroll, that's all. Is everything well with you?"

"Yes."

It was not, I could see, but Sebastian closed his mouth in a tight line. He was about twenty, not much older than the oldest boys at the school. The pupils generally liked him, because he was good-natured, kind, and knew everything there was to know about horses.

A door at the end of the line of stalls led to the quarters for the groom and his stable hands. A man emerged from this door just then. He was tall and burly, with black hair under a coachman's hat.

I stared at him. I recognized him—or thought I did.

He saw me, stopped, then ducked back into the shadows of the doorway.

"Who was that?" I asked Sebastian.

He looked up, puzzled at my tone. "Mr. Middleton," he answered. "The groom."

I had not seen this Middleton since my arrival. I usually visited the stables very early in the morning, and Sebastian alone prepared my mount.

But I knew Middleton. Or at least, I'd seen him before, in London. He had once been the lackey of a man called James Denis.

James Denis was a criminal, or should have been labeled so. He was a gentleman to whom wealthy gentlemen went when they wished to obtain a fine piece of art that was unobtainable, to gain a seat in Parliament that was already filled, to succeed in whatever enterprise they wished. In return, they gave their loyalty and a high percentage of their wealth to Mr. Denis.

I had encountered Denis far more often than I cared to. He had helped me once or twice, but he had also threatened me and once had his lackeys kidnap me and beat me to teach me to respect him. He wanted me to fear him, and my friends, like Grenville, advised me to, but Denis had only succeeded in making me very, very angry.

I watched the door, but the man did not reappear. "What do you know about him?" I asked Sebastian.

He shrugged. "Not very much. He's a coachman, or was. He's very good with horses. A gentle sort with the beasts."

"How long has he been here?"

"Don't know."

I moved to the stable hands still leaning on their rakes and asked them. Like Sebastian, they eyed me in surprise, but answered. Middleton had been employed at Sudbury for six months.

I might have been mistaken, I told myself. I had only glimpsed the man. But I did not think so. Why one of James Denis' men should have taken up a post in Berkshire, at a boys' school, I hadn't the faintest idea. But if I was right, this boded no good.

"YOU sure it was him, sir?"

Bartholomew held my coat in one hand, his stiff-bristled brush in the other. The blond giant had stopped and stared, wide-eyed, when I'd announced what I'd seen.

"No," I answered. I drank the thick coffee Bartholomew had brought after my supper. The quarters allotted to me consisted of a rather plain but cozy room on the top floor of the Head Master's house. My windows looked over the meadows behind the school and the line of trees that marked the canal. "He did not come out again, and I could not go charging in after him. He looked just as surprised to see me."

"But he must have heard you'd come here,"

Bartholomew said. "That's why he's kept scarce whenever you came to take a horse, I'd wager."

"Well, if he is Denis' man, why is he here?" I wondered. "Did Denis send him to keep an eye on me?"

"Could be, sir. Or could be he's quit of Mr. Denis. Or could be he doesn't want Mr. Denis to know where he is."

"True." If I was correct about who he was, Denis had once sent the man Middleton to my rooms in Covent Garden to fetch me. Denis generally employed pugilists and former coachmen to serve as rather menacing bodyguards and lackeys. This one had been no less menacing than any of the others. I had refused the summons. Bartholomew's presence had helped, and the man had left in defeat.

I had never seen him again. Though I'd visited Denis not long ago, while pursuing the affair of the Glass House in London, Middleton, as far as I remembered, had not been there.

"Well, it's interesting," Bartholomew remarked. "What are you going to do?"

I lifted my cup. "I will let it lie for now. He obviously did not want me to see him. But I'll watch. I do not trust Denis, nor any man associated with him."

"No, sir." Bartholomew resumed brushing. "Of course, it does no harm asking about in the kitchens. Why he's here, I mean."

"Your curiosity might prove as dangerous as mine, Bartholomew," I said.

"Yes, sir."

I turned the conversation back to the pranks that Rutledge wanted me to investigate, and frowned in thought. "I wonder whether one house has seen more of the pranks than the other," I mused. "It would be difficult, for instance, for a boy in this house to get into Fairleigh at night."

"The Fairleigh boys would chuck him right out if they saw him." Bartholomew grinned. "And not in a nice manner, would they?"

The houses, the Head Master's and Fairleigh, were similar in amenities and distribution of boys, but the two houses were fierce rivals, each convinced that members of the other were weak and ineffectual. It is common thing among mortals, I had observed, that when placed even arbitrarily into this or that group, they immediately begin to defend themselves against all other groups. I do not exclude myself from this phenomenon. In the army, I valiantly defended the honor of the 35th Light Dragoons, and would have done so with my life. And of course, I esteemed the abilities of the light cavalry over the heavy. Still more serious was the manner in which cavalry viewed the infantry—that body of foot wobblers who could not shoot straight even standing on the ground and dug into place.

I fully admitted to prejudice in my views—I had realized once that if someone were to come along and paint a red or blue spot on each of our foreheads, we who had the blue spots would congregate to other blue-spotters and come up with reasons why we were infinitely better than the red-spotters.

The Fairleighs contended that they were superior to the Head Masters and vice versa. Therefore, if any Head Master boy was caught sneaking into Fairleigh uninvited, said boy had better be fast on his feet and good with his fists. In addition, news of such a break-in would be all over school the next day.

Therefore, the prankster must either be a master of infiltration and deception, or there must be more than one.

I continued to drink my coffee, and Bartholomew and I continued to speculate on the pranks until I sought my bed and slumber. The matter of Middleton, for the time, was dropped.

But the matter reasserted itself almost immediately. Bartholomew woke me early the next morning to tell me that Middleton had been killed in the night, his body fetched up in a lock of the nearby canal.

CHAPTER 2

I had to saddle a horse myself in order to ride out to the canal the next morning because Sebastian and every other stable hand had abandoned their posts. Bartholomew boosted me aboard, then followed me on foot to Lower Sudbury Lock and the crowd gathered there.

This canal was one leg of the Kennet and Avon Canal, which bisected England from Bath to Reading. I was told that over one hundred locks raised and lowered water so that canal boats could navigate across the heartland of England. The intricate locks and arched bridges were fairly new, the canal having been completed and open for use within the last decade.

This morning, my only interest in the canal was in the body of the hapless groom that floated in it.

The gates of the lock were closed, and a barge waited quietly on the lower side. The pumps clanked as the lockkeeper, a fleshy man with lank hair and sweat-stained clothes, turned the sluice wheel. Water noisily drained from the lock to the flat pond that housed the excess water. The parish constable, a sturdy man of about forty years, stood on the narrow parapet of the lock, peering over the side.

Bartholomew fell into conversation with a village lad, then reported what he said to me. "Lockkeeper found him not an hour ago. Came out to open the gates for the barge, and there was Middleton, floating all peaceful. They tried fishing him out with a boat hook, but couldn't catch him. Constable said send in the boat to get him out."

The waiting canal boat was long and narrow, its flat deck filled with goods. One bargeman watched from the tiller, while the other stood on shore, his teeth working a piece of straw. He held the barge horse, a large beast, which lowered its head to crop a patch of grass.

The lock was a simple mechanism, but one that had changed England forever. Locks allowed barges to move up or down hill without having to portage. Locks on this particular canal, I'd read, were a marvel of engineering.

Sebastian the stable hand leaned to watch near me, his swarthy face wan. He wore the same garb as any stable lad, dusty breeches, boots, and shirt, but his blue-black hair, thick-lashed brown eyes, and dark skin betrayed his Romany origins.

The lockkeeper closed the pumps and cranked open the gates. The bargeman slapped the horse's side and guided the boat into the lock.

Relative peace descended, broken by the soft sound of

canal water lapping at the gate. I watched while the man
on the barge dragged the corpse onto its deck. I expected
the boat to back out again, but the bargeman signaled for
the lockkeeper to close the gates. He did so, and then rushing water drowned the silence. The water rose slowly, the
pumps struggling to drag water back in from the pond.

Once the boat was level with the upper part of the
canal, the lockkeeper opened the gates. The horse, used
to the procedure, pulled the boat silently into the canal
beyond.

The constable trudged to the boat, put his foot on the
deck. The bargeman and his partner obligingly hauled
the corpse out onto the green bank.

As one, we crowded round to see. Middleton lay
still, his eyes closed, his body bloated, an ugly gash
across his pale throat. Now that I could look at him
closely, I saw that he was indeed Denis' man.

The constable heaved a sigh, hands on hips. "Nasty
business, eh? Now then, one of you lads run for the surgeon. Though it's obvious he died of having his throat
cut, we might as well get it put down right."

Bartholomew whispered to me, "Think Mr. Denis
killed him?"

"I would be surprised if he did," I answered. "Somehow, I imagine Denis is . . . neater. Likely we'd not
have found Middleton's body at all."

"Are you going to tell the constable who he was?"

"I have no reason not to."

When I could draw the constable's attention, I took
him aside and explained what I knew about Middleton.
The constable showed no recognition of the name
Denis, thanked me for the information, then said that

there was no accounting for the trouble into which foolish Londoners could land themselves.

Bartholomew and I drifted away from the others, looking over the scene.

The lock and pumps stood near the lock house, where the lockkeeper lived. The pond for excess water lay serenely under the clouded sky not far away, a thick stand of trees lining its far bank.

"I wonder that the murderer bothered to drag the man to the lock," I said. "Easier I'd think to drag him to the pond. He'd not be seen in the woods and would not have to pass so close to the lock house and risk awakening the lockkeeper."

"Unless," Bartholomew suggested, "the killer pushed the dead man into the canal, then opened the lock when the chap floated to the gate."

"Which would make still more noise. Unless our lockkeeper is very hard of hearing or an unusually sound sleeper."

"Or he killed the man himself."

I studied the lockkeeper who stood silently outside the ring of men around the body. "Perhaps he did. Although I hardly think he'd hide the body in his own lock. Why not send him downstream? Or not bring him to the canal at all?"

"What should we do, sir?" Bartholomew gazed up at me, blue eyes gleaming with eagerness.

I had asked Bartholomew for help in two previous investigations, and he had obviously decided that he would help me again.

"I think we should have a care," I answered. "Someone near this place does not mind slicing throats."

Bartholomew looked startled, as though he'd not thought of that. "You say truth, sir. Where Mr. Denis is concerned, it's best to go carefully."

He followed me as I moved on, looking about. The Sudbury School rested on a rise of land above the canal. To the west and north, up the canal, lay the village of Sudbury. Trees lined the towpath, the narrow lane that the barge horses traversed with their guides. The canal widened as it curved to the east, shaded by cool trees, its banks shrouded in mist.

The pond that held the water for the lock lay on the west bank of the canal. I rode to it carefully, scanning the undergrowth for any disturbance. I found none. I likewise found nothing in the mud surrounding the pond, except tracks of deer and smaller creatures that had wandered here for a drink.

I suppose I wanted to find two distinct sets of footprints, the dead man's and the killer's, and broken bracken that designated a struggle. A fresh set of footprints leading back to the killer would have been most helpful as well.

A doctor had arrived by the time Bartholomew and I returned to the lock, looking rather nauseated as he stooped over the corpse. I wondered whether he was the sort of doctor who examined his patients from across the room, pronounced what was wrong with them without touching them, and then prescribed an expensive tonic and collected his fee.

The constable set the stable hands and the lock-keeper to scouring the brush and the canal for the knife. He and the doctor decided to wrap Middleton's body and have him taken to the parish church to be held for the coroner's examination. The constable declared his next task was to report to the magistrate and asked me, hesitantly, to break the news to Rutledge.

RUTLEDGE had already heard by the time I returned. He glared at me in utter fury, a vein pulsing in his forehead, when I arrived in the front hall of the Head Master's house.

The prefect, Sutcliff, stood behind Rutledge, his face a mixture of consternation and interest. Fletcher and the mathematics tutor next to him did not bother to hide their curiosity.

"Tell the constable to arrest that gypsy," Rutledge barked. "Bloody thieves will murder us in our beds. Should not even be allowed to walk about. Middleton did a bad day's work hiring him, and he's paid for it. What are you standing there for, man? Go and have done."

I noted a fleeting movement on the stairs high above, heard a faint gasp. I looked up without seeming to and saw who I thought I'd see, Rutledge's daughter, Belinda. She was twenty years old and kept house for her father, rarely leaving their chambers.

"There is no evidence that Sebastian killed him," I pointed out. "We have only a corpse with his throat cut, and not even the knife that did it."

"I do not recall asking your opinion, Lacey. Either you go, or I send someone else."

Rutledge turned on his heel and marched away, growling at a group of boys who had come to see what the fuss was about.

•   •   •

THE constable did arrest Sebastian. I do not think the man would have dared had he confronted Sebastian alone. But in the stable yard, among the group of stable hands who did not much like Sebastian anyway, the constable lifted his chin and told the Romany to come with him.

Sebastian, for the first time since I'd met him, raised his voice. "No. I did not do this."

"Now then," the constable replied, a bit nervously. "Enough of that. Come with me."

A look of abject panic spread over Sebastian's swarthy face. He tried to run. The stable hands caught him. Bartholomew started forward to help the stable hands seize Sebastian, but I grabbed his coat and hauled him back.

"No," I said. "Something is not right here."

Bartholomew looked at me in amazement. "But he's Romany, sir. They're liars and thieves, everyone knows it."

"That may be. But I do not think Sebastian killed Middleton."

"No, sir?"

"Why should he?" I asked impatiently. "Middleton showed kindness, and, I must say, good sense, in hiring him. Not many would hire one of the Roma."

Bartholomew wrinkled his brow, trying to resolve my words with his prejudices.

"I cannot say why I think so," I said. "Perhaps I am foolish, perhaps I like Sebastian because the horses like him, I do not know. But Middleton being Denis' man puts a different complexion on things."

Bartholomew nodded, somewhat dubiously.

Sebastian struggled, but he could not break free. He sent me a look of frozen terror. The appeal in his eyes moved me. I knew that if I tried to help him, I would set myself squarely against Rutledge, but at this point, I cared nothing for that.

RUTLEDGE expected me to take up my duties as usual that day, just as he expected the tutors to continue with their lectures. A corpse in the canal should not, to his mind, interfere with the smooth running of the school.

My regular routine was to write letters for Rutledge after breakfast and before dinner. During this time, I read Rutledge's correspondence, answered what I could, and waited for him to dictate what he needed to answer himself. I also made his appointments, reminded him of upcoming events, and wrote formulaic letters on his behalf to people who had visited or been beneficial to the school.

We worked in a study that was a bright, surprisingly pleasant room, which occupied the end of a wing in the Head Master's house. Windows lined three walls, and paintings of landscapes filled the spaces between the windows. A portrait of a serene woman in a black riding habit and broad-brimmed hat hung over Rutledge's desk. "The late Mrs. Rutledge," my employer had grunted when I'd asked her identity.

Mrs. Rutledge looked as though she'd been far more interesting than her husband. Dark, intelligent eyes above her long nose held good humor and comfort. I found myself looking into those eyes more than once when annoyed by Rutledge. I wondered how she had weathered living with him. Had she met his prickly personality with a fire of her own, or had he cowed her as much as he did his daughter?

Today, though Rutledge wanted to carry on as usual, he was more abrupt and angry than normal. He growled that I was too slow, my writing unclear, my manner offensive. Through it all I ground my teeth and answered him as it suited me. He had already learned that he could not cow me with his abruptness, though he did not like this.

At last, Rutledge, too impatient to sit still, took himself off to harass his tutors. Left alone, I finished my work without interruption and found time to attend to my own correspondence.

I wrote first to Grenville, informing him of the murder and the unusual circumstances. I wrote curtly that I wished he'd apprised me of the true reason to send me down to Sudbury, keeping my sentences short and pointed. I knew I was rude, but my anger at his deception had not abated.

Next I wrote to James Denis. I had never written a letter to the man before, preferring to avoid him as much as possible. But I informed him briefly of the death of Middleton. I wondered what Denis would make of the news, or if he'd indeed had a hand in Middleton's death. If he had wanted Middleton dead, Denis would tell me. He did not bother to lie about his crimes.

I kept my letter short. I sanded it, folded it, and directed it to number 45, Curzon Street, Mayfair.

I had just laid it aside when the door to the room opened. I expected Rutledge, and so kept my eyes on my work, but when I heard no noise, I raised my head.

A young woman peered around the doorframe, her face anxious. Belinda Rutledge had the coloring of her mother, dark hair, dark eyes, and white skin. But while her mother's eyes held a challenge, Belinda's only ever looked timid.

I rose to my feet politely and made a small bow. "Miss Rutledge, good morning. I am afraid your father is not here."

She glanced once behind her, fear plain on her face, then she took a few steps into the room. "Captain Lacey," she whispered hurriedly, "is it true that Sebastian—that the Romany stable lad—has been arrested?"

"Yes," I confirmed.

Her face whitened. "Why? He did not do it." The words were spoken with conviction.

"Why do you say so?" I asked curiously.

"Because he would never have done such a thing." She glanced behind her again. "And, last night, Sebastian was . . . he was speaking to me. Near the canal."

I hid a sigh. She was young, Sebastian was young, she was pretty, he was handsome. It was inevitable that the two should be attracted to one another. They would not have been able to resist the romance of the impossible situation.

Before I could answer, I heard Rutledge's unmistakable tread in the hall, his growl as he dismissed a servant. He tramped into the study and halted, his glare resting first on me, then his daughter. "What is this, Belinda? What are you doing here?"

"Miss Rutledge was looking for you," I extemporized. "She assumed you here. I told her you would be along any moment."

Rutledge did not soften. "Yes? Well, then, girl, what do you want?"

Belinda, pale and shaking, said, "I wish to go into Sudbury and visit Miss Pettigrew."

"Eh?" Rutledge scowled and hesitated as though trying to think of a reason he didn't want her out of his sight. Then he grunted. "Take Pringle with you." Pringle was one of the housemaids, a dour, forty-year-old woman I'd seen determinedly dogging Belinda's footsteps.

Belinda looked dismayed, but she curtseyed and retreated from the room as rapidly as she could.

Rutledge growled. "Ladies can keep nothing in their heads but shopping and gossip."

I knew he wronged her, but I said nothing. I had learned early on that I should not bring up the subject of Rutledge's private life. Rutledge curtailed any interest in his family with blunt, scornful requests to keep my questions to myself.

Rutledge settled himself behind his desk and began to sort through papers that I had already sorted. It occurred to me, as I watched him, that Sebastian had been taken to the constable's house in Sudbury. I'd seen the anguish on Belinda's face, and she had just obtained her father's permission to go to Sudbury. I had a feeling that she would neglect to request Pringle to accompany her.

"Do you need me at the moment?" I asked Rutledge.

He looked up, brows high. "Why?"

"I have a few errands I must run. And letters to post. Including yours."

"Everyone is in such a hurry," Rutledge said. "If

Middleton had minded his job, he'd not have got himself murdered."

I doubted that Middleton had simply been in the wrong place at the wrong time, but I did not say so. I did not thank Rutledge, either. I simply took my leave.

I caught up with Belinda Rutledge when she left the gates to the school's drive and entered the road to Sudbury. As I'd speculated, she did not have Pringle with her, but another of the housemaids, a young woman who looked much more biddable. It was raining. Belinda carried a wide umbrella and wore pattens, shoes with high metal frames that would keep her feet out of the mud.

I had hurried across the grounds to meet her, and my boots were already well caked with mud. "Miss Rutledge," I called.

She turned. She looked alarmed, but she stopped.

"Miss Rutledge," I began at once, "do not try to see Sebastian."

Her look turned panicked. "My father sent you."

I shook my head, water dripping from the ends of my hair. "I have not discussed this with your father. But you must promise me not to visit him. It can do neither of you any good."

"I know he did not kill Mr. Middleton!" Belinda wailed. "They will lock Sebastian in a room for something he did not do. He cannot bear to be locked indoors." Her voice became rapid, pleading. "They will treat him cruelly, because he is Romany."

"But if you attempt to see him, Miss Rutledge, you will give yourself away."

Belinda stopped, confusion in her eyes. "He so fears being kept indoors, Captain. It is torment to him."

I remembered the panic on Sebastian's face when the men had dragged him away. "I also find it difficult to believe that Sebastian killed the groom," I told her. "But you must fix on the purpose of staying well away from him. You can only hurt him if you reveal that you care for his well-being."

Tears darkened her eyes. "How can that be? That caring for someone can hurt them?"

I knew better than she ever would how that could be. But I was twice her age and knew my words would not change her mind. "I will go to Sudbury and inquire after him," I said. "I will see that he is not poorly treated."

Her eyes took on a light of hope. I hid a sigh. I did not want to become her champion. I did not know whether I could succeed in making it clear that Sebastian was not a murderer. The Roma were the enemies of rural people. They stole horses, chickens, and other livestock, and possibly, children. Why should they not murder, as well?

"I would be ever grateful to you, Captain Lacey," Belinda said with too much admiration.

"I will see what I can do. Go back home and stay there. I will let you know what I have done."

"When?" she asked. "You can get messages to me through Bridgett—"

I held up my hand. "I will let you know. You must trust me and say nothing."

She nodded. I thought I understood some of Rutledge's exasperation. Belinda was not stupid, but she was young and romantic. Her father's secretary sending her secret correspondence via a maid would be the height of foolishness. I could be dismissed, or worse, and I hated to think what Rutledge would do to Belinda.

I would not like to see her hurt, but I hoped that when the infatuation between her and Sebastian ended, it would bring her back down to earth.

I said good-bye, touched my hat, and went to fetch a horse to take me to Sudbury.

CHAPTER 3

⚜

THE village of Sudbury lay on a stretch of the canal between Hungerford and Froxfield. The canal and the school had made tiny Sudbury important. Bargemen and parents of Sudbury boys frequented its public houses and inns, and tutors and pupils walked its lanes. The High Street retained much charm of the Tudor age. The half-timbered and stone houses were rather crumbling, but for historians, it was a fine place to stroll and contemplate old England.

I left my horse in the yard at the tavern and approached the constable's house at the end of the High Street. A cat sat square in the middle of the cobbles before the house, washing its face. I bade it a polite good morning.

My knock was answered by a large woman in, of all things, a fine lawn dress with short sleeves. The sleeves cut into the folds of her plump arms, ballooning her skin. She wore a stiff white cap with tapes that were soiled and worn. She regarded me with a wary eye, her lips pursed. She was an unbecoming woman, and I do not mean she was plain. I could see a prettiness that time had marred only a little, but her demeanor had been soured by belligerence.

"What is it?" she snapped.

I removed my rain-drenched hat and made her a polite bow. "Good morning. I am Captain Lacey. I would like to speak to the Romany, Sebastian, if I may."

She folded her arms. "And why would you be wanting to do that?"

"Sebastian was employed by the school, as am I," I said. "Naturally, I am interested in his well-being."

She cast me a questioning gaze, as though wondering why I should bother. "A filthy Romany woman already tried to see him. I sent her on her way."

I wondered who the Romany woman might be— mother, sister, lover? I said nothing, only waited while the woman assessed that I was not Romany but a gentleman.

"You come from the school?" she asked, still doubtful.

"I am secretary to the headmaster."

This seemed to impress her. She opened the door wider. "Mr. Rutledge is a fine gentleman."

I had my own opinion about that.

The woman led me through a low-ceilinged, flagstone hall and out into a courtyard. At the back of this lay a low stone building. It might have been a cheese house were this the abode of a dairy farmer. At one time it probably had been. Now it was used as a makeshift jail.

The plump woman unlocked and opened the door. Sebastian sat on a stone bench in the back of a tiny room lit only by a small, high-set window. I had to stoop to enter, and once inside, I could not straighten to my full six-foot height. Sebastian was as tall as I. He started to stand up, but I gestured him to remain seated.

The young man did not look well. His face was pasty, his breathing shallow. There was plenty of air in the room, if a bit musty; the window was propped open to let in a breeze and hint of spring rain.

The woman did not close the door. She stood in the yard, arms folded, as though she were a sentry. The prisoner would have to go through her, her stance said, if he wanted to escape.

Sebastian may have wanted to escape, but he looked in no condition to do so. He hunkered on the bench, hugging himself.

I looked pointedly at the woman, and she looked back at me, hands on hips. I pulled the door shut, closing it in her face.

She never moved. I imagined her outside facing the closed door, hands on hips, waiting for me to open it again.

I turned to Sebastian. "Are you well?"

"Captain." Sebastian spoke in a low voice, his Romany vowels slurring, "I cannot stay here."

"Well, you will have to at least until after the inquest," I said. "I warn you, you might have to face the magistrate after that. Rutledge has taken against you."

He looked up at me, his face gray. "I will see the magistrate, I will face him, I am not afraid. But I cannot stay here. I cannot breathe. The walls . . ." He gestured with a shaking hand.

I thought I understood. This was more than a Romany man's dislike of being indoors. Sebastian must have an unnatural fear of enclosed places. I had met a man in the army with such a malady, a lieutenant. The man was brave-hearted in battle and could rally his troops like the best general, but put him in a cellar and he developed cold sweats and clawed his way to the door.

"I am willing to help you get out," I said. Sebastian looked up at me with dark-eyed hope, like a seasick man who believes shore might be near. "But you must tell me exactly what you did last night. I need the entire truth."

Hope receded. "I cannot."

I sat on the bench beside him, tired of bending my head. I rested my hands on my walking stick. "Did you meet with Miss Rutledge?"

He looked alarmed. He avoided my eye, bowed his head. "I will not speak."

"Do not be such a pigheaded romantic," I said. "Dying nobly on the gallows to spare your lady's name would be foolish and help no one."

Sebastian stared at me in amazement. Suffering for love was noble—at least that was fashion these days— especially when that love was forbidden.

I softened. "I know, Sebastian. When I was young, I too fell in love where I should not have."

He looked skeptical, but I spoke the truth. My father had expected me to marry a rich man's daughter. I instead had fallen in love with a young woman of little fortune. What's more, I'd eloped with her, with the help of my friend and mentor, Aloysius Brandon.

Carlotta had regretted marrying me almost right away. One day, three years into our marriage, she'd left me. I had not seen her since. James Denis knew where she was. Last summer, he had offered the information of her whereabouts to me. I had refused, knowing that he had only offered to make me obligated to him. He'd told me once that he would win the enmity between us by making me owe him too many favors to oppose him.

Often in the night when I lay awake, fighting off melancholia, I was very tempted to go to Denis and beg for the information. I wanted to find her. I wanted to look into Carlotta's pretty eyes and demand, Why did you leave me?

If I found my wife, I'd also discover what had become of my daughter. Was Gabriella still alive? Was she happy? Would she remember me?

I had not yet succumbed to the temptation to sell myself to Denis, but I was coming close.

"Tell me," I said to Sebastian, my tone severe, "everything you did from the time I saw you yesterday afternoon until now. The entire truth. The sooner you tell me, the sooner you can leave this room."

Sebastian shuddered. His face shone with perspiration. "Very well." He wet his lips. "I did my duties in the stable as usual. I cleaned the tack and brushed the horses, then helped feed and bed them down for the night. No different from any other day."

"And Middleton? What did he do?"

"He asked about you."

I stopped. "Did he?"

"Asked about you and why you were here. Did you know him?"

"I'd met him once," I said carefully. "In London. What was he like?"

Sebastian shrugged. "Kept to himself. Came to Sudbury to enjoy the country life, he said. But he didn't much like dirtying his hands. He left the messy work to us. I didn't mind because I like moving among the beasts. He knew that I could handle a horse, no matter what, better than any of his other lads."

"Did Middleton speak much to anyone else at Sudbury?" I asked. "Rutledge? The pupils?"

Sebastian shook his head. "He watched me and the other stable hands whenever we saddled horses for the students. Sometimes he'd talk to the boys while they waited, but not much. Only one of the tutors rides much, Tunbridge, I think his name is. And Miss Rutledge rides."

His eyes took on a soft look. I imagined that was how he and Belinda had met, Sebastian saddling her mount and her looking on, young and pretty in her riding habit.

"What happened last night after you finished your duties?" I persisted.

Sebastian took a breath. "Mr. Middleton said he was going into Sudbury to the pub, and not to look for him until late. I was glad, because Miss Rutledge sent word that she wanted to see me. I went to her."

So Belinda had indicated. "You are a pair of brave fools," I said. "What time was this?"

He thought. Sebastian would probably not own a watch and likely could not read the time anyway. "The clock at the school struck ten, I think. I walked to the canal and down the towpath. Miss Rutledge had told me to meet her around the first bend past Lower Sudbury Lock. There is a stand of trees there that would screen us from the school."

"How did she send the message? Did she write you?"

He shook his head. "I cannot read. She sent her maidservant."

"Unfortunate," I said.

He looked indignant. "Bridgett loves Miss Rutledge."

"Perhaps, but even if Bridgett would die for her mistress, tongues slip. But go on. Did Miss Rutledge meet you as planned?"

He nodded. "She came late. The clock had struck the half hour before I saw her. Bridgett came with her. I was glad. I would not have liked her out in the dark, alone."

"In that case, you should have sent word for her to stay home."

His eyes were anguished. "But I craved to see her. Her father guards her well."

In a school filled with boys and a handsome young Romany in the stables, I could hardly blame Rutledge. I reflected, though, that in this instance, he'd not guarded her sternly enough.

"So, she arrived, and you met her. What did you speak about?"

He smiled. His smile was dark and roguish, and had my daughter lived with me, I'd certainly set a guard on her day and night. "In truth, sir, little. My heart was full, I couldn't think of what to say."

I would have accused him of reading too much poetry had he been able to read at all. "I must ask you directly, are you and she lovers?"

He looked almost shocked. "No, sir. She is an innocent. I would never touch her, never."

The pair seemed too romantic to be true. I had been
a bit romantic about Carlotta, but my craving for her
had not been merely in my heart. I'd proposed to her in
a Norfolk meadow; when she'd said yes, I'd laid her
down and made sweet love to her then and there.

But then I'd married her right away. Our families
had been furious, but society had accepted the marriage—we'd been of similar background and class, and
our alliance was no worse than any other. Sebastian and
Belinda, on the other hand, would be thoroughly condemned. Belinda would be ruined, received nowhere,
her family could shun her—living death in a world that
valued honor and social standing above all else. Sebastian's own family would likewise not be pleased.

"Well, at least you were sensible in that regard," I
said. "How long did you stand and gaze at each other?"

His face darkened. "Not long. We were together
twenty minutes, I think. She was gone before the clock
struck the hour again."

That took us up to eleven o'clock. "What did you do
then?"

"I stayed near the canal. I did not want her reap-
pearance at the school to be connected to mine, if
someone should see her return from her late walk."

"Very sensible of you. How long did you stay?"

"I do not know. I was deep in thought. Then I decided not to return to the stables, but to visit my fam-

ily." He gave me a defiant look, as though I would not believe him. "I knew they were moored down the canal near Great Bedwyn, so I walked that way. I boarded their boat, and we shared food and wine and conversation. It was good to see them."

Some Roma traveled up and down the canals in boats with all their worldly goods, much like other Roma traveled overland in caravans. They would take odd jobs and buy food and wine from any that would sell it to them.

I sometimes envied the gypsies their freedom, although I knew it was not true freedom—they lived hand to mouth and could not give it up when they liked.

"Did you stay with them all night?"

"A good part of it," Sebastian said. "I argued with my uncles—they do not believe I should work for the . . . English." He paused before he said *English*, and I knew he'd suppressed a more derogatory, Romany term. "But I want to have maybe a better life. Not hungry, not stealing."

"I understand," I said. "What then?"

"We argued for a while, then I left the boat and walked back to the stables."

"What time did you arrive?"

He bowed his head, stared at his fingers. "I think the clocks had struck two."

"Did you see Middleton?"

He looked at me, shrugged. "No. I thought he'd gone to bed. It was very quiet. I went to sleep."

He'd have had no reason to check that Middleton had actually returned. I let that go.

Sebastian went on. In the morning, he'd began his

duties as usual, turning the horses out to the yard while he mucked out stalls. At about dawn, one of the stable hands had dashed in, looking horrified, and said that Middleton had been found dead in the lock.

Sebastian's story sounded plausible and was probably true. Unfortunately, however, the story provided ample gaps of time in which Sebastian could have met Middleton, killed him, and disposed of his body in the lock.

Even if Belinda dared admit that Sebastian talked with her between ten-thirty and eleven o'clock, there was still the time he waited on the canal bank, the time it took him to walk to his family's boat, the time he'd spoken with them, and the time he'd walked back to the stables. He had stood right next to the lock in question, lost in thought, which was not good. A canny magistrate could poke plenty of holes in his story.

On the other hand, his very vagueness spoke of his innocence. If Sebastian were guilty, would he not come up with a story that accounted for his whereabouts every minute?

His family would no doubt confirm that Sebastian had visited them, but would a magistrate believe them? Would a jury?

I sighed. "Did you see anyone, anyone at all in your journey up and down the canal? Hear anything?"

Sebastian shook his head. "I heard only noises of the night. I saw no other person."

Most helpful.

I rose, remembering in time to duck my head in the low-ceilinged room. "I will do what I can to help you, Sebastian. I cannot promise it will be easy, but I will help."

"Do not tell the magistrate about Belinda," Sebastian pleaded quickly.

He was a handsome lad. A girl constantly bullied and sheltered by her father would seek solace in the smiles of an attractive man who admired her. But theirs was a doomed love.

"I hope we do not have to." I paused. "Who was the Romany woman who tried to visit you?"

Sebastian started. "Woman?"

"The constable's housekeeper told me that a Romany woman came to visit you, but the housekeeper would not let her see you."

Sebastian's mouth was open. He looked pale, but that might still be his fear of the enclosed room. "My mother, most like," he whispered.

I could always ask her. Questioning the Roma would be my next task.

"A piece of advice, Sebastian," I said. "When you face the magistrate, tell the truth. Stick to the truth, do not try to embellish, and do not avoid answering a question. If you stay with the truth, the person lying will eventually be revealed. Do you understand?"

I do not think he did, but he nodded.

I gave him a few more reassuring phrases, then I departed.

The door opened for me easily enough. The woman had not locked us in. She was waiting, though, in the yard, ample arms folded. As soon as I emerged, she slammed the door and shot home the bolt, as though fearing that poor Sebastian would leap from his den and murder us both.

CHAPTER 4

❧

I returned to the tavern to collect my horse, intending to ride down the canal from here to Bedwyn to look for Sebastian's family.

The tavern, called the Boar, was the tavern to which Middleton apparently had been making his way to last night. I inquired of the hostler whether he had seen Middleton the night before. The man shrugged. I decided to discover what the landlord knew and ducked my head to enter the warm, dark interior of the taproom.

Despite the excitement of the murder, the tavern was quiet, the people of Sudbury having gone about their business. They had not forgotten, however. When the landlord approached me, he expressed his views.

"Gave me a turn, hearing we had such a brutal murder so close to home. The lads hereabouts are all looking out for the murderer, I can tell you."

I asked him if Middleton had come to the tavern the

previous night, and he shook his head. "Never saw him. Not last night. Came in here from time to time, he did, but didn't talk much with us. Kept to himself. Looked on in kind of a quiet way. But last night, no. Didn't darken the doorway."

I wondered why Middleton had set off for the tavern and never reached it. Had the killer lain in wait for him and dispatched him at once, or taken him somewhere?

Someone waved to me from a dark corner. I recognized Simon Fletcher, the Classics tutor. I moved across the room to him, and he grinned and gestured to the chair beside him.

"Sit down, Lacey, and share a pint. Poor old Middleton," he said jovially as I took a chair facing him. "One day saddling your horse, the next dead in a canal. You never know what the world will send your way, do you?"

"Did you know him?" I asked.

Fletcher shook his head. He had lank brown hair that was wearing thin and rather flat brown eyes. His face was long, horse-like, but his mouth curved into ready smiles that made his otherwise dull eyes twinkle. "I never went to the stables much. Not a horse man. I trust my own shanks or ride a coach if I need to go farther afield. Don't much understand the beasts."

The landlord's wife brought me an ale. I much wanted to be on my way scouring the canal for Sebastian's kin, but Fletcher could possibly tell me much. I took a fortifying sip of ale and found it spicy and warm, pleasant after the chill rain outside.

"What do you think happened?" I asked.

Fletcher looked mildly surprised I should ask him. "Good lord, I have no idea. Probably he met up with some ruffians who tried to rob him. Is there not a band of Roma wandering about?"

"They've arrested Sebastian, the Romany stable hand."

Fletcher nodded. "I heard. Some of the lads are unhappy. They like the fellow. Others say he should be stoned to death." He made a face. "Bloody little beasts boys can be."

"One of them put a garter snake in my bed," I remarked.

Fletcher barked a laugh. "That would be young Ramsay. He enjoys greeting the newcomer with reptiles."

"Ramsay is the towheaded boy about thirteen years old? A bit nervous?"

"Oh, yes. Looks as though he is quiet and innocent, but is a little devil in fact. Smart, though. Sits through his Latin studies and soaks it up. His father is filthy rich, filthy. Owns half of London, I wouldn't wager."

"But he is a prankster."

Fletcher chuckled. "They all are. But if you mean, is he writing letters in blood and setting servants' rooms on fire or murdering grooms, I'd say no. He hasn't got the ballocks for it. It's garter snakes and toads and beetles down the younger boy's backs. Annoying things. Harmless."

When I'd suggested to Rutledge that the snake was harmless, he'd gone purple with rage. Fletcher, closer than Rutledge to the boys, agreed with me.

"If you had to choose which boy was perpetrating

the more harmful pranks, which would you say?" I asked.

Fletcher's eye gleamed. "Ah, Captain, that I cannot answer. You are Rutledge's man. First thing you learn when you're inside is that you do not peach on your fellows."

"I am hardly Rutledge's man," I said, slightly offended. "He employs me, as he employs you."

"The school employs me. And you. And Rutledge."

"I am not his man, Fletcher," I repeated.

He nodded. "I know. Sensed that when I met you. In Sudbury, you are either for Rutledge or against him. No middle ground. He's a bastard, but he knows what he's doing running a school. Have to say that much for him."

He slurped the last of his ale, waved aside the publican's wife who advanced to ask if he wanted more. "I have Latin lessons to grade." He grimaced. "A task that requires two pints of ale, no more, no less. To answer your question, Captain, I am hard-pressed to say. There are a fair number of little beggars that I'd like to see the back of, but none that I'd call cruel. Or mad. No, depend upon it, it's a servant causing these problems. Or a tutor." His eyes twinkled.

I admitted, "I had speculated that the tutors would have access to the places in which the pranks were played."

"A fair statement," Fletcher agreed. "I will protest my innocence, however, Captain. I have no time to play pranks, and what little time I find on my hands, I spend here or flat on my back with my eyes closed. When I sleep, the boys could burn down the entire school without me being the wiser."

He smiled, as though he'd think it a good joke.

"I imagine the other tutors have similar impediments."

Fletcher nodded. "Oh, yes. Rutledge believes idleness is the refuge of weak minds and all that. We barely have souls to call our own. Only the occasional pint." He smiled at his glass. "Tunbridge does extra tutoring, but God knows where he finds the time."

"And he rides," I commented, remembering what Sebastian had said.

"Oh, he likes a hack across the fields. He fancies himself a gentleman and a man of sport."

And, I thought, he'd have occasion to know Middleton and his habits.

"Is Tunbridge a good tutor?"

"One of the best, according to Rutledge. And himself. But I know for a fact he's no better or worse off than the rest of us, despite his airs." Fletcher shook his head, turned his empty glass. "Ah, the joys of teaching. Joy is all we get; the income is certainly shallow. But one day, Lacey . . ." He gave me a wink. "One day, I will be quit of all this. I'll have my fortune, retire to a grand house in the country, and enjoy the amenities of life denied a conscientious schoolmaster."

I smiled, nodding in sympathy. It was unlikely a fortune would drift my way, either.

"Shall we stroll back together?" Fletcher suggested, rising.

"No, I shall ride along the canal. Perhaps we can meet for port some evening," I said.

"Never a free moment to myself, I'm afraid. But we'll retreat here for a pint soon, I promise that."

He nodded to me, gathered up his robe, which had
lain on the seat next to him, and a book, which he
clutched to his chest, and departed.

I took a long drink of my ale, deposited a few coins,
and left the tavern, setting my hat at an angle against
the rain.

I rode up and down the canal to no avail. I saw many
barges traveling from Avon to London, but none with
Roma. Like the villagers in Sudbury and Great Bedwyn, the bargemen I spoke to talked of the murder with
interest and faint horror. In a small place like this, murder was an extraordinary thing—a thing of dangerous
places like London, although highwaymen still appeared now and again. The farmers and villagers of
Sudbury had spread the word to their friends and neighbors, who told the lockkeepers, who in turn told the
bargemen as they traveled through the locks.

The horror was mitigated a bit by the fact that a man
had been arrested. Quick work—at least we can all
sleep in our beds tonight, was the general feeling.

For me, the unease had not gone away. I truly did not
think Sebastian had committed the crime—his arrest
was just to soothe Rutledge's pique. Someone who had
brutally cut the throat of a large man who had been
used to danger was still walking about. I wondered
whether Middleton had simply been unlucky and come
across a robber or madman. But if that were the case,
would we not have found him where he'd been killed?
Instead, his body had been placed in the lock and all
traces of the murderer's trail obliterated.

I believed Middleton had known his killer. Probably had not feared him, which was why he'd allowed the man to get behind him with a knife. They had met somewhere between the stables and the village of Sudbury, walked together to another location, and Middleton had died. Whereupon the killer had taken Middleton to the lock and rolled him in.

Why? A quarrel? Over money, a woman? Or had the man planned to kill Middleton all along? Again, why?

One man I could easily picture cutting Middleton's throat was Rutledge himself. He was large enough and strong enough, and he had the devil's own temper. But I had asked Bartholomew to discover from Rutledge's servants what he had done the night before, and they had all sworn that Rutledge had retired to his bed at ten o'clock and had not left it until rising as usual at six the next morning.

Again, no reason presented itself, at least on the surface. If Rutledge had found out that his daughter and Sebastian were yearning for each other, I could imagine him wanting to kill Sebastian. But Middleton? As far as I could see, the two men had had little contact.

I rode back to the school, unsatisfied. I knew so little. I would have to discover everything about Middleton—his connections and his friends and his enemies. I would have to pry into his life with Denis and beyond.

I would have to discover why anyone would bother cutting the throat of a man who'd simply come to enjoy working with horses in peace of the Berkshire countryside.

•   •   •

I had no time to investigate that afternoon, because Rutledge spied me returning. Angry that I'd disappeared for so long, he piled me with work until supper.

I managed to speak briefly with Belinda after I left the study and before I returned to my own rooms for my meal. I'd spied her in Rutledge's garden, and I slipped out there, pretending to take a short, leg-stretching stroll and encounter her by chance. Swiftly, while I tipped my hat and bowed, I told her that Sebastian was well and that, at this point, she was to say absolutely nothing about meeting him the night before the murder. I would give her further instructions later.

I walked away as she drew breath to ask questions. I knew it cruel, but I could not chance that her father would note any lengthy conversation with her.

After Bartholomew fed me supper, removed the tray, and served me claret that Grenville had sent with me, I went over things with him. Bartholomew had already made friends with every other lackey about the place, and likely knew the gossip upstairs and down about the inhabitants of each house. I told Bartholomew what Fletcher had talked about, and I asked if he had learned anything from the other servants about the boy called Ramsay.

"Yes, sir," Bartholomew said, dribbling wine into my glass. "From what I gather, he's a quiet tyke. Not the mischievous kind, I'd've said, but not cowed much by the others, either. The tutors call him Ramsay *minor.* That means he has an older brother, that they called Ramsay major, even though the older brother's gone off to work for his father. No one called me and

Matthias *minor* and *major*," he went on, chuckling. "Mostly they just shouted at us to bring their boots."

"Which of you would be major?" I asked curiously. The brothers looked much alike and were roughly the same age. I'd long thought them twins, but Grenville had told me they were not. Grenville did not know himself which was the elder and which the younger.

Bartholomew cleared up the matter. "Matthias is older," he said. He caught up one of my boots and leaned against the table to clean it. He spat on the leather and scrubbed busily with a brush. "But not by much. I popped up less than a year after he did. We have two more brothers, younger than us, about one year apart." He grinned. "Our mum and dad, they were much partial to each other."

I smiled, imagining the four brothers in a rough and tumble but happy household. "Ramsay is a normal boy, you'd say?"

"I wouldn't call any of the lads here *normal,* sir. Their fathers' arses are all planted on piles of money so high they must go dizzy. Ramsay's dad is rich as sneezes, they say. Like them Rothschilds."

"Ramsay is in this house, am I correct?" I inquired.

Bartholomew spat again, brushed vigorously. "Stands to reason. It's much easier for him to get up here to put a snake in your bed than if he were at Fairleigh."

"Do you think you could get your hands on young Ramsay? I'd like to ask him a few questions."

Bartholomew set down the boot. "Right now, sir?"

"Yes, unless he is meant to be doing something else. I do not wish to get the boy into trouble with Rutledge."

"You leave it to me, sir."

Bartholomew left the room, a spring in his step.

I envied his energy, and his youth. I had to say, however, that so far my stay in the country had been good for me. Riding each morning was beginning to harden my muscles again, and the fresh country air renewed my appetite, which had never been light to begin with. I liked it. I stared into the flames and contemplated the differences between life here and my life in London. I really ought to return to Norfolk, I thought. My home was there, and so were my memories.

My memories. Memories were why I had gone to London and not east and north to the fens when I had returned to England. There were certain memories I did not want to face in Norfolk, even after all these years. I felt them there, waiting for me. Here in Berkshire, on the border of Wiltshire, the tentacles of the memories were weaker. But I'd felt them even in India, strive as I might to break them off.

What I ought to do was return there with part of my new life, with a person who could banish the memories. Louisa Brandon could do that. She was stronger even than memories of my father and my deep boyish hurt when I'd realized as a child that he'd hated me. Louisa could look at me with her wise gray eyes, put her hand on mine, and say, "It does not matter any longer, Gabriel." And thus it would be true.

Of course, I could not be traveling to Norfolk any time soon. Here I was in Berkshire, earning money to stave off poverty, investigating vicious pranks and a murder. Norfolk, and memories, would have to wait.

Bartholomew was a long time in returning, so I rose

and limped across the room to refill my glass. I noted my boots positioned neatly on the floor. They had never been so shiny until Bartholomew had come to work for me. I'd had a batman in the army, but his idea of shining boots had been to bang off the mud and most of the dung and toss them into a corner. At the time I hadn't cared—they'd simply get muddy again.

I heard Bartholomew's tread in the hall as I sat down again. He opened the door and pushed young Ramsay inside with a beefy hand on the boy's shoulder. I greeted Ramsay and offered him a glass of claret.

He accepted. He walked quickly to the chair by the fire, seized the glass Bartholomew brought him and took a long gulp.

Ramsay minor was at the age of just before he would shoot into his full height and his voice would drop. He had very light brown hair and blue eyes and pale skin. He held his claret glass with a practiced air, but he did not relax.

"What is your other name, Ramsay?" I asked pleasantly. "The one your mother calls you?"

He assessed me over the rim of his glass. "Didius, sir."

"Didius," I mused. "Very Latin."

"Yes, sir."

"Nothing to be ashamed of. My Christian name is Gabriel. Very Biblical, I've always thought. I hope Bartholomew did not frighten you when he persuaded you to come to see me?"

Ramsay cast a glance at Bartholomew, who grinned back at him. The boys as a whole seemed to like Bartholomew, who was good-natured and friendly.

Bartholomew knew his place, at the same time offering his own brand of wisdom in his deferential way. He also towered at least six and a half feet high and had biceps that bulged and flexed in an alarming fashion. I'd spotted more than one boy feeling his own arms after seeing him.

"No, sir," Ramsay said.

"Good. Now, Mr. Ramsay, why did you decide I was a lover of reptiles?"

Ramsay jumped, looked guilt-stricken. "It was just a bit of fun, sir. You know."

I tried to sound reassuring, but had already realized, during my brief stay here, that I had no idea how to talk to boys. "I do know, Ramsay, I've been to school. How did you manage it? You have to walk right past Rutledge's sitting room to get to my stairs."

Ramsay's gaze went to the window. "Climbed the tree outside."

I was impressed. "And no one saw you?" My room overlooked a bleak hill that led to the canal. The path below was much frequented, and the boys played cricket in a field not far from the walls.

"It was dark already."

"Are you telling me you climbed up that tree, in the dark, carrying a snake?"

"Yes, sir."

I raised my glass. "I commend your ability and bravery. The snake did not frighten me, Ramsay."

"I know, sir."

I took a contemplative sip of wine. Ramsay did the same. "The other events here," I said slowly, "have not been quite as harmless."

Did I imagine a glint of apprehension in his eye? Or would any boy look so, while questioned by the secretary to the headmaster?

"No, sir."

He could not seem to drop the *sir*. Ramsay could have addressed me as he would other servants—by last name alone. Perhaps something in my air prompted the *sir*. My late father would have had apoplexy that Ramsay dared address me at all. The boy's family, despite their great wealth, were merchant class, their status below my family's landed gentry. My father would not have even spoken to Ramsay or his father had he met them. He would have snarled something about upstart burghers and crossed the street to get away from them. Even as he'd owed half the bankers and money-lenders in London, he had despised them.

"I will tell you the truth, Ramsay." I leaned forward, resting my elbows on my knees. "Rutledge has asked me to look into the pranks. But I am not Rutledge's toady. I will learn all I can, and then decide what to tell him."

"Yes, sir."

I could not discern whether he believed me or not. "Nor will I reveal to him the source of my information. So I wonder if you will tell me, what are your own opinions on the matter?"

Ramsay looked at me in surprise. I suppose he'd thought I was leading up to accusing him of the crimes. He took a fortifying drink of claret. "I really couldn't say, sir."

"I know you do not want to peach on your fellows, but I will keep anything you suggest to me in confidence. I am not certain how to convince you that is true, but I will give you my word, as a gentleman."

Ramsay looked doubtful. "Were you in the war, sir? Some of the lads said you were in the cavalry."

"In Portugal and Spain. Not at Waterloo."

Most people looked disappointed when I told them that. I had fought the entire savage war on the Iberian Peninsula, the six years we had pushed Napoleon from Spain, step by bloody step. But because I had quit the army and returned to London after Bonaparte's abdication, I could not wear the Waterloo cross and so was considered somewhat second-rate.

Ramsay, on the other hand, simply nodded. "My father says that the war was won because of English bankers, not soldiering." He paused, looked at my raised brow, and finished, "My father is an ass."

I strove not to laugh. "Arthur Wellesley was a fine general. He knew how to make the most of a situation and how to persevere with what he had. He set out to wear down Bonaparte, and he did it."

"Yes, sir."

"I beg your pardon, Ramsay, I did not mean to lecture. Well, if you do not have any views on the prankster, perhaps you do have views on the murder this morning."

Ramsay again looked startled. "It was horrible."

"It was. Do you, like all the others, believe it was Sebastian?"

Ramsay immediately shook his head. He did not even take time to think. "No, sir. I put the blame on Freddy Sutcliff."

I stared at him in surprise. Bartholomew, who was

brushing my clothes on the other side of the room and pretending not to listen, froze.

"Sutcliff?" I repeated. "The prefect?"

Ramsay nodded. "Yes, sir."

I thought about Frederick Sutcliff. He was tall, nearly as tall as I was, but with the thin, spidery look of a young man not yet grown into his body. A prefect was employed to keep the other boys in line when they weren't overseen by the house master. From what I had seen of Sutcliff, he'd used his post to become a brutal little tyrant.

"Does he have a violent nature?" I asked.

"I wouldn't have said so, no," Ramsay said. "Though he doesn't hesitate to box a chap's ears whenever he likes."

"What makes you think he killed Middleton? Murder is a bit different from boxing a chap's ears."

"Because I saw him, sir. He left the house last night and hightailed it toward Sudbury."

"He did, did he?" I asked, alert.

"Yes. I saw Middleton the groom leave the stables. He walked on the road, toward the village. Not long after, I saw Sutcliff go over the wall. He ran across country toward the road. To cut him off, like."

I grew excited. "Did you see them meet?"

"No. Too many trees in the way."

"Are you certain it was Sutcliff? Were you looking out of the window of your bed chamber? He must have been a long way from you if you watched him climb the wall."

Ramsay flushed. "I wasn't in my chamber." He tightened his lips, then decided to plunge in completely. "I was on the other side of the wall myself. I started to climb back, then I heard someone coming up on the school side. I hid in the brush. I saw Sutcliff vault over, then melt into the shadows. 'Twas him, all right."

"Interesting," I said. "And what were you doing on the other side of the wall, if I may ask?"

"Went to share a cheroot with some other lads. They started another, but I came back. Timson was one of them, and he was already drunk. He's disgusting enough when he's sober. He likes to rag on me, anyway."

I sat back, wondering. Sutcliff could have been pursuing his own business and might have nothing to do with Middleton. Or, he could have followed Middleton, as Ramsay thought. Why, I could not fathom. I would simply have to ask Sutcliff. I had difficulty imagining the lad killing the canny Middleton, but strange things happen. If nothing else, Sutcliff might have seen Middleton meeting with his killer without realizing what he'd seen.

"I appreciate your candor, Ramsay," I finished. "Bartholomew, would you bring the box that Grenville sent with me?"

Bartholomew, knowing what I wanted, grinned. He fished in a drawer of the writing table and came back with a polished box. Inside rested an assortment of small iced cakes that Grenville's chef had prepared before I'd left London. Grenville knew I did not have much of a sweet tooth, but Anton, the chef, had insisted I would waste away in the country if I did not have a box of cakes to help me between meals. Because Anton was a chef of fine caliber, I did not decline the offer.

I offered a cake now to Ramsay. "Take one," I said. "I guarantee it is better than Timson's cheroots."

"Did you say Grenville?" Ramsay asked, eyes wide. "Thank you, I must say. Mr. Grenville, he's . . . well, he's that famous, isn't he? In all the papers, and his caricature all over London."

"He is that famous," I answered. "Rutledge went to school with him."

Ramsay looked at me, wide-eyed. "S'truth! Must have been a dashed odd school, then, to turn out Mr. Grenville *and* the headmaster."

"It is a dashed odd school," I remarked. "It's called Eton."

He did not smile at my feeble joke. "As you say, sir."

I let it go. "Why does Timson rag on you, Ramsay? I've seen him. Looks a perfectly ordinary little devil to me, no better or worse than you."

Ramsay shrugged, unembarrassed. "Because my father is wealthy. Timson and his mates think I will buy my way to prefect, like Sutcliff. Not bloody likely. Sir."

"Did Sutcliff buy his way to prefect?"

"His father did. Sutcliff will have all his father's money once his father turns up trumps. Sutcliff reminds us every day."

"I see. A braggart."

"An awful one, sir." Ramsay reached in, snatched the topmost cake. "Thank you, sir. Sorry about the snake."

"No harm done." I snapped the box shut. "But no more of them."

Ramsay shook his head, clutching his precious pastry. "No, sir. I'll spread the word. You're not to be touched."

CHAPTER 5

❧

THE next morning, I received a letter from James
Denis. He briefly thanked me for telling him of
Middleton's death. He also asked that I furnish him
with the complete details of the inquest and anything I
discovered about the murder. He stressed that it was
most important. "Middleton sent me several letters
about the dangers there. Guard yourself."

I viewed the last sentences with surprise and some
mild annoyance. I agreed with Denis that danger lurked
here, and that blaming Sebastian for Middleton's death
was not the right solution. But I wished Denis had been
clearer about what dangers Middleton had hinted and
who I was to guard against.

I tossed his letter aside and opened one from
Grenville. Grenville professed amazement at the murder and asserted he wanted to come down as soon as he
could get away. He was distracted at the moment, he
said, by the disappearance of Marianne Simmons.

I stopped, brows rising. Marianne had lived upstairs from me in London for the first year or so I'd lived in rooms above a bake shop. She was an actress by trade, making her living treading the boards at Drury Lane. With her golden curls and childlike face, she also lived by enticing foolish gentlemen to give her more money than they should.

Grenville himself had given her money; in total, twenty gold guineas, though I tried to tell him not to waste his coin. A few months ago, Grenville had taken Marianne from Grimpen Lane and deposited her in a gilded cage on Clarges Street, a fine Mayfair address. He'd given her every luxury, but she'd chafed at her confinement and had amused herself by torturing him.

Now, it seemed, she'd broken out of the cage and flown. Grenville wrote of it in terse sentences. She had disappeared a few days before. He had searched, but had not found her. He had decided to hire a Bow Street Runner.

I blew out my breath, picked up a pen, and prepared to write back that he should not do such a damn fool thing.

I hesitated. It was not my business. I was not terribly worried for Marianne's safety; she had often vanished from her rooms for weeks at a time and returned without any harm done. If Grenville hired a Runner to drag Marianne home, she would simply leave again and find a more clever way of escaping. This was a game he could not win.

Why he was so adamant on keeping her confined, I could not understand. Grenville was usually the most rational of gentlemen, but where Marianne was concerned, he had certainly lost his head.

I turned his letter over and wrote on the back, "Let her go. It can only do you harm if you find her. Your motives are the best, I know, but you cannot bind her if she does not want to be bound."

I knew Grenville would not want to read those words or heed them, but I wrote them for what it was worth.

As I sealed the letter, I remembered something that I'd pushed to the back of my mind. A few days ago, during my morning ride, I had taken the horse as far as Hungerford. At the end of the High Street, I had seen a woman who'd looked remarkably like Marianne duck back inside a house. At the time, I'd thought nothing of it, believing Marianne safely in London with Grenville.

Hungerford would certainly be a place to hide from Grenville. But why should she hide herself here in the country, so close to the Sudbury School, where she knew I'd gone? I had assumed, and apparently Grenville did too, that she'd gone to visit a man. I was in all likelihood mistaken about the woman I saw, though it could not hurt to discover whether I was in error.

My next letter was from Lady Breckenridge. I opened it carefully, as though it might sting me, and well it might. Lady Breckenridge's letters to me so far had been filled with barbed witticisms about various members of the *haut ton*. The letters amused me—I shared many of her opinions—but they did leave me to wonder what barbed witticisms she made about me in my absence.

This letter urged me to cease praising the beauty of the Berkshire countryside and write of something more interesting. "Really, Lacey, you are a man of intellect, and what's better, common sense, and yet, you address me as though I were an inane debutante who would want to hurry down and do a watercolor of the place. Amuse me with anecdotes of the silly things country people and merchant schoolboys get up to, for heaven's sake."

As usual, with Lady Breckenridge, I did not know whether to laugh or grow irritated. Donata Breckenridge was thirty, black-haired, blue-eyed, and sharp-tongued. I had disliked her when I first met her—over a billiards game in Kent—but she had rendered me assistance during the affair of the Glass House not a month ago. I'd come to see that she could be kind-hearted beneath her acid observations. I had also kissed her, and the memory of that was not disagreeable.

I laid her letter aside, reflecting that she might find news of the murder a little less inane than my descriptions of country meadows.

I had left the next letter for last. Louisa Brandon had not yet written me since I'd arrived in Sudbury, though I had written her twice, and I'd feared she would not correspond with me at all. But now she had—three thick sheets full of her slanted writing.

I broke the seal, sat back in my chair, and prepared to savor every word.

I was still savoring the letter later, when I rode my usual horse to Sudbury for the inquest that afternoon. Louisa had said nothing out of the ordinary, nothing that one acquaintance might not say to another. She'd described a tedious supper she'd attended with her husband with veterans from the Peninsular War, "during which the colonels congratulated one another on the depth of the dung they had stood in and the viciousness of the flies that had bit them while they waited for the French to shoot at them."

I smiled. I could imagine Louisa politely containing her boredom, while the retired officers relived the hardships of the Peninsula as though it had been the finest of holidays. The more venomously they'd complained at the time, the louder the laughter and the longer the reminiscences would be. Poor Louisa.

She'd said little more than that. Only that she'd shopped and gossiped with Lady Aline and visited a girl called Black Nancy, who was doing fine as a maid in an inn near Islington.

She apologized for going on about trivial matters that would bore a gentleman, but I imbibed every word as though they were the finest brandy. This is what I wanted with Louisa, the small things, the friendly discussion, the sharing of lives. What she termed trivial, I called pleasure beyond price.

The inquest for Middleton was held at the magistrate's house in Sudbury, a fairly large brick dwelling half a mile on the other side of the village. Behind it a slope of damp green ran down to brush that lined the canal.

We sat in a large hall in the middle of the house, almost a square room with benches all around. The coroner sat on a landing a few steps up from the rest of us, the magistrate next to him. The magistrate reminded me of Squire Allworthy in Henry Fielding's humorous novel *Tom Jones*; he was rotund, with a pink and benevolent face.

I learned quickly that the magistrate's flesh did not house a warmhearted being but a man slightly harassed that he had a murder on his hands.

The coroner, who was thin and cadaverous, the opposite of the magistrate, called the proceedings to order. Rutledge, looking annoyed that he'd been pulled from the important business of running the school, identified the body as Oliver Middleton, who had come to work in his stables six months before.

The coroner had examined the corpse, he said, as had the local doctor. The coroner announced that Middleton had met his death from a knife across his windpipe, and then he had been pushed into the lock, where he had lain underwater for some time, four hours at the very least. The coroner could not be certain how long Middleton had actually been dead, but certainly no more than eight hours before he'd been found.

Since Sebastian had told me he'd been speaking to him at ten o'clock, and Middleton had been found at six o'clock in the morning, this information did not seem particularly helpful.

According to the stable hands, Middleton had left the stable yard about ten o'clock Sunday evening and said that he was off to Sudbury and the tavern. The landlord of the tavern stood up and told the coroner what he'd told me, that Middleton had never arrived.

"Very well." The coroner looked vacantly about the room. "Where is the man who found the body?"

The lockkeeper shuffled forward and said in his taciturn way that he had gone out to open the lock for an early barge about six o'clock. He'd seen the dead body, recognized Middleton, sent word up to the school, and sent for the constable. They'd tried to fish the body out, then decided to send the barge through and drag Middleton out with it, as I had witnessed.

The coroner called Sebastian next.

Every person in the room craned to watch Sebastian walk forward. He looked pale, but otherwise well. In fact, he seemed relieved to be here in this open hall, out of his prison, no matter what happened to him.

Belinda Rutledge had not attended the inquest. I assumed her father had forbidden her to come, something I would have done in his place. A coroner's inquest was no place for a young girl, and she might have betrayed herself in agitation over Sebastian.

"Your name is Sebastian?" the coroner began. The magistrate next to him leaned forward, like a bull lowering its head, and watched.

"Sebastian D'Arby," Sebastian answered, his voice subdued.

The coroner gave him a sharp glance, as though not believing he had a surname at all. "You were employed by the Sudbury School to assist in the stables?"

"Yes."

The coroner looked annoyed that he'd not appended a *sir* to the *yes*. "No doubt the residents of the Sudbury School were pleased to know that a Romany was looking after their horses," he said.

A titter ran through the room. Many people considered the Roma criminals simply for existing, and most believed they were horse thieves. Sebastian did not smile. "I am good with the horses."

"Yes, yes, of course you are. Tell me, did you get along with Mr. Middleton and the other stable hands?"

"Well enough."

The coroner moved a sheet of paper. "And yet, one of the stable lads reported to the constable that he had heard you and Middleton arguing, quite loudly, just before Middleton left the stables that night."

Sebastian stared. I stared as well. Sebastian had mentioned no quarrel with Middleton, and I had not heard that any of the stable hands had witnessed such a quarrel. I wondered where the coroner had obtained this information.

I waited, suddenly uncomfortable. If Sebastian had lied to me, I could not help him.

"He makes a mistake," Sebastian said weakly.

The coroner looked displeased. "Mr. Middleton left the stables at about ten o'clock," the coroner went on. "Said he was heading for the public house in Sudbury. At a little past ten, you yourself left the stables, according to the other lads. Where did you go?"

Sebastian wet his lips. His black hair glistened in the chunk of sunlight that slanted through a tall window. "I went for a walk. Along the canal."

"Along the canal. In which direction?"

"South. Toward Great Bedwyn."

"And you returned, according to your statement, at two o'clock?"

"Yes."

"A long walk, Mr. . . . er . . . D'Arby, wouldn't you say?"

"I visited my family."

"Yes, so you said. Interesting that the constable has

not been able to find a trace of your family, on the canal or off it."

Sebastian's eyes flickered. "They move all the time. They could be in Bath by now."

"Be assured, we are still looking. Now, did anyone see you on this walk? Did you speak to anyone who would remember you walking about between the hours of ten and two?"

Sebastian glanced once at me. I kept my expression neutral. "I saw no one."

The coroner looked pleased. "And so you walked back to the stables and went to bed."

"Yes. And rose in the morning as usual."

"Whereupon you learned of the death—yes, you told the constable." He shuffled papers again. "When you walked along the canal, did you go anywhere near Lower Sudbury Lock?"

Sebastian looked startled. "Of course. I had to walk past it to reach the stables."

"And you saw nothing amiss?"

"No."

"Very well, Mr. D'Arby, you may sit down."

The room rustled as listeners stirred and whispered to their neighbors. The coroner took his time about calling the next witness, giving everyone, including the jury, plenty of time to speculate.

The next witness proved to be the stable hand called Thomas Adams, who claimed he'd heard an argument between Sebastian and Middleton. "Tell us, in your own time, Mr. Adams, what you heard when the gypsy and Mr. Middleton argued," the coroner said smoothly.

The stable hand was about fifty years old with iron-gray hair. He looked uncomfortable standing up in front of the coroner and magistrate as well as the rest of the men crowded into the hall. "I was just going up the stairs to me bed, in the loft," he said, carefully pronouncing each word. "I heard Middleton down in the stable yard, shouting. He said, 'I don't care what you do, I'm quit of you.' Then the other fellow said, 'Where are you going?' Middleton, he says, 'Down pub. Where I can drink with real men.'" Thomas cleared his throat, looked nervously at the magistrate. "Then the Romany man, he says, 'No, you're going to hell.'"

The coroner perked up. "And what did Mr. Middleton say to that?"

Thomas looked apologetic. "Mr. Middleton said, in so many words, that Sebastian should fornicate himself. A might more vulgar than that, you understand, sir."

The coroner nodded. "And then?"

"Middleton stormed across the yard and out of the gate to the lane. A few minutes later, I see Sebastian also let himself out the gate. I figured they would shout at each other all the way to Sudbury, and I went to bed."

The coroner nodded and dismissed him. As the man shuffled back to his bench, Sebastian sprang to his feet. "He is lying. I never said these things to Mr. Middleton. I never shouted at him."

"Mr. D'Arby, you have had time to tell your story. Sit down."

Sebastian remained standing, quivering. Several of the jury looked alarmed. I caught his eye, made a *sit down, for God's sake* motion with my hand. Sebastian saw me, lowered himself reluctantly to the bench once again.

The coroner turned to the jury. "Now, gentleman," he began.

He was finished. No more witnesses. The coroner, I could see, had made up his mind. I rose to my feet. "May I speak?"

The coroner looked at me, surprised and slightly irritated. "Yes, Mr. . . ." he peered at me shortsightedly, realized he did not know me.

"Captain," I said. "Captain Lacey."

"Yes, Captain Lacey?"

"I would like to point out that I knew this man, Middleton, in London. He used to work for a gentleman called James Denis."

I do not know what I expected. Gasps, perhaps. The magistrate and the coroner simply looked at me.

Rutledge, on the other hand, reacted. He flushed until his face grew mottled, his brows thunderous.

"And how long ago was this?" the magistrate asked.

"Before he came here. Last summer, at the least."

"Last summer? Eight months ago? I beg your pardon, Captain, but I hardly understand how can it be connected with what happened here."

"This Mr. Denis is a dangerous man," I said. "I am suggesting that a connection in London, possibly one through Denis, caused Middleton's death. Perhaps some person followed him down here from London and killed him."

The coroner considered this. He took his time. "And why do you suppose that this person, whoever he is, waited eight months?"

"I have no idea," I said. "It is merely a suggestion."

"A suggestion." The coroner wrote something on the ivory colored paper before him. "And I have noted it. Thank you, Captain."

He turned his back and prepared to address the jury. I remained standing a few seconds longer, then realized there was no point. I sat down as the coroner began his summing up and instructing the gentlemen on their duty.

I waited in the chill room with everyone else while the jury conferred in low voices in a corner. I felt Rutledge's glare on me, but I did not acknowledge him. I simply coughed into my handkerchief, the dampness getting the better of me.

The jury at last returned, and their verdict was no surprise. They found that Oliver Middleton, head groom to the stables of the Sudbury School, had been deliberately murdered, and they named Sebastian D'Arby, a Romany, as the one who should be examined by the magistrate for the crime.

The constable came for him. Sebastian, on his feet, clenched his fists and shouted, "I did not kill him. I did not!"

The constable and another large man subdued him and led him away. The magistrate would try him, and very probably hold him until the assizes, where he would face a criminal trial. The inquest was at an end.

CHAPTER 6

❦

I found myself plagued on all sides the rest of that day and into the next. I rode back to the school, annoyed at what I'd learned at the inquest, that Sebastian had quarreled with Middleton. I wondered why Sebastian had omitted this crucial fact when he'd told me his story, and I wondered why I had not heard the stable hands speaking of it. I supposed the stable hand could have invented the quarrel—Sebastian had seemed surprised and adamant that it had not happened. But why should the man, Thomas Adams, invent the altercation? I had no answer. I also had no satisfactory answer as to why Sebastian had not told me of it.

My thoughts bothered me, and so I was in no frame of mind to contend with all that came next.

The first plague to set upon me was Rutledge. As soon as I entered the quad after leaving my horse at the stables, Rutledge bellowed to me.

I forced myself to turn and meet him. He came striding through the gate, plowing through boys in their dark robes like a cat scattering sparrows. He stepped up to me and spoke in thunderous tones.

"Damn you, Lacey, why did you not tell me about James Denis?"

I sensed the lads' curious stares all around us. I said to him, "Perhaps we should speak of this privately."

Rutledge opened his mouth to roar again, but just then young Timson strolled by, his mild brown eyes fixed on us with obvious interest. Rutledge noted him, snapped his mouth shut, and commanded me to follow him to his rooms.

Once in the study, Rutledge commenced shouting. I sat down, relaxing my stiff leg, and balanced my sword stick across my knees. I waited until he ran out of breath before I attempted to speak.

I said, "I had not met Middleton here until this Sunday afternoon. And I could not be certain he was the same man I'd seen in London. Before I had time to discover anything, he was dead."

"You ought to have come to me at once," Rutledge growled. "How did you know him in London? Were you in league with the man?"

"I did not *know* Middleton in any sense," I said impatiently. "I had seen him during my dealings with James Denis. That is all."

Rutledge's face grew still redder. "James Denis is not a gentleman with whom another gentleman has dealings. That you do speaks volumes. I cannot fathom why Grenville never mentioned this. He has sorely deceived me."

"Perhaps he did not think it relevant," I said.

"Not relevant? Denis is . . ." He spluttered. "He has a foul reputation. No one can deal with him and maintain his respectability. Why the devil did you seek him out?"

"I did not," I said. "He came to me. You flatter me if you believe I can afford his services."

"He came to you?" Rutledge gave me an incredulous look. "Explain what you mean."

"I cannot explain. He has assisted me in several small ways and sometimes requests my assistance. I avoid the man as much as possible, believe me."

"He asks for *your* assistance?" Rutledge exclaimed.

"Yes."

In fact, Denis had once told me, in his cold, calm way, that he wanted to own me utterly. He wanted me in his power, under his obligation, wanted me bound to him. Needless to say, I resisted with all my might. Still, he had manipulated me more than once to do what he wanted. It was a tense game between us.

Rutledge was looking at me as though he needed to reassess me. The look in his eye, I was delighted to see, was one of trepidation, almost fear. I wondered very much whether he had crossed James Denis in the past.

Rutledge did not press me. He told me to go away in his usual irritable manner, but his tone was wary.

MY second plague was Belinda Rutledge. She accosted me, or rather her maid Bridgett did, and bade me follow her.

Bridgett led me up several flights of stairs to a darkened hall, the servants' quarters, I surmised. She took me to a servant's room containing two plain bedsteads and a washstand.

Belinda sat on one of the beds. She rose when I entered. Her eyes were red and puffy, her face wet.

"Miss Rutledge," I began, trying to sound severe. Her insistence on meeting me in clandestine places would not help matters.

"They arrested him." She sniffled. "They arrested him, Captain. You said you would help him."

I grew irritated. "I cannot simply make the coroner or the magistrate do as I like, Miss Rutledge."

She looked at me, wide-eyed, then her face crumpled.

I tamped down my annoyance and gentled my voice. "I told you that I would assist you, and I will. I am putting things in motion even now. I assure you that we will have him free before the assizes."

My voice rang with confidence, but even I did not much believe it.

"He cannot bear to be confined," she whispered.

"I know. But you and he must be patient. I have friends in London who can help."

"My father wants him hanged. He hates Sebastian."

I had to admit that had Sebastian cast his eyes at my daughter, my attitude toward him would not be as benign as it was currently.

"Many do not like the Roma, Miss Rutledge. You must be prepared for that." I paused. "I suggest that even when I do get him released, you steel yourself to send him away."

She looked up at me, eyes wide, tears on her face. I saw, though, behind her immediate pain and worry, that she knew I was right. Though Belinda was downtrodden by her father, she was not stupid. She knew that an association with Sebastian would ruin her. Her hesitation in sending him away would only put off the inevitable.

"Think hard on it," I said. "Imagine yourself at my ancient age and decide what would have been best."

She sniffled again, gave me a watery smile. "You are not ancient, Captain."

I would have been flattered, had I not suspected she spoke out of pity. "I will do what I can, Miss Rutledge. And I will let you know of any outcome. Do not seek me out again. Your father will not like it."

Her misery returned. "It is difficult to wait and do nothing."

"Yes, but it must be done." I made her a bow. "Good afternoon."

Bridgett made to lead me back downstairs again, but I told her I'd find the way. I left her to comfort Belinda and made my way back to the lower floors.

Boys were pouring up the east staircase when I strolled down it. I spied Sutcliff the prefect giving a dressing down to one of the younger boys, who listened in sullen resentment.

Sutcliff, turning away, saw me, and gave me a curious look. Then he moved his lanky shoulders and swung away down the hall, his black robe billowing behind him. I had not forgotten Ramsay's conviction that Sutcliff had followed Middleton the night of the murder. I wanted to speak to him and moved to follow but I lost sight of him in the sea of boys.

• • •

THE third plague did not come upon me until the next morning. I woke early, determined to continue my investigations. I wanted to find Sutcliff and ask him why he'd followed Middleton—if indeed, Ramsay had been correct. I wanted to find Sebastian's elusive family, and I wanted to question the stable hand Thomas Adams myself about the quarrel he'd overheard.

I downed some bread and coffee and set off for the stables through a thick white fog. Thomas Adams was not in the yard when I arrived. A younger stable hand was there to help me saddle the brown gelding I usually rode.

"Did you hear them?" I asked him. "Middleton and Sebastian arguing?"

The young man looked phlegmatic and shook his head. "I was round t'other side. Drawing water. Didn't hear a word."

I questioned the other two stable hands, but they, too, had not heard the quarrel, neither of them having been in the yard at the time.

I gave up, mounted my horse, and rode off.

The fog became denser as I approached the canal, but the towpath was clear. I followed this path past the Sudbury lock and the lockkeeper's house. The lockkeeper was just opening the gates for a barge heading south, toward Bath. Several men stood on the deck of the narrow barge, but they were not Roma, not Sebastian's family.

The countryside was quiet, the muddy path muffling my horse's footsteps. The silent canal flowed on my right, high hedges and trees lined the path to my left. Sometimes the hedges broke, allowing me to glimpse green fields brushed by tendrils of fog. Sheep wandered across the greens, trailed by spring lambs.

As I neared Great Bedwyn, the trees became larger and more evenly spaced, the terrain flattening somewhat. I began to pass boats drifting up from Great and Little Bedwyn, the bargemen and their families continuing their journey toward Reading and the Thames.

When I reached Great Bedwyn, I saw, on a flat path on the other side of the canal, the woman I'd seen in Hungerford, the one I'd mistaken for Marianne. She wore a bonnet, and her head was bent so that I could not see her face. The gathered curls at the back of her neck were bright yellow, and her dress was fine, too fine for muddy walks through the Wiltshire countryside.

At the next bridge, I turned the horse across the canal and urged him into a trot. The woman glanced over her shoulder and saw me. She hurried off the road and into a stand of trees.

Marianne or not, her mysterious behavior intrigued me. I slowed my horse and ducked under the trees. There were enough saplings and overgrown brush here to make going precarious. I quickly spied the woman, and she spied me. She broke into a run.

"Stop," I called. "You will injure yourself."

She did stop. She stooped to the ground, dropping her basket. She came up, her hands full of mud and pebbles, and she flung them at me.

I swore. The horse, struck in the face, bucked and bolted. I strove to hold him, but my injured leg gave, too weak to help me. I lost my balance and fell heavily to the ground.

I found myself on my back, the wind knocked out of me. The horse trotted off, empty-saddled, my walking stick hanging from its pommel. As I struggled for breath, the woman loomed over me, her hands filthy, her eyes wide with alarm.

"For God's sake, Marianne," I gasped.

Under the bonnet, Marianne Simmons' doll-like face was as sharp as ever, her pretty eyes wary. "Lacey! What are you doing here?"

I pushed myself into a sitting position. My left leg throbbed and hurt. "I ought to be asking you that. I have taken employment at Sudbury. Did you not know?"

"Yes," she snapped. "I have heard the full details from *him*. I thought that if I bought myself a deep bonnet and only went about in the small hours of the morning, I could avoid you. I might have known."

"Why should you avoid me?" I demanded. "And why should you be here at all?"

She looked away. "I have told you so many times, Lacey, it is none of your business where I go and what I do."

"At least assist me to rise, please. Else I'll have to crawl all the way back to Sudbury, to the ruination of my trousers."

"They are already ruined," she said, unsympathetic. But she reached down to help me stand.

Once I was on my feet she said, almost contrite, "I would not have flung the mud if I'd known the horse would throw you. I thought I'd killed you for a moment."

"He did not throw me," I said. "I fell off."

"There is a difference?"

"Yes."

Even a very good horseman could be thrown by an unruly horse; an incompetent one simply toppled off. The horse had not been that frightened.

"I will have to lean on you," I said.

"Oh, very well." She retrieved her basket and allowed me to drape my arm across her shoulders. Surprisingly, she snaked her arm about my waist, supporting me while I hobbled painfully out of the trees and back toward the path. My horse, sadly, was nowhere in sight.

"I suppose you will rush home and write to *him* of this," Marianne said. Her words were muffled by the huge bonnet. "And tell him where I am."

"I do not report to Grenville," I said. "He will arrive in Sudbury soon in any case, because he wants to know all about the murder."

"Yes, I heard of it, and of the arrest of the Romany. My landlady in Hungerford speaks of nothing else."

"Things are not as straightforward as the landlady in Hungerford believes." I glanced down at her. "Did you walk all the way here from Hungerford? I must ask why."

"To confuse you," she said.

I professed myself confused. "Grenville is worried about you. He is on the verge of hiring a Runner to look for you. He will likely choose Pomeroy, my former sergeant. Your fate is sealed if that is the case."

She stopped walking, her eyes sparkling with anger. "I will return to London and to him when my business is finished. Why can he not let me be?"

I tried to mollify her. "I do agree that he should not try to keep you confined. But I must wonder, Marianne. He has been kind to you. In return, you treat him callously. He is a very powerful man, and he could make your life miserable if he chose."

"He treats *you* kindly," she said. "And some days you can barely bring yourself to be polite to him."

I had to acknowledge that. "He does like to control people and events, I admit. But at least he is benevolent."

"Is it benevolence?" she almost spat. "To have me dragged back to London by Bow Street? What happens if he decides to bring suit against me—accuse me of stealing from him or—or perhaps he'll force me to pay for the house and the clothes and the meals he's given me."

"I very much doubt that," I began, then broke off. I'd seen Grenville angry only a few times. He was a man who held himself in check, hiding his emotions behind a cool facade. His sangfroid made him enviable, and even feared, among the *haut ton*—a gentleman could lose the respect of others forever at one quirk of Grenville's eyebrow. I held such power in disdain, but I could not deny that he had it.

"You see." Marianne looked triumphant. "You cannot be certain what he will do. You must help me."

"Tell me what you are doing here."

"Damnation, Lacey."

My exasperation rose. "My help has been begged in the past several days by people who refuse to tell me the truth. If I am to assist, I must have complete candor. That is my price."

She glared at me. "And I could simply leave you here to take root in this meadow."

"Marianne, Grenville will hire a Runner, though I advised him not to. I imagine he has done so already."

Marianne bit her lip. I had never seen her look so anguished, not even when I'd spoken to her in Grenville's house a few weeks ago, where he had more or less confined her and assigned a maid and a footman to dog her footsteps. She'd been angry then, but now, she looked frightened. "I am not certain I can trust you."

I hid a sigh. "You will have to trust me. Who are you in Berkshire to meet? A man?"

"No. I've told you."

I shook my head. "You quite baffle me, Marianne. Any money Grenville has given you has disappeared with nothing to show for it. If you do not give it to a man, what becomes of it?"

She held up her hand. "Stop. Cease questioning me. I am not certain what to do. I must think."

She was trembling. I tried to conjure sympathy for her, and I really did wish to help her. Marianne struggled through life even more than I did. Grenville had offered to become her protector, to give her every luxury, but she fought him. Marianne loved her freedom, even if it brought her penury.

We walked for a while in silence. The path led behind the hedges and trees that screened us from the canal. I wished we could come upon a bridge over which to cross back to the towpath, which would be much easier to traverse. The track on this side was little used and often plunged right into undergrowth.

Marianne was lost in thought, and so was I, so nei-

ther of us at first heard the curious drone that came
from behind a clump of brush. When I did hear it, I
stopped, puzzled.

Marianne gave me an impatient look. I stepped away
from her, walked a little off the track, and parted the
grasses. I froze.

"Whatever is the matter, Lacey?" Marianne asked. I
heard her behind me, then she peered past me, and
gasped.

A horde of flies and other insects buzzed about a
knife that was half-buried in the grass. It was long and
serrated, the kind a butcher might use to cut up a car-
cass. The blade and the mud and grasses around it were
caked with brown stains. The flies swarmed around it
all.

I looked up. The canal was not five feet away, but
thick scrub and trees screened it from view. We were
perhaps half a mile from Sudbury in one direction, and
half a mile from Lower Sudbury Lock. "Middleton was
killed here," I breathed.

Marianne's hand went to her mouth. She looked
green. "How awful."

I reached down and lifted the knife. I had no doubt
that Middleton's lifeblood stained it. The killer had
lured him here. Or—thinking of Middleton's past—
perhaps Middleton had been the one who lured his
killer to this spot, then the tables had turned.

Ramsay had told me that Sutcliff had run after Middleton in order to meet him on the road to the village.
But this spot was in the opposite direction, south of the
lock. What had made Middleton come this way?

The brush was much broken here. I stepped over the

bloodstained grass and slipped and slid down to the bank of the canal.

A barge was drifting past the far bank, on its way to Lower Sudbury Lock. The man at the tiller stared at me curiously as I came plunging out of the brush, but lifted his hand in a courteous greeting.

I waved back, but my heart was beating excitedly. No wonder we'd found no signs of the body having been dragged through grass or mud near the Lower Sudbury Lock.

"He was taken to the lock in a boat," I announced to Marianne.

Marianne looked puzzled. "You mean a bargeman obligingly gave a murderer and his corpse a ride to the lock? Or do you think he was murdered by a bargeman himself?"

I climbed back to her. "Not a barge. A rowboat. There are ample places to tie a rowboat at the bank. The man murdered Middleton, tipped the body onto his boat, rowed up the canal, and heaved him into the lock. Then he could row back down to Great Bedwyn, hide the boat, and go about his business, or even portage around the locks so the keepers would not see him. He could be far, far away by now."

Marianne gave me her hand to help me to the top of the bank. "Surely someone would have noticed."

"Not in the middle of the night. It would be dark as pitch along here. Most barges tie up for the night near towns, not out here. This stretch would have been empty, and were it foggy, I doubt that anyone would even see a boat go past. No, he had perfect cover."

Marianne's face was still white. "It is gruesome."

"I know." I wrapped the knife in my handkerchief. "I must take this to the magistrate in Sudbury."

"Which you could do if I hadn't frightened away your horse," she said, looking chagrined.

"If I'd been on horseback, I'd never have found this spot."

I borrowed Marianne's handkerchief, tied it to the closest tree to mark the place, and then we resumed our slow progress up the trail.

"Why would he not take the knife away with him?" she asked as we made our way along. "If he took such trouble to remove the corpse, why not the knife?"

I considered. "Perhaps he was too agitated. Or perhaps he dropped it in the dark and could not find it. But do you see, Marianne, no matter what he did with the knife, that the rowboat is significant?"

"The rowboat you think he used," Marianne corrected me. "Why should it be significant? "

"Because it means that the meeting was planned. They either rowed here together, or they met here. It is unlikely anyone would chance upon each other in this bleak spot in the middle of the night. The boat was brought so that the murderer could get away without leaving a trail."

"I suppose," Marianne said doubtfully.

"Middleton did not meet a man on the road, quarrel with him, and fight to a deadly end. This knife is large—it's a butcher's knife, not a paper knife or a cutting knife that a man might just happen to have in his pocket. Someone fetched it specially. Just as they fetched the rowboat specially. So you see," I finished, "the murder was thought out, not done on the spur of the moment. That means that the idea that it was a continuation of Sebastian's quarrel with Middleton in the stable yard will not wash."

Marianne raised her brows. "You sound certain."

"I am certain. Someone who knew Middleton, wanted him dead. Someone he was not afraid to meet in the dark on the side of the canal."

"He was a fool then," Marianne observed.

"He was not afraid. But perhaps, working for James Denis, he'd become confident that he could face any man who challenged him."

Marianne shook her head. "The Romany man could have done it, Lacey. Easy for him to steal a boat and a knife and arrange the meeting."

I disagreed. "Sebastian is big and strong and young. Even Middleton might think twice about confronting him alone in an isolated spot. Besides, they worked in the stables together—why would Middleton agree to meet somewhere else in the middle of the night? No, it was someone who did not want to be seen at the stables, and someone Middleton considered weak." My heart chilled as I spoke the words. "Such as one of the students."

"Or a tutor," Marianne said. "I've seen some of them. They look a bit spindly and colorless."

"Or a tutor," I glumly agreed.

"But would a lad or a spindly tutor have been strong enough to kill him?"

"Possibly, if they took him by surprise. The boat points to a person not as strong as Middleton. That person already knew he could not carry the corpse away, and so provided the boat."

"You are on flights of fancy, Lacey," Marianne said skeptically. "Why not simply slide the body into the canal and have done?"

"To point attention away from the spot, perhaps to incriminate someone else. The lockkeeper, for instance, is a large and strong man. The body is found in the lock—there is the strong lockkeeper living next to it. Probably the constable was supposed to suspect him. But Rutledge muddied things by insisting that Sebastian had committed the crime."

Marianne did not answer, merely kept her head bent, her gaze on the trail. When we at last turned onto the narrow track that passed the lockkeeper's house and led to the stables and the school, Marianne stopped.

I looked at her. "You will come no farther?"

"No, thank you."

She looked so downcast, so worried, that I wanted to pat her shoulder, but I knew she would not accept such a thing. "Grenville will be here soon," I said. "You must decide whether you will let him see you, and what you will tell him. If you wish to speak to me of it, or wish me to help you, send word to me.

"It is not a simple matter, Lacey."

"I see that."

She gave me a belligerent look. "I know you will tell him. You are loyal to him. Why should you be loyal to me?"

"Marianne," I said impatiently. I was much more interested at the moment in getting the knife to the magistrate than in her feud with Grenville. "I am beginning to believe that you and Grenville are a pair of fools. I give you my word I will say nothing to him until you give me leave. But I wish you would confide in him. It would, at the very least, make things more comfortable for me."

Her glance turned ironic. "And certainly I wish nothing more than to make you comfortable." She sighed. "I will send for you . . . perhaps."

She began to walk away.

"Where do you lodge?" I called after her.

She turned to face me, walking backward a few steps.

"Shan't tell you."

She swung around again, skirts swirling, and tramped on toward the canal.

I found my horse, the sensible beast, in the stable yard. Thomas, the stable hand, was just pulling off the saddle.

"One moment," I said. "I must ride on to Sudbury."

Thomas blinked once, twice, then fastened the saddle back in place without a word. I was in a hurry, but I took the time to ask Thomas about the quarrel he claimed he'd overheard between Middleton and Sebastian.

"It were him," he insisted, when I suggested he'd been mistaken.

"Where were you standing?"

Thomas pointed. At the end of the yard, a door led to a tiny hall and a stone staircase that led to the rooms over the stables. A small window broke the wall above the door. I peered at the dusty pane which overlooked the yard below.

"They stood by the gate," Thomas said, motioning across the yard. "Shouting. Could hear them clear as day."

"It was dark. You could not have *seen* them clear as day."

Thomas looked impatient. "Mr. Middleton was tall, wann't he? So is Sebastian. The tallest men in the stables. No mistake."

He was certain. I knew a suggestion that it had been another tall man, not Sebastian, would not be welcomed. I let it go and had him boost me onto the horse.

I rode to Sudbury and the magistrate's house. He and the constable were as excited as I to see the knife and hear what I'd told them about the spot near the canal. We went together back to the place I'd marked, the constable on foot, the magistrate driving himself in a one-horse cart.

The two men speculated over the crushed, blood-stained grass, and I showed them exactly where I'd found the knife. I told them my theory that the murderer had taken the body up the canal in a small boat. They were less inclined to believe that, but agreed that they could see no evidence that the body had gotten into the lock any other way.

They also agreed with me that the knife was made for butchering or cutting up meat for cooking. The constable was given the task of wandering through Sudbury and the nearby villages inquiring who had lost a knife.

I could do little more than point them to the spot and tell them what I thought. They were much interested in the area, less so in my opinions.

I left them, rode back to the stables, deposited my horse with the lads, retrieved my walking stick, and made my way back to the school.

When I reached the quad, I found commotion. The morning was fully upon us, light flooding over the eastern wing of the Head Master's house. In the middle of the quad stood Simon Fletcher. His brown hair was awry, his robe kilted back on his shoulders. He stared down at what lay in the middle of the circle of curious boys.

It was a pile of books, Fletcher's, I guessed by the look on his face. They were charred and still smoldering. The wind stirred sparks that whirled in tiny, bright flashes.

On the cobbles next to the pile of books was a placard, ill-printed, containing a foul-worded invective against boys learning Latin.

Fletcher lifted an anguished gaze to me. "My books," he mourned. "My entire library. Gone. I'll never replace them."

He kicked aside a scorched tome, scattering sparks and blackened paper.

At that moment a cultured, well-bred voice said coolly from the arched portico, "Good lord. Have I arrived at a bad time?"

CHAPTER 7

GRENVILLE'S sudden arrival provided a better diversion for the boys than a pile of burned books. They swarmed out to his traveling coach, marveling at its polished sides and mahogany inlay, the perfectly matched horses, his coachman in fine livery.

Grenville himself looked slightly alarmed as the gangly youths rushed past him. He dabbed his lips with a handkerchief and strove to maintain his mask of sangfroid. I saw, however, that his cheeks were pale and his eyelids waxy, and I knew that the journey from London had brought on his motion sickness.

"You need brandy," I remarked.

"Good of you to notice." His dark eyes took in the quad, Fletcher wringing his hands, the scattering of charred books. "What has happened? Where is Rutledge?"

"I imagine he will charge along any moment now," I murmured.

I was not wrong. Rutledge emerged from his house just then, Sutcliff at his side. He swept his gaze over the tableau, assessed the situation, and stormed to the middle of the quad. "Bloody hell, Fletcher."

"Ruined," Fletcher moaned. "I can never afford to replace them all."

Rutledge gazed at him in baffled outrage. "Are you telling me, man, that you never noticed somebody carting off a load of your books and setting them alight? Or were you off at the tavern nursing your day's dozen pints?"

"I was having breakfast in the hall," Fletcher said, thin-lipped. "We heard shouting in the quad. We came out. Found this." He gestured at the pile of books.

I looked at the sad heap on the stones, a light rain hissing on the smoldering pages. The books lay haphazardly, some having skittered a few feet from the main pile, some flopped open upside down. The pile was anything but neat. Yet, all had burned.

I turned and peered up at the south hall, windows open to let in the mild spring air. "They were not placed here," I said. "They were dropped. Probably from that window." I pointed to an open window above the ground floor, right over the clump of books.

Grenville gazed upward, tilting back his curled-brimmed hat. "But surely someone would have seen that."

Rutledge turned a cold eye to Grenville, just noticing that he stood among us. "Good God, what the devil are you doing here?"

Next to him, Sutcliff glanced sideways at Grenville, taking in his black coat and gray trousers, his ivory and yellow striped waistcoat, and his cravat with its perfect, and simple, knot.

Grenville ignored them both. "It would take daring," he said to me.

"The boys were breakfasting," I said. "As were the tutors. The quad would be deserted." I peered up at the window again. "What is in that room?"

Grenville adjusted his hat, lifted his walking stick. "Let us have a look. With your permission of course, Rutledge."

"By all means," Rutledge growled. "Let Captain Lacey indulge himself."

Grenville gave him a half-smile. The smile shook a little; he must have been in a bad way on the journey. "Captain Lacey's guesses have been correct before. Only a few short weeks ago, he looked upon an anonymous body fished out of the Thames and was able to pinpoint the killer in less than a fortnight."

Rutledge's brows knit. "Well, he's been here almost that amount of time and has done nothing useful."

"Give him a chance, my dear Rutledge," Grenville assured him.

I was ready to tell the both of them to go to the devil. But I was curious to see that room. We all entered the chill darkness of the south hall; me, Grenville, Rutledge, Sutcliff. Fletcher, still wretched, followed us. "I can tell you what's there already," Fletcher said as we climbed the main stairs. "Nothing. It's a small room, and we store things there. No one ever goes in it."

"Is it kept locked?" I asked.

Rutledge answered. "No. Why should it be?"

We moved down the corridor that ran the length of

the house. Rutledge opened a door partway along. "You see?"

The room was indeed small and filled with junk. Broken chairs, half-painted drapes obviously used as scenery backing, old bookcases, a few crates, empty bottles, battered books—things that might be useful to someone if they cared to come here and root around.

Grenville moved through the junk to the window. It was open, and rain pattered on the sill. "Well, well," he said. "Lacey was correct." He leaned down, retrieved a few objects from the floor. I moved closer.

He held a piece of flint, a spill, and a small, pocket-sized book, half-burned. "Someone stood here and struck a spark and then calmly set the books alight. Probably piled them on this . . ." He kicked at a velvet drape lying in a wrinkled mass next to the window. "And tipped them out below. From here, he could make certain no one was in the quad. A quick rain of burning Latin texts, and then he nipped out of the room again, probably back to breakfast." He turned to Fletcher. "Did anyone come in late?"

Fletcher shrugged tired shoulders. "I did not notice."

"Or," I suggested, "he could have run outside and began the shouting. Does anyone know who shouted first?"

"By the time I reached the quad, most of the boys were there, and the tutors," Fletcher said.

"There were only a handful when I came out," Sutcliff volunteered. "But I really didn't see who. Ramsay was one, but I couldn't say which were first. I saw what had happened then ran to fetch the headmaster."

"Leaving us with a large number of suspects," I

mused. I shifted my gaze to Rutledge, and he glared back at me.

Grenville let the spill fall to the floor, and we went out again.

As we clattered down the stairs, I reflected that a boy could easily rush from this place without detection. He could run out into the quad, as I suggested, or he could stay beneath the portico and hurry past a windowless wall to the gate, or he could duck inside the east wing of the Head Master's house without anyone being the wiser. He did not necessarily have to "discover" the fire; he could have bolted back to his own room and innocently run down when the shouting began.

Outside, the rain had begun to stream down. Fletcher wandered back to his ruined books and stared at them morosely. Most of the boys had dispersed, hounded by the tutors to lessons. Sutcliff hurried off, too, his robe flapping.

"I believe you offered me a brandy, Lacey." Grenville gave me a pointed look. "You needn't worry, Rutledge, about putting me up here. I'll take rooms in Sudbury."

Rutledge grunted. "You're welcome to stay here. Food isn't much, though. Not what you're used to."

I imagined Rutledge was thinking that having someone like Lucius Grenville as a visitor to the school could not hurt its reputation. Grenville might be a fashionable dandy, but he was also quite wealthy and made plenty of investments. The men of the City of London approved of him.

Grenville laughed lightly. "I am not likely to find the best in cuisine at the public house in Sudbury. I will take up your offer, Rutledge. It will take me back to our carefree days at Eton."

Rutledge looked as though his carefree days were the last things he wanted to remember. He nodded once. "I'll have my daughter set up a room for you. Fletcher," he called. "Cease your weeping. You have lectures this morning. Get to it, man."

He walked away, leaving Grenville and me alone in the rain.

ONCE upstairs in my cramped quarters, Grenville let his mask drop. He exhaled sharply as he leaned back in the wing chair and gratefully accepted the brandy I handed him. "The road from London has more twists and turns than I remember. Thank God I wasn't going all the way to Bath."

"Next time, try a canal boat," I suggested. "They seem to move slowly and smoothly."

Grenville grimaced, took a long draught of brandy. "A strange sight I would look, perched atop a pile of cargo. But I suppose no less strange than lying in my coach, gasping and praying that the journey will end soon."

"I would think you would be used to traveling by now." I sat facing him with a glass of brandy, perfectly happy to take time from my duties. "Have you not stood outside the emperor's city in China, bought sandalwood from the natives of the Cook islands?"

"It was pure misery. But worth the trouble, I assure you." He made a face. "Although I do not recommend weevil-ridden biscuit for a daily diet."

I smiled because he expected me to. "I wrote you yesterday afternoon of the inquest. Did you receive the letter, or shall I explain it all again?"

"I did not receive your letter. I left late last night to arrive this morning. I imagine the letter is waiting for me on my bedside table to peruse when I return. Please." He took a sip of brandy. Color slowly returned to his face. "Regale me with the details."

I went back over all that had happened during the inquest and since, including my interview with Didius Ramsay and my finding of the knife and the place Middleton had died, omitting, of course, that Marianne had been with me. He listened attentively and asked pointed questions, as though he were a scholar taking notes.

"This prank is a little different from the others," he mused. "It was malicious, but not dangerous, after all. It hurt only your poor tutor in his pocket, though it did disrupt things."

"Yes, poor Fletcher," I agreed. "He has no money besides the income he gets from the school. In the brief time I've known him, he's lamented it."

"Well, I might be persuaded to purchase him a few new tomes. I always hated my Latin tutors. I wanted to revel in the lurid adventures of Jason; they wanted declensions."

"Perhaps they found excitement in grammar," I suggested. My mood became reflective. "Being here does odd things to my memories. I left Cambridge to join the army. Harrow seems another life. I had forgotten much about it and the lads I counted as friends, until I arrived here and began to remember. An odd feeling."

Grenville gave a half-laugh. "In my case, somebody reminds me every day at White's of some damn fool thing I did while at Eton. My cronies have long memories. The boy I fagged for now has gray hair and side whiskers, and he still reminds me I was not very good at blacking boots."

I raised my brows. "Somehow I cannot picture you slaving. I thought you'd have had the entire school dancing to your tune."

He shook his head. "Not a bit of it. When I arrived, I was small and dark and ugly. The perfect quarry for every bully. And then, one day, I grew tired of it. I had discovered that sarcasm and wit could be far more effective than fists. The duller-brained the boy, the more others laughed at my *bons mots*. And so I became a nasty bit of goods in my own way, fighting with words where I could not fight with fists." He smiled ruefully. "Not that I did not receive my share of black eyes."

"Whereas I never learned the art of words." I studied my large hands. "I relied only on my fists. In the world today, I believe you are the stronger."

"You flatter me." He finished his brandy, set aside his glass. "Tell me, Lacey, why do you believe that Sebastian is not the murderer?"

"I like him," I said at once. "Then again, perhaps I simply feel sorry for him, a downtrodden soul. He is a warmhearted, if somewhat foolish, young man. I can imagine him arguing with Middleton, perhaps even knocking him down, but luring him to the canal and slicing his throat? I am not so certain."

"But you can imagine James Denis hiring someone to do such a thing."

I rubbed my chin. "Yes, indeed. Or, perhaps some-one hired by Denis' rival."

"You refer to Lady Jane?"

I nodded. When Grenville and I had investigated the affair of the Glass House, we came across an individual called Lady Jane. She was a ruthless business-woman, and James Denis considered her a rival. Why she would bother to have killed a man who had not worked for Denis for six months, I did not know, but I could not rule out the possibility.

"An odd business, this," Grenville mused. "When I suggested Rutledge employ you, I never dreamed things would progress to brutal murder. I assumed the pranks to be the work of a lad with a strange sense of humor. I thought you would quickly sort it out."

"It's more of a mare's nest than that. If you reasoned it would be simple, why send me? Why not offer to hire a Bow Street Runner to poke about here and find out the truth?"

Grenville twined his fingers together. "Because London was doing nothing for you. I thought I would do you a favor, send you to the peace of the countryside and a problem that would intrigue you. I suppose I thought that here in the country, you would find some-thing missing in your life."

I gave him a faint smile. "I have. Knee-deep mud. A foul murder. A man who is a boor running a school for appallingly rich bankers' sons."

Grenville snorted. "Yes, Rutledge can be an ass. You would not think he comes from one of the finest families in England. Why he decided to take up a post as head-master, I never understood. But he seems to enjoy it."

Grenville crossed his ankles on the ottoman, giving me a view of his extraordinarily clean boots. Rumor had it that he had his right boots and left boots made by two different boot makers so that they'd fit his feet perfectly. I doubted that—Grenville was not frivolous—but the leather did conform to the shape of each foot and was shined with care. Even after a journey of sixty miles, the boots were nearly free of mud.

"Are you certain you want to lodge here?" I began. "While the accommodations in Sudbury are not elegant, they are at least quiet."

"Ah, but here, I am in the thick of things."

I wondered whether Marianne knew he'd arrived. Had she seen his coach as she'd hurried across the fields toward Hungerford?

As though reading my thoughts, Grenville glanced at me, slightly defiant, and said, "I hired the Runner."

We regarded each other in silence. We were so different, the pair of us, he a smallish man with clean dark hair brushed in the latest style, his dark eyes quick and lively. I, on the other hand, was a tall man, muscular from my days in the army, brown from the same, although my tan had somewhat faded. My hair was only a shade lighter than his, but wiry and thick and never stayed down, no matter how much I might slick it with water. My eyes, too, were a shade lighter brown than his, too light, I thought for that lively look he had.

I did not think either of us had a face to attract a lady's attention, but Grenville had a constant string of admirers. His status as the most eligible bachelor in England caused every mother in the *haut ton* to eagerly plot. Grenville neatly avoided their snares by rarely appearing at Almack's, the rooms in King Street where each Season's crop of debutantes were paraded. Admission to this bastion was more difficult to obtain than presentation at court. The hostesses expected applicants to conform to a strange and stringent code of behavior and ancestry that few could meet.

Needless to say, I had not been granted a voucher to purchase a ticket to Almack's. I refused Grenville's offers to intercede for me. I was too old to care for attending, and in any case, I did not have the clothes for it. Ironically, my lack of interest in Almack's had made me a focus of social curiosity. As a consequence, I had more invitations to events in the *ton* than did other hopeful nobodies.

Grenville was everything to the polite world. And yet, he faced me now, caring that he had my disapproval.

"I am concerned for her well-being, Lacey," he began.

"She is a resourceful woman and survived long before you knew she existed," I countered.

His eyes darkened. "If you can call it survival."

Marianne and I had lived in identical rooms in Covent Garden, hers above mine. "I do," I said stiffly.

"Damnation, Lacey. If I defend myself, I insult you. You are making this bloody difficult."

"If you had read my letter, you'd know I advised you to let her go."

"I did read it," he growled.

We regarded one another again.

After a time, I said, "I should not interfere in your business."

"You are making it your business," he snapped. "The devil if I know why."

"Perhaps because you like to stride over people, and I understand how that feels. Your intentions are always benevolent, of course."

"Of course? What would you have me do, Lacey, cease bestowing money on the London poor? Because they might take offense? Or fear that I am interfering in their business?"

I shook my head. "The situation is not the same. When you give money to the poor, you hand it to the parishes to use as they see fit. You do not enter into each person's life and tell him or her how to live it."

"And you claim I am doing so with Marianne?"

I tried another tack. "Marianne has survived on her own for a long time. She has had other protectors, some of whom did not treat her well. You cannot blame her if she has learned to distrust."

Grenville thumped the arms of his chair. "The pair of you will drive me mad. I am not an evil villain of the stage. I have given her a house to live in and clothes to wear and money to spend. A woman with those amenities should be content to stay at home."

I smiled dryly. "It is apparent that you have never been married."

"I have kept mistresses in the past, Lacey. Even the most greedy and extravagant of them lived quietly in my houses."

"Because those ladies stood in awe of you. Marianne never will. She's been knocked about most of her life, many times by wealthy gentlemen. Why should she trust you?"

He looked offended. "I have shown her nothing but kindness."

"Perhaps, but also great irritation when she does not do exactly as you like."

He threw up his hands. "I have never attempted as benevolent an act that tried me as much as this one. So you would like me to cease looking for her? Cease wondering whether she is with a brute who is even now beating her because she will not give him the money that I handed her? Cease wondering whether in her haste to run away she did not fall among thieves who abandoned her somewhere along the Great North Road?"

I felt suddenly cruel. I knew good and well that Marianne was safe. But I could not tell him this; I had given her my word.

I wished she had told me her secret so that I might know whether holding my tongue helped or hurt. I wished still more that she'd simply confide in Grenville herself. I would be saved much trouble, and so would they.

"If you will trust me," I said, "I will make certain she is restored to you."

He stared. "How?"

"You must dismiss the Runner," I answered, "or you will make a muck of things."

"But how can you—" He broke off, and his eyes went black with anger. "You know where she is."

I said nothing. I turned my brandy glass in my hands, not looking at him. I sensed his rage grow.

"Damn you, Lacey."

"I will see that she returns home," I interrupted.

"You must not ask me to choose which view I will take in the matter. I choose no views. Trust me to restore her to the Clarges Street house, and then the two of you may come to your own arrangement."

I had rarely seen Grenville angry, and never this angry. He remained still, his fingers white upon the arms of the chair. His dark eyes were sharp, tense, regarding me with fury.

The mantel clock chimed nine, notes of small sweetness. In the silence that followed, I grew to respect Lucius Grenville. At that moment, he might have chosen to quit me, to leave behind our friendship forever. By speaking a few words at White's, he could ruin my character. He could make certain I was received nowhere, simply with the lift of an eyebrow, the shrug of a shoulder.

He also could have shouted at me, accused me of all kinds of things, just as Colonel Brandon did whenever I angered him, which was often.

Grenville did neither. What he did instead was sit still and let his anger course through him. Then, quietly and slowly, he mastered his emotions. I watched his gaze cool as he drew upon his sangfroid and good breeding, becoming more and more remote as his grip on the arms of the chair relaxed.

"I will send word to Bow Street," he said quietly, "and tell them I no longer need the services of a Runner."

I gave him a quiet nod. "I will make certain she returns home. Although I cannot guarantee the state of her temper."

He rose from his seat and casually poured out another glass of brandy. I admired him greatly at that moment.

"I am certain she will be quite annoyed," Grenville said, returning to his chair. "But let us speak no more of it." He gave me a wry smile. "Let us return to the somewhat safer topic of murder."

In some relief, we both reimmersed ourselves in the problem at hand. We talked over everything I knew and the steps I had begun to take. We did not mention Marianne again.

Later, a servant came to tell Grenville that rooms had been made ready for him. Grenville left with the servant to seek rest, and I made my way to Rutledge's study and the day's correspondence.

Rutledge was disinclined to talk of the morning's events. Instead, he growled as he read his morning's post and dictated responses in a rush. He was already receiving letters from worried families about the murder. He told me to answer all with a statement that a Romany had been arrested and all was well. He eyed me balefully and read over each letter I wrote for him, as though fearing I'd put forth my idea that Sebastian did not commit the crime. The wealthy men whose sons attended this school would not care who did the murder, Rutledge implied, as long as *somebody* had been arrested.

Rutledge had made arrangements for Grenville to take luncheon with him in his private rooms. He grudgingly invited me along, but I declined, knowing he did not truly want me. I made my way instead to the common dining hall, where I seated myself next to a still-morose Fletcher.

"I suppose it does not matter," Fletcher sighed as he

scraped the last of his stew from his bowl. "I should never have become a tutor, but I much needed the post. I was a translator, you know, in London. I translated books from fine Latin and Greek into raw English so that the great unwashed could understand them. Sacrilege, but one must eat."

He ate the remainder of his soup now, hungrily.

"Do you lock your rooms?" I asked him.

"No, why should I? Servants have to tidy and lay the fire, do they not? Anyone is free to enter, including those bent on destroying perfectly innocent books." His mouth quivered. "A good book is like a good friend, do you know, Lacey? One you can turn to when the night is cold and you are lonely. And there is old Herodotus, standing ready to regale me with tales of his travels."

"Yes," I said sympathetically. "Grenville has offered to help you replace some of the books."

He brightened. "Good heavens, has he? How noble of him. Well, I shall toast Mr. Grenville." He lifted his port glass.

I drank with him to Grenville. "Why should anyone burn your books?" I asked presently. "I mean *your* books in particular, rather than, say, Tunbridge's math texts?"

Fletcher shrugged. "Science and mathematics are all the rage, you know. But who has time for good old Horace? I managed to save one." He patted his robe. "In my pocket at the time. One, when I had so many."

"I am sorry," I told him. "It was a rotten thing to do."

He heaved a long sigh. "Ah, well, Captain, God sends us trials, does he not? But one day, one day, I shall buy an entire library of everything I want. And then I shall sit back in a room filled with so many, many texts, and read to my heart's content." He smiled a little, enjoying his dream.

I noted Sutcliff watching us from his place at the head of his table. When he caught my eye, he nodded, lifting his glass. Then he turned away to snarl at a younger boy down the table, who had not finished his stew. A Rutledge in the making, I reflected.

When the meal finished and we all left the hall, I caught up to Sutcliff and touched his shoulder. "Mr. Sutcliff," I said. "Could you spare some time to speak to me and Mr. Grenville?"

CHAPTER 8

❦

SUTCLIFF agreed to meet with Grenville and myself for a glass of claret that afternoon. His tone when he delivered his answer told me that he never would have accepted had Grenville not been involved. Gabriel Lacey might be a gentleman, his look said, but Gabriel Lacey could barely afford the clothes on his back.

My own father would have thrashed him soundly just for that look. Lucky for Sutcliff that my father was dead.

At three o'clock, Sutcliff reported to Grenville's rooms, and Grenville, now rested and bathed and dressed again in a fine suit, received him.

While Didius Ramsay was a usual sort of boy trying to fit in with his fellows, Sutcliff was a few years older than the rest, and definitely Rutledge's man. He regarded everyone about him with a sneer and considered himself higher than all except Rutledge. Sutcliff's father, I had learned from gossip, one of the wealthiest men in London, had risen from assistant clerk at a warehouse to become the owner of a fleet of merchant ships and several warehouses. Goods from all over the world—and the money those goods made—had passed through his hands. Sutcliff stood to inherit all that money, and he made certain, with every gesture and turn of phrase, that we all knew it.

I wondered, however, how much money he truly had at present. His father likely gave him an allowance, but even wealthy fathers could be stingy as a way to teach their sons to respect money. Sutcliff's clothes were not shabby, but nor were they the equal of Grenville's, or even small Ramsay's. Perhaps his papa held the purse strings tighter than Sutcliff liked.

Sutcliff seated himself on a Turkish sofa in Grenville's rather grand rooms and accepted the glass of claret that Matthias, Bartholomew's brother, whom Grenville had brought with him, served us.

When Matthias had drained the bottle, Grenville told him he was finished with his duties and suggested he find Bartholomew and take him to visit the pub in Sudbury. Matthias thanked him, said a cheerful good afternoon to me, and departed.

Sutcliff gave Grenville a look of mild disdain when he'd gone. "They get above themselves, you know, if you allow it."

Grenville nodded as though Sutcliff had said something wise. "Indeed, my servants ever take advantage of me." He studied the fine color of his claret before taking a sip. "Now then, Mr. Sutcliff, what do you think of Sudbury School? It has a fine reputation."

Sutcliff arched a brow. "What do I think of it? You hardly plan to send your sons here, do you?"

"I am interested."

Grenville was holding himself in check. I'd seen him turn the full force of his cold and satirical persona to others, observed peers of the realm wilt before him, seen powerful gentlemen fear to come under his stare. Grenville needed only to imply that a gentleman purchased his gloves ready-made or did not pay his servants or had bad table manners, and that gentleman would be forever marked. Sutcliff was unaware of his danger.

"It's a tedious place, if you must know," Sutcliff said. He gulped his claret, and then helped himself to more. "But at the end of this term, I will be finished, thank God."

"I agree, being buried in the country is not stimulating to the intellect," Grenville said. "What do you do for diversion?"

"Oh, we amuse ourselves. Games and whatnot. The younger boys smuggle in spirits and dice and believe themselves sophisticated. Of course, I report all that to Rutledge."

Grenville smiled in reminiscence. "When I was at school, we knew a house nearby that didn't mind offering cards and other vices to us as long as we could pay."

Sutcliff snorted. "Nothing like that in Sudbury. Or even Hungerford."

"And yet," I broke in. I knew Grenville was leading up to the question in his own way, but my impatience got the better of me, as usual. "There must be a reason that you climbed the wall on Sunday evening, shortly after Middleton the groom left for the village."

Sutcliff's glass froze halfway to his mouth. He stared at me for a long moment, while Grenville shot me an annoyed look.

"Who has said this?" Sutcliff asked stiffly.

"I am well informed," I answered.

Sutcliff clicked his glass to the table beside him. "Did Rutledge ask you to spy for him? To follow his pupils and report what they do?"

I shook my head. "I can hardly run about after you on a game leg, can I? You were seen, Mr. Sutcliff. Where did you go?"

His lip curled. "Not to the village, certainly. It is quite dull on a Sunday night."

"Ah, you know this."

His eyes sparkled with anger. "See here, Captain Lacey."

Grenville broke in with a soothing gesture. "Who is the lady, Mr. Sutcliff?"

Frederick Sutcliff stopped, flushed.

I grew irritated with myself for not having thought of it. I had been so fixed on the murder, that I forgot that young men sneaked away from school for other reasons, one of them being female companionship.

Sutcliff's tone was a bit less disdainful. "You are a gentleman of the world, Mr. Grenville. I say, you will not peach to Rutledge, will you?"

"I assure you, I have no wish to tell your secrets to Rutledge," Grenville said. "Neither does Captain Lacey. We are simply interested in Middleton's murder."

"I see. Well, this can have nothing to do with it." He lowered his voice, looked at us as though we were co-conspirators. "I do have a lady, gentlemen. She stays in Hungerford. She is French."

He sat back, quite proud of himself. For a moment, I wondered what lady would want him, then I remembered that Frederick Sutcliff's father was enormously rich.

"You said she *stays* in Hungerford," I said. "She does not live there?"

He gave me a half-smile. "She lives where I tell her to live. This term, I have hired rooms for her in Hungerford."

I had a awful thought. Marianne was staying in Hungerford. This could not be her secret could it? That she was mistress to a stripling man with a spotty face? But Sutcliff's potential of a vast fortune might attract Marianne. Grenville had a fortune, too, of course, but I imagined Marianne would find Sutcliff much more controllable than Grenville. I could only hope I was wrong.

"You visited her late Sunday evening, then?" I prompted.

He gave us a self-important smile. "I confess, gentlemen. I walked to Hungerford and stayed with her most of the night, if you know what I mean. I returned just before dawn. Good thing I did because at first light, all sorts of ruckus was raised about the dead groom, and I might have been seen creeping back in."

Grenville sipped his claret and gave him an indulgent nod. "Yes, your timing seems to have been excellent."

Sutcliff preened himself.

"While you were traveling to and from Hungerford," I broke in, "did you happen to see Middleton? Or anything unusual?"

Sutcliff frowned. "No. What does it matter, in any case? The Romany killed him."

"Did he? There was no sign of blood on Sebastian's clothes. He was absent from the school when Middleton died, yes. But so were you."

Sutcliff gaped. "Are you accusing *me?* How dare you? I am not a dirty Romany."

"I did not say you were. I said that there was as much evidence to convict him as you."

"Rutledge told me you were far too impertinent. And why do you care about his clothes? Doubtless he stripped off his bloody clothes and threw them into the canal. His kind are not stupid."

"Why did he return to the stables, then, if he was so crafty?" I plunged on. "He could have met up with his family, disappeared with them. He could be far away by now. But he chose to return to his room."

"There would have been a hue and cry after him if he'd run away," Sutcliff said. "The entire countryside would be turned out to find him. He'd know that."

"And so he stayed put where he was immediately arrested? No, Mr. Sutcliff, you cannot argue that he was simultaneously crafty and a fool."

His eyes flared. "What is your interest? He is Romany, for God's sake."

"I am interested in the truth. I do not like to see an innocent person hanging for someone else's crime."

Sutcliff regarded me in dislike. "You certainly are

easily agitated. Perhaps you are a radical, ready to let the mob and the Jew and the Roma rule us?"

"The mob and the Jew will likely be customers for the goods you ship, and you will employ them in your warehouses," I pointed out. "The Roma, of course, will not be allowed to work for you."

"Good God. You *are* a radical."

"Not so. But perhaps I have sympathy for those crushed underfoot. I do not have to be a radical to wish a man to pay for his crimes."

Sutcliff sat forward, his long nose flaring. "The Romany is to blame, and he will pay. Do you know, my father would tan my hide if he knew I'd spoken to a radical. The mob overthrew the aristocrats in France, you know. You have more to fear than I." He climbed to his feet, his large hands red below the cuffs of his jacket. "Good afternoon, Mr. Grenville. I am afraid I do not think much of your claret, or your friends."

Grenville and I watched him as he strode across the room, dodging furniture like a young hound not yet accustomed to his body. He went out and slammed the door, the sound echoing from the dark beams.

Grenville, to my surprise, chuckled. "The poor chap. This claret is the finest money can buy. A man who cannot recognize quality when he tastes it will not make a very good merchant."

I glanced at the closed door. "We did not obtain the name of the French lady who is willing to live in Hungerford for him."

"That is not a bother," Grenville answered. "Hungerford is not a large town; I imagine the entire population knows who this woman is and where she resides. I do not know why he thinks he can keep such a secret from curious neighbors. They will have found out, one way or another, and be happy to confide the information."

I raised my brows. "You sound as though you speak from experience."

"I have a country estate located near a town about the size of Hungerford. The most entertaining activity there is gossip. A stranger is dissected down to his boots. They are hospitable people, but secrets are impossible to keep." He drained his glass. "If you like, I'll pursue the mystery of the Frenchwoman while you do your duties with Rutledge."

"No," I said immediately.

He looked surprised. "Why not?"

I certainly did not want him in Hungerford to trip over Marianne. "I'd rather have you here, speaking with the lads," I extemporized. "They will admire you and be thrilled to speak to you. You might be able to pry more information from them than I. I will attend to the French lady of Hungerford."

He watched me with curiosity in his black eyes, then he grinned. "Ah, of course, you would want to interview the lady. Your affinity for the fair sex eclipses me every time."

I opened my mouth to argue with him, then closed it. Let him think what he liked. I did not want him near Hungerford until I was certain that the "French" lady was not Marianne, and until I could persuade Marianne to go sensibly back to London.

He put his hands to his chest. "Command me. What would you have me do?"

I thought. "Speak to what students you can, then search Middleton's rooms in the stables. I have not had chance to do so. No groom has been hired to replace him, but I am certain Rutledge will not wait long. And speak to a lad called Timson, the one Ramsay smoked cheroots with the night of Middleton's death."

Grenville reached out an elegant hand and poured more claret. "I will endeavor to charm Mr. Timson. Has James Denis sent you any more warnings, by the bye?"

"No, as a matter of fact. Not since he wrote asking me to look into Middleton's death."

"Hmm. I wonder what danger Middleton had mentioned. The pranks?"

"My greater wonder is that Denis should ask me to take care. Why should he?"

"Because he knows you could be a valuable resource to him."

I lifted a brow. "James Denis knows I will not work for him. I am investigating this death because I wish to help Sebastian, not because Denis has asked me to."

Grenville made a placating gesture. "I know. But see it from Denis' point of view. You are intelligent, you have been right more times than not, and you persist until you know the truth. You could be quite an asset to him."

"He is a criminal," I said quietly, "though the magistrates fear to arrest him. He procures artwork, however dubiously, for vast fortunes, owns Members of Parliament and peers outright, and once murdered a coachman who worked for him because he was displeased. I hope I will never be an asset to him."

"And yet, many men would envy your exalted position," Grenville said. "No, do not grow angry with me. I admire your resistance. Not many a man could, or would. He could pay you quite well, I imagine."

"I imagine he could," I agreed. "But I should lose myself, Grenville. My dignity is all I have left, and even that deserts me now and again. Shall I give up that as well, and become another of Denis' anonymous lackeys? Sell my soul for a handful of coins? Maybe I am a fool. I do not know any more."

Grenville studied his wine, not looking at me. I must have embarrassed him. I'd certainly embarrassed myself.

"I do not believe you a fool." He raised his eyes, but they were shuttered. "In fact, Lacey, I always considered myself a wise man until I met you. And then I realized that I have been looking at my life the wrong way round."

I stared at him. "The wrong way round? What does that mean?"

"It means you are the wise man, and I am the fool. But enough." He set aside his glass, rose. "Let me find and interest the boys, and you go in search of your French lady."

HUNGERFORD had once been used by Charles I as a base from which he fought battles with Cromwell's army. One could picnic now at the battle sites, as I imagined that one day Spanish ladies and gentlemen would picnic at the sites of Talavera and Abuerra and other gruesome chapters in the war against Bonaparte. The locals also proclaimed that Queen Elizabeth had some time rested here on one of her progresses to and from London.

Hungerford's High Street was long and backed onto the canal. This late in the afternoon it was crowded with those purchasing goods for their afternoon meal. The sky was leaden, but the rain had ceased. Mud coated the street, and a passing cart threw more upon my boots.

Grenville had been correct about the ease with which I discovered the rooms in which Sutcliff had placed his paramour. I stepped into a tavern that smelled of stale beer and yesterday's roast, and nursed an ale while the publican's wife told me everything I wanted to know. I finished the ale, thanked her, and went off in pursuit.

At the end of the High Street, I found a small lane branching from the main road. At the end of this, just as the publican's wife had indicated, sat a square brick house, not very large, surrounded by an untidy garden.

Two women had taken rooms to live here. The woman who owned the house, a widow by the name of Albright, offered the rooms to bring in extra money. The renters were expected to find their own meals and pay extra for a maid to clean their rooms and remove their night soil. According to the publican's wife, the house attracted only those who knew they would not be welcome at other, more respectable lodging houses.

One woman at this house was Miss Simmons, an actress from London. The other was a young woman named Jeanne Lanier. She was French, the daughter of French émigrés, and, I had no doubt, Frederick Sutcliff's lover.

Mrs. Albright wore a brown dress with rents in several places mended with clumps of black thread. She had brown hair the same shade as the dress and faded blue eyes. When I asked to see Miss Simmons, she gazed at me doubtfully but ushered me into a small, stuffy sitting room and departed to find her.

Dust lay thick on the furniture, and the windows must not have been opened for a long while. I had given Mrs. Albright my card, and as the minutes ticked past, I wondered if Marianne had seen it and fled the house. After a time, however, I heard her step.

She entered the sitting room alone. "You gave me a fright, Lacey," she said, closing the door. "I thought you'd brought him with you."

I had risen at her entry. "You know he's arrived, then."

"Oh, yes. I saw his coach. You were correct about him flying down here on the moment. He cannot keep his long nose out of any business."

"Grenville has been most helpful to me in the past," I told her, my tone cool. "I welcome his help now."

"Yes, yes, he is your dearest friend."

I ignored this and motioned for her to sit on one of the chairs. She glanced at it in disdain, brushed it off with her hand, then sank into it.

I seated myself, facing her. "Have you decided to confide in me?" I asked.

Marianne studied her hands. In the dim light of the room, the hair on her bent head looked more silver than blonde. I realized, studying her, that though she dressed in a young woman's clothing and wore her hair in ringlets like a girl, Marianne was not as young as she pretended to be. She had the gift that some women had of maintaining a young face no matter how much time passed, but I saw in the droop of her shoulders the tiredness that years bring.

"I have decided," she said. She looked up at me, her blue eyes hard. "I will tell you everything."

CHAPTER 9

SHE had no intention of telling me there and then, however. "I will show you," she said. "That will be easier than explaining. Tomorrow, when you go out for your preposterously early ride, meet me by Froxfield Lock."

"Froxfield?" I asked, surprised.

"Yes. I will not tell you any more, so do not press me. If you want to know, you will meet me; if not, then I will tell you nothing."

"Very well, you have convinced me." I wanted to shake her, truth to tell, but I could see she was troubled and a bit frightened.

"I have another errand here," I went on. "I came to see Jeanne Lanier."

Marianne looked surprised. "What on earth for? She would not suit you, Lacey."

I ignored her needling. "What do you know about her?"

Marianne shrugged. "She is French, but she has lived in England all her life. She's young, pretty, wants money. Typical."

"Typical of what?"

"Fallen ladies, my innocent friend. I do not mean she walks the streets; but she makes contracts with gentlemen to keep her. Her current protector is quite young, only nineteen, I think, although she is not much older than he is, in truth."

"Yes, he is a student at the school," I told her. "A vastly wealthy one, or at least his father is. Do you know whether he visited her Sunday night? About ten o'clock it would have been."

Marianne nodded. "Oh, he was here all right. I never saw him, but I heard them." She grimaced. "I put my pillow over my head and went to sleep. So I cannot tell you what time he departed, if that is what you want to know."

"Could you be persuaded to find out? I mean, could you keep an eye on Jeanne Lanier and let me know if she says anything unusual about Mr. Sutcliff?"

"In case he had anything to do with the murder?" She tipped her head to one side, and her childlike look returned. "I might be persuaded."

"For a reasonable fee, of course," I said. "But please be discreet."

"My dear Lacey, I am discretion itself. Were I not, many a gentleman in London would fall. I am amazed at what they confide in me."

I could imagine. Gentlemen said things to their lovers that they told to no other.

Marianne agreed to fetch Jeanne Lanier for me, and I waited while she made her way upstairs.

I had always wondered about Marianne's origins. She spoke well, as though she'd come from at least a middle-class family, and she did know manners, if she did not always use them. At the same time, she could swear volubly with words even an army man would hesitate to use. Her knowledge of men, and her frank admission to manipulating them through their desires, could be a bit embarrassing. And yet, she put herself above the street girls who lured men to their dooms, and even above the other actresses with whom she shared the stage.

Asking direct questions of Marianne had never gotten me far, however. When she wanted me to know about her past life, she would tell me.

After a few more minutes, Jeanne Lanier arrived.

Marianne had been correct when she said that Jeanne was not much older than Sutcliff. I put her age at about twenty, possibly a year less. Dark brown ringlets trickled down her neck from under a small white cap. She had a pretty face that was not beautiful but pleasing. Part of its pleasantness came from her dark-lashed blue eyes and wide mouth.

She made a curtsey, held out her hand. "Captain Lacey?"

I bowed, took her hand, and said, "I've come from the Sudbury School. Mr. Sutcliff told me about you."

She smiled wisely. "Ah, Mr. Sutcliff. Please sit down, Captain. The chairs are horrid, but I can offer you no others, unfortunately. Your leg must be tired from the ride."

She spoke with a very charming accent. Most children of French émigrés that I had met, born and raised in England, spoke English in a manner quite the same as any English person. But perhaps Jeanne Lanier had learned that a gentleman finds a slight misuse of English intriguing.

"I would offer you refreshment, but again, I fear . . ." She shook her head. "You would do better to visit the tavern on the way out of Hungerford."

I returned the smile. She was indeed quite charming. "I am sorry you must stay in such accommodations. Mr. Sutcliff should do better for you."

She waved this away. "When we are in London, I assure you, my accommodations are quite fine. Here in the country, one takes what one can find. Mr. Sutcliff is most generous. He is not to blame."

I had difficulty reconciling young Sutcliff, the lanky youth with his nose in the air, with this quiet young woman. Their ages were close, and yet, Jeanne Lanier was far more sophisticated than Frederick Sutcliff would ever be.

"It is of Mr. Sutcliff that I wish to speak to you," I said. "To ask you, specifically, if he visited you here on Sunday night."

Her smile turned coy. "He visits me nearly every night, Captain, so indeed, he visited me on Sunday."

"Will you tell me what time?"

"You wish to know because that was the night the murder happened?" she asked, her expression intelligent. "Let me see, he arrived a little after ten. He stayed quite late—or quite early, I should say. I believe he left for home when the clock was striking four. He made certain everyone at the school would be asleep before he went. If his headmaster found him sidling back into the school . . ." She made another gesture, but smiled as she did it, imagining Rutledge's explosion.

"Thank you, that is most helpful."

"But why do you ask? I thought the murderer had already been found."

"A Romany has been arrested, yes. But I like to put everything in order."

She cocked her head. "So you must have learned in the army. I admire a man who puts things in order."

I wondered whether, had I confessed to a chaotic life, she would have admired that instead.

"Did Mr. Sutcliff ever speak of the incidents at the school?" I asked. "The pranks and so forth?"

She spread one long-fingered hand on her knee. "Goodness, yes. He finds them most annoying. As prefect, he must make the younger boys behave, and he is distracted to know who is doing these dreadful things. Mr. Rutledge is quite put out with him."

"Mr. Rutledge is put out with everyone," I remarked.

Her smile deepened, a glint of true humor in her eyes. "That is so. I have not met Mr. Rutledge, but Mr. Sutcliff tells me much."

"How did you meet Mr. Sutcliff?" I asked, curious.

Her gaze shifted, though her charm did not diminish. "Oh, in the usual manner."

I had no idea what was the usual manner, never having looked for a contracted paramour myself. Only very wealthy gentlemen were so able. She must have guessed this, because she added, "My former protector introduced us. He thought Mr. Sutcliff would suit me."

I had heard, through Grenville, that when a gentleman tired of his mistress, he sometimes introduced her to a friend and more or less suggested that she try her luck with him. The previous gentleman said his good-byes at the same time the next gentleman would offer her *carte blanche*. I wondered what kind of man would suggest his mistress take up with a schoolboy, even if the schoolboy, at nineteen, was a little older than his fellows.

"Mr. Sutcliff will become quite a wealthy man, I understand," I said.

"Oh, indeed." She radiated pride. "He will be able to purchase the City of London twice over, I think."

"But not until the sad day that his father passes away."

She nodded. "He will come into more money when he reaches his majority. But his father is rather horrible. He does not allow Frederick to have all that he could, does not trust him, he says. Frederick is quite annoyed. His father has even kept him in the school longer than most of the young men. He says that Frederick must learn to be a man before he can come into the business with his father. But I ask you, Captain, can a boy learn to be a man in the company of boys?"

I had wondered why Sutcliff was a bit older than his schoolmates. A boy could leave school when he or his father felt him ready for university, at seventeen or eighteen. But Sudbury was not a preparatory school. Most of the young men at Sudbury would never attend university; they would slip right into the family business and not seek the esoteric studies of theology and law at Oxford or Cambridge. Perhaps Mr. Sutcliff wanted Frederick to learn all he could learn before he took part in the making of the family fortune. Sutcliff's disdain might extend from anger at his father's lack of belief in him.

"Frederick will be quite wealthy one day, however," Jeanne went on. "He is amazed at the vastness of his father's wealth."

"When my father died, I was truly amazed at the vastness of his debt," I said with a smile. "Mr. Sutcliff is a fortunate young man."

"Indeed, he is."

I did not add that she was a fortunate young woman to have found Sutcliff while he was still hungering for his wealth. Later, when he realized just how much power his money gave him, he might seek out a lady more expensive, more sophisticated, one who hadn't known him as a callow youth.

But Jeanne Lanier did not look troubled. She was shrewd and no doubt knew exactly how to obtain as much as she could from Sutcliff before her *carte blanche* ran out.

She began to converse with me then, as though I'd come to pay a social call. She asked me about the army and mentioned gentlemen of various regiments until we discovered one or two with whom we were both slightly acquainted. She asked more and more questions, prompted more and more stories, until I suddenly found myself speaking to her freely and at length.

She listened to me with avid attention, smiled at my attempts at wit, laughed at my anecdotes. I found myself speaking to her quite frankly of things that I had never discussed with anyone but Louisa.

She knew how to put me at my ease, how to enter-tain, how to make me feel as though she would like nothing better than to sit in this dreary parlor and converse with me all afternoon. I could well understand why Sutcliff was taken with her.

Though I knew Jeanne was practiced at chatting with gentlemen, I had not so enjoyed a conversation in a long while. Because we did not know one another, she was easy to speak to; no tension existed between us. Louisa and I had used to converse as freely, but now I felt strain when I spoke to her, much of which was my own stupid fault. My conversations with Lady Breckenridge were always a bit odd. Lady Breckenridge was clever and knew it and had never learned the art of pleasing. I admired her frankness, but her frankness could cut.

So, as the hour drew to a close, I found myself wanting to stay. I nearly asked to see her again. *Just to talk,* I wanted to say. *To talk to someone who enjoys listening.*

Without doing anything so foolish, I rose and took my leave. She had charmed me today because it suited her, nothing more.

She said good-bye to me very prettily, letting me bow over her hand. I thanked her for passing the time with me and made myself depart.

WHEN I reached the school again, it was in commotion. Rutledge was in an uproar, although most of the students were swarming about snickering behind their hands.

Grenville informed me that, apparently, the good-natured Simon Fletcher had lost his temper during a lecture and given Frederick Sutcliff a sound thrashing.

"Fletcher did?" I asked Grenville in amazement. Grenville had come to my chambers high in the Head Master's house, looking relieved to escape the lower floors. Bartholomew and Matthias had followed him.

"Yes." Grenville turned away from the window, through which he'd been studying the canal and the overgrown strips of land that lined it. "He was incoherent as to why. Something about not regarding Virgil with proper respect."

"An odd reason to lose one's temper." I accepted the cup of coffee that Bartholomew had been trying to press into my hands since we'd entered the room. "I never thought Fletcher much for thrashing. He never struck me as being cowed by the boys. More indifferent to them, I thought."

"Well, he certainly took a cane to Sutcliff," Grenville said. "Rutledge is furious. I imagine the Sutcliff money funds much of this school. Drink it yourself, Bartholomew. I am not in the mood for coffee." Bartholomew turned away, apologetic.

"Mr. Fletcher is sulking in his rooms," Matthias offered. "At least, that's what his maid says. Won't come out."

"What about Sutcliff?"

"In a towering fury," Grenville put in. "He's going about as usual, in high dudgeon. Implying that Fletcher will be sacked, and so forth."

Bartholomew grinned around the coffee cup. "The other boys are in transports. They hate Sutcliff. I'll wager every one of them has wanted to thrash 'im

themselves. They're likely having their own little cele-
bration." He chuckled.

"I am not entirely surprised the other boys do not
like him, from what I've seen," Grenville said. "Does
he have *any* friends here?"

Bartholomew shook his head. "He is loathed by one
and all, sir. My mam would take a stick to him, that's
for certain."

"His mam will likely be dependent on him one day
and knows it," I put in.

"True, poor woman," Grenville agreed.

I drank my coffee. It had begun raining again, and I
was cold, my muscles stiff. Between sips, I informed
them of all Jeanne Lanier had told me.

Grenville listened, interested. When I asked what he
had done, he confessed he'd chatted with some of the
boys, but had not yet had the chance to search Middleton's quarters. I suggested that while everyone in the
school was up in arms about Fletcher and Sutcliff that
we take ourselves there.

Grenville and I walked through rain to the stables by
ourselves, leaving the two footmen to gossip with servants and find out more about Fletcher's outburst.
Grenville carried a large black umbrella, held over his
costly suit and greatcoat.

As we walked, Grenville told me what he'd learned
from young Mr. Timson. He'd found Timson to be a typical bully with a few hangers-on and a cowed younger student who acted as a veritable slave for him. Bribed with a
flask of brandy Timson had admitted to sharing a smoke
with Ramsay on Sunday night. Ramsay, he'd said, had
turned tail and run after the first cheroot.

Timson had seen a man pass on the road, on the other side of the brush, but he could not say who. He'd not set eyes on Sutcliff. Neither had Timson's friends.

I mused, "I wonder why Ramsay, whose father is almost as wealthy as Sutcliff's from what I understand, needs to obtain his cheroots from Timson. Can he not purchase his own?"

Grenville gave a pained laugh. "I know exactly why. To keep Timson from despising him."

I raised my brows. Grenville's black umbrella was beaded with water, and beneath its shadow, he wore a rueful grin. I disliked umbrellas and was letting the rain do its worst to my hat. "Why on earth should he care whether Timson despised him?"

"Twenty-five years ago, I was Ramsay," Grenville said. "Or very like him. I was the son of the man with the most money. I hated that. I just wanted to be one of the chaps."

"So Ramsay puts up with Timson so that he can be one of the chaps? I suppose that makes a sort of sense."

Grenville nodded. "Better to grin and take Timson's sneers with the others than to be universally despised, like Sutcliff. Good lord, I would have."

"I am beginning to wonder how any of us survived to adulthood," I remarked.

"My father told me that the boys I'd meet at Eton would be my cronies for a lifetime. Quite frightening, I thought. Perhaps it was that which spurred my fondness for travel." He chortled.

"With your fondness for travel," I said, "I am surprised you've remained in England for this long."

He looked at me in surprise. "It has been only a year or so, Lacey."

"I read a newspaper article about you not long ago, in which the writer made the same observation. He implied that you rarely stayed in England above six months at a time."

Grenville shrugged. "I am getting old, belike. I become ill when I travel, as you know, and comfort is beginning to have greater importance."

"But you are growing tired of London life," I said. We had reached the stables, and I stopped outside the yard. "You long to be off, exploring distant realms. That is why you hurried down to Sudbury the minute something sordid happened. This murder should not interest you much. There has been an arrest, and all agree Sebastian the Romany is guilty."

"Except you," Grenville said. "Hence my interest. "But you might be correct. One can only stand in White's and pass judgment on knots in others' cravats for so long. I am fond of Egypt, as you know. Perhaps, when I take the fit to travel there again, you would accompany me?"

I blinked. I had toyed with the idea of offering to be his paid assistant or secretary when he traveled again, but I'd thought I'd have to persuade him. Now he offered it between one breath and the next. He was offering to pay my expenses, because he knew bloody well I could not.

"How would we fare as traveling companions?" I asked. "I am not the easiest man to live with."

"Nor am I. We would arrange something so that we

were not in each other's pockets. I would be lying ill in my cabin for most of the voyage, in any case. Do consider it."

"Unfortunately, at present, I am busy with my duties at the Sudbury School," I said.

He threw me an accusing glance. "I know. I apologize, Lacey. I had forgotten what an idiot Rutledge could be. I truly thought you could uncover his problem, and he would shower you with gratitude." He sighed. "My benevolence seems to have backfired."

His contrite look did not quite make me forgive him, but I decided not to be surly. "Rutledge is not your fault, and the problem is much more subtle than it first appeared. Shall we commence with Middleton's chamber?"

CHAPTER 10

꧁꧂

THE stable hand Thomas Adams grudgingly pointed us the way to the room Middleton had occupied during the six months he'd lived here.

The stable hands slept in a sort of dormitory above the stables, with bunks along the walls. It was warm there, the horses in their boxes below lending their heat and fragrance to the air.

Middleton had had a room to himself, more of a walled off portion of the dormitory. The room was simply furnished. He'd had a low-post bedstead with a straw mattress, a table and a chair, and hooks for his clothes.

The clothes had gone, but the table still held a pile of papers, weighted down by a large book.

The one window looked out over the stable yard and the land beyond. The canal was a flat, gray line across the green. I could see the lock and the lockkeeper's house. A low barge was floating toward the lock, slow-ing as it approached. The lockkeeper emerged from his house, brushing off the front of his coat, and trudged to meet it.

"This is interesting," Grenville said behind me.

I turned from the window. Grenville had moved the book and was now leafing through the pile of papers. He unfolded one and spread it across the table.

I moved to him and looked over his shoulder. "What is it?"

He had spread out a finely detailed map of the Kennet and Avon Canal. The map depicted the portion of the canal from Kintbury in the east to Devises in the west. Every village was marked, as was every lock and every bridge on the canal. A solid vertical line marked the boundary between Berkshire and Wiltshire.

"Was Middleton interested in canal navigation?" Grenville wondered aloud. "He was a horseman, was he not?"

I flipped through more papers. These were also maps, sketches of the canal and the lands beyond, each focusing on a small fragment of canal. On two maps, a line of another canal intersected the main canal, one at Hungerford and another at Newbury.

"But there are no canals there," Grenville said. "Are there?" He looked at the main map. It showed only the Kennet and Avon Canal, with no offshoots. "I admit I do not know the layout of every waterway in England," he said, "but I am fairly certain there are no branches of the canal there."

"Perhaps they are old maps with proposed routes that were never finished," I suggested. "This canal was only opened completely end to end seven years ago."

"But why would Middleton be interested in the canal before or after it was finished? And keep detailed maps of it in his room?"

I touched the drawing of the canal offshoot from Hungerford. "Perhaps it one of Denis' schemes. Something Denis asked him to look into."

Grenville frowned. "It is most bizarre. Shall we go to Hungerford and see whether this map is true?"

"Now?" I asked, alarmed.

"Why not? The rain is slackening, and we have the remainder of the afternoon. Unless Rutledge is screaming for you to write more letters."

For the first time since I arrived, I hoped he was. I did not want Grenville wandering about Hungerford with Marianne there. Although, I reasoned, if Rutledge detained me, Grenville would likely traipse off to Hungerford alone.

Grenville rolled up the Hungerford map and tucked it inside his greatcoat. "Shall we borrow a few horses? I hate to rouse my coachman for the chaise and four for such a short journey."

"Very well," I said, my voice hard.

His brows rose. "You do not sound keen, Lacey. You are usually quite bursting with curiosity."

I was, but I still did not want Grenville at Hungerford.

I hid my foreboding and descended with him to fetch the horses.

OUR journey to Hungerford proved fruitless. The map was so well marked that we found the spot of the pro-

posed canal without difficulty. It lay near Hungerford
Marsh Lock on the common lands where farmers could
still graze their animals without fear of landlords or en-
closure.

We found the place all right, but no sign of any
canal, new or old. Grenville dismounted his horse,
walked about the tall grass, trailing the reins loosely
behind him. "I see nothing," he said. "Not even a stray
surveyor's stake or mark."

Still in my saddle, I saw nothing either.

We searched the area, Grenville walking with his
head bent, studying the ground minutely.

"Bloody mystifying," he said, remounting his patient horse. "Why draw a map of something that does
not exist?"

"Perhaps it will exist one day," I said.

"Hmm. I suppose we could check in London to see
whether someone is funding a new offshoot of the
canal. Perhaps you are right and Denis is involved. He
is good at having his finger in moneymaking pies.
Canals make money."

"Yes," I answered. "Or perhaps Middleton wanted to
be free of Denis. He comes here to see whether the
canal offshoot will actually happen, so that he can invest."

"Well, he must have been disappointed," Grenville
said. "There is no sign that there will ever be any canal
building here. Shall we return to the rigid atmosphere
of the school? Or wet our throats in a tavern?"

"The school," I said promptly. When he raised his
brows, I feigned a smile. "The claret you brought with
you is much finer than anything we'll find in a tavern."

"True," he conceded. "We'll shut ourselves in my chambers and refuse to answer the door."

"Like Fletcher," I mused, and then we rode back.

AT least we saw no sign of Marianne. We had been poking about to the west of Hungerford, and her lodgings were on the east end of the town, but even so, I held my breath until we gained the stable yard again and dismounted.

I tried to see Fletcher while Grenville took himself back to his chambers to change from his riding clothes to his sitting-and-drinking-claret clothes. Fletcher opened his chamber door to my knock and peered out. He smelled heavily of port.

"Hallo, Lacey," he said, breathing hard. "I do not wish to talk about it."

"Are you well?"

The eye he pressed to the crack was puffy and red. "As well as can be expected. Good afternoon." He shut the door in my face.

There was nothing for it, but I should leave him alone.

Grenville and I had our claret, then I went down to take supper in the hall while Grenville remained in his rooms. He wanted an early night, he said.

Fletcher did not make an appearance at supper. Rutledge glared at Fletcher's empty chair. Sutcliff, his face white, his nostrils pinched, ate rigidly at the head of his table. There was much nudging and tittering among the boys when Rutledge's eye was not on them.

Rutledge took me to his study after supper and bade

me write more correspondence for him and help him go over expenses. He was in a foul mood and found fault with everything I did, but I chose not to heed him. The fact that I did not cower or shout back enraged him even more, I believe.

His wife smiled serenely down while he spluttered. When he caught me returning the smile, he let out a string of vile invectives and dismissed me for the night.

I simply neatened the papers on my desk, stood, and left him alone.

I imagined Rutledge still cursing when I rose earlier than usual, dressed and shaved myself, and went out to meet Marianne.

I had to wait for her. The early morning air was cold, and I hugged my greatcoat close. Several boats moved along the canal, bathed in mist. The horses plodded on the towpath, heads down, led by equally plodding men. Bargemen on the backs of the long, narrow boats steered through the waters. The towropes hung slack then went taut, then slack again.

Marianne arrived on foot. She wore a long mantle and another deep-crowned bonnet. She marched across the bridge and down to where I waited on the west bank.

She looked carefully past me. "You did not bring *him* with you, did you?"

"I agreed that I would not."

She tilted her head back, eyeing me with a hard gaze. "Gentlemen have broken their words to me before. They laugh about it."

"But not I."

"Still, I am not certain it is a good idea."

I grew impatient. "If you do not wish to tell me, I will not press you. You are correct, it is not my business."

She regarded me a moment longer. "You are disarming with your show of honor, did you know that?"

"Not everyone finds me so."

"More fool they. My feet hurt, and it is a long walk."

I nudged the horse to her, removed my foot from the left stirrup, and held my gloved hand down to her.

She lifted her skirt, giving me a glimpse of a long slender leg, then she thrust her foot into the stirrup and vaulted upward, clinging to my hand as I pulled her into the saddle.

She was evidently used to riding in front of gentlemen, because she settled herself easily on the pommel of the saddle, clutched the horse's mane, and returned the use of the stirrup to me.

I nudged the horse into a walk again. She gave me the direction, and we rode off past Froxfield and down a track that led west of the town. Marianne's bonnet bumped my chin, and I had to twitch sideways to avoid it.

She directed me to a lane that led behind hedgerows. We rode along this for about two miles, then the lane began to rise, winding through taller trees and scrub.

Marianne told me to turn onto a barely marked path between the trees. I guided the gelding slowly, ducking beneath low branches.

She spoke little, except to guide me. I could not imagine why we'd come back here, far from any farm. But she offered no explanation.

The path finally died out in a small clearing. Here, on a bleak pocket of land, stood a tiny house. The cottage's roof was in ill repair. The two windows and door sagged, and neither had seen paint in a long time. Noises came to us from within. We heard a woman shouting, and then a wail, long and winding and shrill. Marianne slid from the saddle and ran inside the house without a word.

I dismounted more slowly, looped the horse's reins over a branch, and stooped beneath a low lintel and into the cottage.

I found what I expected to find. A kitchen occupied the entirety of the cottage's ground floor, with a stair in the corner that led to a room or rooms above. The place was clean, though the cavernous fireplace smoked a little. The kitchen table was littered with fruit, an open bag of flour, and a pot of coarse salt.

The room was deserted, the back door open. I ducked through and found myself in a surprisingly neat garden surrounded by a crumbling wall.

Three people ran through the tall grasses beyond the wall; Marianne, a plump woman who strove to keep up with her, and a small person I could not well see, sprinting far ahead.

I moved through the garden gate after them. The large woman gave up, stood panting, hands on hips. When I reached her, she stared at me, startled, but was too out of breath to ask who I was.

Marianne eventually caught up to the child she chased. Her bonnet tumbled off in the wind and fell to the ground before the lad. His wails abruptly ceased. When he stooped to grab the bonnet, Marianne swept him into her arms.

Astonishment kept me in place as she walked back to us. The lad had long legs that reached to Marianne's knees, and a square body, slightly running to fat. His hair was wheat-colored. He laid his head on Marianne's shoulder and did not lift it when she stopped before us. He seemed content to lie there and let his limbs go slack while she swayed with him, back and forth.

She looked at me over his head. "He is mine," she said, almost fiercely. "His name is David."

The boy lifted his head. His lethargy seemed to leave him, and he squirmed to get down. Marianne set him on his feet.

I put the lad about seven years old, and when I saw his face, I realized what Marianne had hidden.

I had seen children like him before, and they generally did not live very long. His nose was too broad in his round face, especially at the bridge, where it flattened out into his forehead. Low brows jutted out, giving him a frowning look over rather vacant eyes.

"Shake hands," she told him.

David stared up at me, his mouth open. His teeth were dirty and stained. He wore clothes that were soiled, but the dirt came from his recent run through the field, plus flour from the kitchen. The clothes had been fine ones, carefully mended.

I held out my hand to the boy. He continued to stare at me, as though he could not look away from my face. Marianne took his hand, guided it to mine. I shook it. The hand slid away, slack, as though he hadn't noticed.

"Marianne," I said.

The child, without breaking his unabashed stare, suddenly slurred, "Who's he?"

"He is Captain Lacey," Marianne said. "My friend."

Whether the boy registered this or not, he continued to stare at me in blank fascination.

The plump woman was still out of breath. She was not much older than Marianne, and her face was red and creased with worry.

"I am sorry, madam," she said. "He was trying to grub up the pies before I even made 'em, and then ran away when I shouted at him." She looked apologetic, but not contrite.

"Never mind, Maddie," Marianne said. "Let us return to the house. He's filthy."

Her own dress was ruined with mud from his little boots. She took the lad's hand and pulled him around. He planted his feet and would not move until I took his other hand and walked along with them.

Once we'd gained the house, Maddie dragged the lad to the fireplace and started stripping off his clothes, to his squealing protest.

Marianne sank to a bench set against the wall, looking exhausted. I sat next to her, resting my hand on my walking stick. We waited in silence while Maddie cleaned David's face and redressed him in a fresh shirt. He screamed for a while, then as she swiped his nose several times, hard, he began to laugh.

Maddie led David to a stool and sat him there. She told him to stay, and then she returned to the table and her pies.

David remained on the stool for nearly ten minutes, sitting motionless. Then he climbed down, curled up on the floor, and went to sleep. Marianne continued to sit silently.

"I can brew tea for you, if you like," Maddie said to me as she worked. "You're the captain what lives downstairs from Miss Simmons are you not? Not that she's polite enough to introduce ye."

Marianne gave her an irritated look. "Yes."

"No cause for anger," Maddie said. "From what you say, he's a kind gentleman."

"Do not tell him so, he will become arrogant," Marianne answered.

I declined the tea. Maddie shrugged as though it made no difference to her, and began to mix butter into the flour with her fingers. Marianne remained fixed in place. Maddie worked. David slept.

I let questions spin through my head and then fall silent. I thought I knew now where Grenville's generous gifts to Marianne had gone. They'd gone here, to Maddie, to buy food and clothes for David.

I suddenly understood Marianne's grasping selfishness, her economies that included borrowing my candles and coal and snuff. I knew now why she did not want to be shut up in Grenville's elegant house in Clarges Street. From there, she could not visit David, could not make sure he was cared for.

From the slump of her shoulders, I guessed that she was in no way proud of her sacrifice. She was tired of it; she hated it. And yet, she must love David enough to continue caring for him, to continue paying Maddie to look after him while she worked in London.

I let out a small sigh. Marianne shot a glare at me. She rose from the bench and stalked from the cottage without a word. Maddie looked up from her pies but simply watched her go.

I took up my walking stick, said good-bye to Maddie, and followed Marianne.

She waited for me by the gelding, absently stroking his neck. The horse stretched to yank leaves from the tree, most of which it dropped.

"Marianne," I began. "You must tell Grenville."

She turned to me, her face a study of misery. "Would you? If you had a half-wit child, would you tell him?"

I was not certain what I'd do, but I pretended that I would. "Grenville is a generous man. He can help you. I know you are proud, Marianne, but you need his help."

She gave me a defiant look. "He is *not* generous. He gives me money only because I fascinate him, no more. What do you think he'd do, did he know that his money went to another man's child?"

I could not guess that, and she knew I could not. "He deserves to know," I said stubbornly. "You are using his coin."

She walked away from me, swiftly, without looking back. I untied the horse, turned him, followed.

"Suppose he does prove to be generous?" she snapped when I caught up to her. "You know what his generosity is like. He will consider this cottage wretched, try to take David away from it. He'll lock him away somewhere, perhaps in a private house where David will be shut away from all eyes, including mine."

I could not disagree with her. Grenville did like to be high-handed, and he was not always predictable.

Still, I tried to defend him. "You are supposing ahead of yourself. If Grenville wishes to put David in a fine house with every comfort, where is the harm?"

She swung to me, her eyes moist. "Because here, he is happy. He can run about and not be bothered. Maddie does not mind him; she knows how to care for him. I do not want him bewildered by a pack of jailers."

"I agree with you," I said. She looked surprised. "But I still believe he deserves to know."

"You may think so," she said savagely.

"You cannot keep lying to him and hiding, Marianne. He will grow tired of it and decide he's had enough."

She began walking again. "Well, it is simple enough to unravel the tangle. I will cease accepting his money and living in his house. I will be quit of him. Then he can spend his money on some other lady who will be grateful for soft quilts and silk dresses."

Her voice faltered at the end of this speech. She walked along, her head down, her hair hiding her face. She had left her bonnet behind.

"That is not fair to him," I said. "Nor to you. I believe that you care for him."

Her flush told me I'd guessed correctly. "It is useless for me to care for anyone. As you saw."

"Who is David's father?" I asked.

She looked up. "What?"

"Who is David's father? He ought to be giving you coin and making certain his son is well. Name him, and I will drag him here by the neck and shake him until his pockets empty."

She gave me a faint, ironic smile. "Are you not the gallant gentleman? It truly does not matter. I bore David eight years ago, and his father died of a fever seven years ago, the bloody fool."

"Well, then, his family ought to help you," I persisted. "David is their kin."

"A by-blow and a half-wit? Oh, certainly, any family would be pleased to hear of it."

I stopped again, turned her to me. "You should not have to do this alone, Marianne."

"Do not pity me, Lacey. I am finished with pity. I have been taking care of him for eight years now. I am used to it."

"But you no longer need do it alone."

She looked at me in alarm. "Damn you, Lacey, you gave me your word you would not tell him—"

I held up my hand. "I did not mean Grenville, I meant me. I know about David. I can help you."

She stared. "How on earth can you? You barely have two coins to rub together yourself. And in any case, why should you?"

"Do you judge a gentleman only on what he has in his coffers? That is rather irritating of you. I can at least let you talk about David. I can offer my advice, for whatever it is worth, and my ear when you need it."

For one moment, I thought I saw her soften. Marianne Simmons, who turned a hard face to the world, looked for a brief moment, grateful.

The moment did not last long. "I told you, I do not want your pity," she snapped. "David is happy. He does not know that there is anything wrong with him."

"I am pleased to hear it. I am offering you friendship, Marianne. It is all I have to offer. You may take it or leave it alone, as you wish."

She turned away and remained silent while I got myself awkwardly mounted, and boosted her once more into the saddle.

She said, her voice sour, "You must have had a fine upbringing, Lacey, to be so damn obliging."

"I had a terrible upbringing," I said, turning the horse to the road. "But I am determined to be nothing like my boor of a father. You will simply have to bear the brunt of it. You have forgotten your bonnet, you know."

She touched her hand to her bare, golden head. "Leave it," she said. "I hate the bloody thing."

CHAPTER 11

I took Marianne all the way back to Hungerford. We were silent most of the way. Mist hugged the canal, and we rode along the towpath through a hazy world of water and greenery.

We reached Hungerford's High Street and went on to the lane at the end. Before we reached the house, Marianne said, with some of her usual acerbic manner, "By the bye, Mr. Sutcliff visited again last night. He was not pleased to discover that you had spoken to Jeanne Lanier."

"You heard him say that?"

"Certainly, I did. He said so at the top of his voice. The scullery maid in the kitchen must have heard."

"What did Jeanne say to that?"

"I could not hear her as well. But she tried to soothe him, from the sound of it. Said things like, 'it does not matter' and 'you must not take on so.'"

"I wonder," I mused. "Was he speaking in jealousy,

or was he afraid she might have revealed something to me?"

"Well, I cannot tell you," Marianne said. "I could not press my ear to the door, because Mrs. Albright was standing in the hall. She was listening, too, if I am any judge. Neither of us heard enough to satisfy our curiosity."

"Did he stay long?" I asked Marianne.

"Most of the night. That is, if the creaking of the bed frame was any indication. I had to sleep with my pillow over my head again."

I did not wish to think about Sutcliff in bed with the gracious Jeanne Lanier. I murmured, "I wonder how long it creaked on Sunday night?"

Marianne shrugged. "All night, hard and long, as far as I know. And her gasping and moaning. I don't know when he left, but I could find out if you like. Mrs. Albright is a nosy old body; she likely knows. Or I can ask Jeanne directly. Women like to chat about their men, you know, either to claim theirs is better or to disparage him."

I tried not to shudder at the thought of ladies sitting nose-to-nose comparing the faults of their gentlemen. "Very well, but have a care."

"I always take excellent care of myself, Lacey."

We reached the house. She slid from the horse. In the polite world, she would have invited me in for breakfast or coffee, but this was far from the polite world, and doubtless she wanted me to leave her alone. Revelations about one's inner secrets can be rather embarrassing.

As the door closed behind her, I spied Jeanne Lanier

looking out of a window in the upper story. Tree branches grew against the house, and she peered through them as though wondering who had ridden to the door. When she caught my eye, she smiled and nodded a greeting.

I tipped my hat to her, then turned and took my leave.

I rode back along the canal, preferring the quiet, cool green of the towpath to the main road where I'd have to dodge the mail coaches and other wagons. More boats plied the canal now, floating silently along the smooth trail.

When I approached Lower Sudbury Lock, I heard argument. The lockkeeper stood on the bank, hands on hips, and directed his invective to a boat beyond the lock. I rode past on the towpath to look.

A narrow boat had sidled up to the lock from the south and west. This one was full of people, children with brown faces, women who covered their heads with gaily covered scarves, and one young man who lounged in the stern smoking a long-stemmed pipe. A goat stood tied in the bow, nibbling in a bored manner on straw.

An older man, his skin brown with sun, his steps slow and sure, led a fat horse along the bank

The man leading the horse stopped at the lock. The barge continued its forward momentum until it bumped the gates. The lockkeeper was glaring at the bargeman, not moving to turn the cranks. "Best go back," he spat. "Don't want you up here. Your kind have already done enough."

The Romany man simply stared at him, black eyes enigmatic.

"Let him through," I said on impulse.

The lockkeeper glared at me. "Rutledge wants them cleared out." He curled his lip as though to say I ought to have known that.

"I will explain to Rutledge. I wish to speak to them."

The lockkeeper looked as though he'd like to hurl me into the canal and let the Roma fish me out. He settled for a black stare, then turned to the pumps.

The lock gate slowly opened. The Romany led his horse forward, and the boat coasted gently inside. While the lock filled with water, lifting the boat, women, children, goat, and all, I asked the Romany man point-blank whether Sebastian D'Arby was his relation.

He looked at me. Intelligence glinted in his eyes. "He is my nephew."

He must be the uncle who so disliked Sebastian working at the Sudbury School. "You know that he has been accused of murder," I said.

"I heard," the man responded dryly. "I knew that no good would come of him mixing with the English."

"You told him so," I said. "Did you not? On Sunday night. You spoke—or rather, argued—for a long time."

"Aye." He did not ask how I knew.

"Where did he meet you?"

"Down past Great Bedwyn. We moored there for the night."

"What time did he reach you?"

The man shrugged. "The Roma are not interested in time. We know morning, afternoon, night."

I gave him a skeptical look. He caught my gaze, and his lips twitched. "Perhaps half past ten," he said.

"How long did he stay?"

"It is important, is it?"

"I wish to help Sebastian," I said impatiently. "I seem to be the only person in Sudbury who does not believe he murdered Middleton."

The Romany looked me up and down. He looked neither angry nor pleased. "He stayed a good long time. Until just before sunrise."

"Sunrise? Are you certain?"

Sebastian had told me he'd returned at two o'clock, long before sunrise. He'd sworn so on oath to the coroner.

"Aye," he said. He smiled, showing brown teeth. "I do recognize sunrise, Englishman."

I ignored that. "What did you do when Sebastian left you?"

He shrugged. "Pulled up our mooring and started west. I was angry at young Sebastian, did not much want to see him. So we went back down, toward Bath."

"We didn't," said a voice behind him. "We didn't right away."

We both turned. A woman stood on the deck of the barge. She was younger than the bargeman and wore a bright blue shawl around her shoulders. "We did not turn to Bath right away. We floated Sebastian up toward Sudbury, at least as far as Lower Sudbury Lock."

She had a fine voice, soft and contralto. The voice did not match her face, which was quite plain. She had thin lips and a narrow nose, nothing remarkable. Her dark eyes, however, reminded me of the those of ladies in Spain, who watched soldiers march by and promised them delights if they turned aside.

"At sunrise?" I asked.

The older man scowled at her. She gazed back at him, undaunted. "Just before. It was still dark, the sky just gray."

"You did not call the lockkeeper to open the lock for you?" I asked.

"We had no need. Sebastian stepped off the boat, and we went back the other way. The next lockkeeper down let us through."

So they had been at Lower Sudbury Lock at sunrise. And the lockkeeper had not heard them? Nor had he heard Middleton's body being deposited in the lock.

"We move like ghosts," Sebastian's uncle said. He smiled again.

The lockkeeper bent over his wheels, cranking them to shut off the pumps. He turned the gear to open the gates. "Bloody Romany," he muttered.

The Romany moved the horse slowly forward, pulling the barge into the canal. I turned my horse next to his.

"Then you were at the site of the murder," I said. "Tell me what you saw."

The Romany raised his grizzled brows. "Nothing to see. Canal quiet, land waking to the day. Nothing more."

"A shadow," the woman said. Again Sebastian's uncle glared at her; again, she took no notice. "A shadow by the lock gate. Someone staying hidden. I could not see who."

Not Sebastian. The murderer? Why the murderer, though? The doctor had said the body had been deposited at least four hours before it was found, and it was found at six o'clock, just after daybreak. Why should the murderer linger?

"If Sebastian was with you at sunrise, according to your evidence, he could not have placed the body in the lock," I said. "He could not have killed the groom. Will you tell the magistrate this?"

The Romany spat. "Will the magistrate listen to me?"

I thought of the magistrate and his treatment of Sebastian. I thought of Rutledge and the constable. They all believed the Roma to be liars. Sebastian's uncle was no fool. "I know a magistrate who might," I said slowly.

I was thinking of Sir Montague Harris, the magistrate of the Whitechapel house in London. He had intelligence, and he actually listened to my ideas, as farfetched as they were.

Sebastian's uncle faced me, angry. "Sebastian has forsaken us. He does not like Romany ways. He would rather be a slave to Englishmen and lust after a girl with pearl-white skin. What need has he of us?"

The woman looked sad. "Must we abandon him?"

"He has abandoned us," the Romany said fiercely. The children on the boat had gone quiet, watching their elders with large eyes. "He has abandoned you."

I tried to placate him. "I am certain Sebastian does not mean to desert you entirely. He seems fond of you all."

"Does he?" The Romany looked me up and down, black eyes snapping. "Then why does he refuse to return to us? That night I argued with him long, yes. And he agreed to nothing. Not anything I said could persuade him, nor could his spending the rest of the night with his wife."

I stared at him, dumbfounded, while his last words struck me. "His wife?"

The Romany jerked his thumb over his shoulder, and I looked again at the young woman standing patiently on the deck. "Aye. Young Megan. She is Sebastian's wife."

I left the Roma on the bank of the canal. I forgot all about breakfast and charged back to Sudbury to persuade the constable's housekeeper to let me see Sebastian.

Sebastian looked slightly better but still gazed longingly at the door when the plump woman let me in.

I called Sebastian a bloody fool, and then told him why. He flushed and would not meet my eyes. "It is true, then," I said. "She is your wife, and you were with her that night."

"She is not my wife," he growled. "We were never married in a church, with an English license. My uncle decided she should be my wife about one year ago and brought her to live with us."

I remembered the first time I had visited Sebastian here, remembered the constable's housekeeper telling me that a Romany woman had tried to see Sebastian. Sebastian had blushed and said it had been his mother. I knew now that the visitor must have been Megan. She must have come to see whether he was all right. A wife who loved her husband would do that.

"And you spent all of Sunday night with her?" I asked. "On your family's boat?"

"Yes," he said.

"Then why the devil did you not say so?"

He looked at me as though I'd gone mad. "In the magistrate's court? With Miss Rutledge's father looking on, to take her the news of all that happened?"

I let out a sigh. "So you lied because of Miss Rutledge. I take it from your reluctance that Miss Rutledge does not know about Megan?"

"No," he said.

"Good God, Sebastian. You cannot have it both ways."

He looked at me defiantly. "That is why I took the post at the Sudbury School. To work and have money so that I no longer have to be Romany."

"Megan seems to care about you."

"Megan is an obedient woman. She does what her father tells her, she does what my uncle tells her."

Belinda Rutledge, on the other hand, must seem like a tragic heroine to him, a pretty young woman dominated by her father and chafing at her bonds. Why settle for dutiful kindness when one can have romantic devotion?

"Megan said that she would be willing to tell the magistrate that you stayed with her," I said. "That you did not return to the stables at two o'clock, but left your family at sunrise."

Sebastian's brows knit. "I do not wish her to."

"You would prefer to hang for a murder you did not commit?"

He shook his head, a little desperate. "No."

"You are the most stubborn young man I have ever

met, Sebastian. I like you, but your head is in the wrong place."

He gave me a pleading look. "The magistrate will not believe Megan, in any case. She is Romany."

"That is possible. What you need is an independent witness." I thought a moment about the shadowy figure Megan had seen hovering near the lock. I had some ideas about that. I also thought about Megan and her patient eyes. Sebastian was an idiot.

"You are a romantic fool, Sebastian," I told him. "Did you plan to elope with Miss Rutledge? Even if you managed to marry her, your family would never accept her, and her family would banish her. Life is long, my young friend. Do not make it more difficult than it already has to be."

He, of course, did not believe me. "I love Miss Rutledge," he said stubbornly. "I would die for her."

"Perhaps. But would dying for her do her any good? Duty is difficult, and well I know it. But sometimes it is all we have."

Sebastian studied his strong, brown hands. I was asking him to chose between losing his life and losing the woman he loved. To him, at twenty, each choice was equally foul. To die in ignominy or to live in wretchedness must seem the same to him.

"I believe Megan will try to make you happy," I suggested.

He looked up at me, a rueful smile on his lips. "Then you do not know her."

I was puzzled. "She did not seem a shrew to me."

"No. She is quiet and obedient, as you say."

Still his eyes held a glint of something I did not understand. I conceded that I knew little of Megan save my brief conversation with her. But perhaps I'd grown jaded and bit cynical about love. A quiet, plain woman determined to do her duty seemed a restful choice over storms of emotion.

Sebastian looked at me across twenty years, and did not agree.

I tried another tactic. "If you take the blame for the murder, Sebastian, then the true killer will go free. He could be at the school, right now, or in the village of Sudbury. Do you think Miss Rutledge will be safe? What if he decides she knows you did not kill Middleton and wishes to keep her from speaking? Or what happens if he decides your family is a danger?"

Sebastian looked at me in alarm. "You must look after Miss Rutledge. You must tell my family to get away."

"I cannot be everywhere. And I cannot live at Sudbury the rest of my life."

He looked away, eyes troubled. "The magistrate will not believe me, or my uncle, or Megan."

"Leave that to me," I said. "Now, tell me the truth this time, when you arrived at Lower Sudbury Lock, did you see any person, or any activity out of the ordinary?"

He shook his head. "I wished only to reach the stables before the others stirred. I never noticed."

"A pity, but never mind." I rose, leaned on my walking stick in the low-ceilinged room. "If you truly love Miss Rutledge, you will let her go. Let her marry a gentleman who will take her to live in a dull house and talk of dull things. She will be cared for, in that way."

He looked at me, eyes full. "You are wrong. Her father will marry her off to a man just like him, one who will make her miserable."

Sadly, I suspected he was right. If Rutledge allowed Belinda to marry at all, he'd likely find someone as bullying and tyrannical as he was.

I sighed, put on my hat, told Sebastian good morning, and let myself out of his cell.

UPON my return to Sudbury School, I found breakfast just ending and tutors and pupils scurrying to lessons. Grenville emerged from the dining hall among the crowd and hailed me.

"I breakfasted with Rutledge in the dining hall," he said. "Fletcher was there." He nodded toward the lean man who stalked down the corridor to his lecture hall. "He spoke to no one. Mr. Sutcliff still seems subdued. In my opinion, Sutcliff needed the thrashing."

"I have no doubt he did. But I wonder what provoked it."

"I could not get close enough to Fletcher to ask." Grenville looked me up and down, taking in my muddy boots and breeches. "What did you get up to this morning? Rutledge demanded I tell him your whereabouts, and I was forced to answer that I did not know. I must say, it has been a long while since a headmaster called me on the carpet."

"I found the Roma," I said evasively. "Sebastian stayed with them the night of the murder. I would tell you more, but Rutledge is glaring." I tipped my hat. "I will see you at dinner."

Grenville looked annoyed, but he could say no

more. He would simply have to wait until I could tell him the tale.

In Rutledge's study, I removed my hat and gloves, seated myself, and gave myself to my duties. Rutledge entered soon after I did, gave me a long, loud-breathed stare. He strode to his desk and sat down.

"You missed breakfast," he observed.

"I was riding."

He said nothing. He opened ledgers, shuffled papers. "Presently," he said, "I plan to sack Fletcher."

I stopped writing, raised my brows. "Does he deserve that?"

"Of course he does. Getting his books burned in the quad, losing his temper with a pupil who can make a large difference to this school."

I wondered suddenly if Sutcliff had demanded that Fletcher be sacked.

Rutledge glared at his ledger. "Damn difficult to find another Classics instructor. Fletcher at least knows his subject."

"Then why let him go?"

He did not answer. "I would ask Grenville for a recommendation," he said in a surely tone. "But he's already landed me with a damn fool secretary."

"I had thought you satisfied with my work."

"Oh, I have no quarrel with your *work*, Lacey. But your tongue is sharp, and you have difficulty with respect. Did your regimental colonel never beat any into you?"

I was torn between anger and amusement. "My regimental colonel did not. And I do have respect, sir, for a man's deeds and his comportment. I cannot respect a man simply because he was born into the correct family or has a large fortune."

"Huh. You are egalitarian, like the damned Frenchies. You do not respect me."

"Not true. You have a difficult job, and you carry it out with efficiency. Even if you are a bit ruthless."

His grizzled brows rose. "High praise from my impudent secretary."

"I beg your pardon if I am impudent. At times, in the army, if a man did not speak his mind, it could be life or death for his men. I came into the habit."

"Humph. Grenville ought to have warned me."

"Yes, he ought." I finished the letter I was copying, laid down my pen, sanded the sheet. "I would like to journey to London tomorrow."

Rutledge stared. "Eh? What for?"

I had known he'd balk, so I was prepared. "When I arrived, we agreed that I should have a holiday once a fortnight. Tomorrow is a fortnight since my arrival."

He gave me a sour look. "I wonder why I do not sack you."

I met his gaze with a tranquil one of my own. "Grenville would not be pleased."

"No, he would not. Grenville's approval is much sought after these days, is it not? I must be able to say that Sudbury School has it. You have a powerful friend in him, you know, Lacey."

"I know." I felt somewhat ashamed of myself for deliberately baiting Rutledge, but I was in a foul mood, and tired of trying to please people. I was angry at Sebastian for lying, and angry that I would have to hurt Belinda Rutledge in order to set him free. Her life was not tranquil, and I hated to destroy her one bit of happiness, as tenuous as it was.

"Very well, take your holiday," Rutledge grumbled. He looked back at his ledger and muttered, "Dear God, but I am besieged by fools."

I knew precisely how he felt.

CHAPTER 12

❧

I left for London the next morning with Bartholomew.
After a long discussion with Grenville that escalated
into near argument, he agreed to stay and keep an eye
on things in Sudbury. I knew he was worried about me
visiting James Denis alone. James Denis and I always
stood on precarious ground, and Grenville feared that
I'd overstep my bounds and Denis would retaliate. I
promised I'd be cautious, and Grenville at last conceded.

I had reported to him about what I had learned from
Sebastian and his family. His reaction was similar to
mine—surprise and annoyance. He agreed to watch
over Belinda Rutledge and also to continue investigating in my absence.

I sent a message to Marianne explaining that I was
traveling to London and that Grenville was remaining.
I half-hoped she would seek out Grenville while I was
gone and confess her troubles to him. Neither of us

could predict what Grenville would do, but in all fairness, I ought to give him a chance. So should Marianne.

I had planned to go post, but Grenville insisted I take his traveling coach, and I did not argue with him too heatedly. So, at five o'clock in the morning, Bartholomew and I departed Sudbury and rode in luxury to London.

Grenville, as always, had stocked the coach well. A compartment held port and crystal glasses, and Bartholomew had procured a bit of roast from the Sudbury School kitchens in case we grew hungry on the road.

He also reported to me what the constable had discovered, that the knife that I had found in the brush had come from the kitchens of the school. The cook, a very fat woman of about fifty years, was most distraught. Knives, she'd snapped to Bartholomew, were very dear, and why did the Romany have to steal one from *her* kitchen?

The information was useful. Sebastian had never been allowed on the grounds outside the stables, and no one, Bartholomew said, had ever seen him near the kitchens. A point in Sebastian's favor if I could get Rutledge and the magistrate to believe it.

Bartholomew and I ate and talked, drank and rested through the long ride. By the time we reached London later that afternoon, the roast was a bone and the port gone.

Grenville had insisted I spend my visit to London in his house in Grosvenor Street. Bartholomew charged inside when we reached it early that afternoon, shouting orders to get rooms ready for me. To my discomfiture, the maids and footmen scurried about the place as though the Prince Regent had come to call.

Bartholomew took me to the huge guest room that I had used once before, unpacked my clothes, shined my boots, and told me that Anton, the chef, was creating a midday meal especially for me. I resigned myself to sleeping in a soft bed and eating fine food, though I felt a bit of a fool eating by myself in the palatial dining room while a maid and two footman hovered near to serve me.

After I thanked them and showered compliments on the chef, I at last persuaded the eager staff that I had to go out.

There was nothing for it but that I use Grenville's town coach, they said. This I did refuse, preferring to be inconspicuous on my errands. The servants looked bewildered, but Bartholomew assured them that I was investigating and needed to be cautious, and so they at last let me depart.

My first visit was to Sir Montague Harris in Whitechapel. Sir Montague, a man I'd helped earlier that spring with the affair of the Glass House, greeted me effusively. Sir Montague was rotund and had silver hair which he wore in an old-fashioned queue. I had written him, outlining the situation at the Sudbury School and keeping him informed of what I'd discovered. He began discussing things even as his servant bustled around to bring us coffee.

"A pretty problem," Sir Montague said, his eyes twinkling. "You will make yourself unpopular if you champion this Romany, you know."

"I am already unpopular," I said dryly. I accepted the coffee, sat down. "But I have found no connection between Sebastian and Middleton except that they worked together in the stables. The Roma's evidence shows that Sebastian was with his family on the barge when Middleton was getting himself killed. They could, of course, be covering up for him, I cannot deny that. Also, Sebastian swears he did not quarrel with Middleton."

"That quarrel seems odd to me," Sir Montague said. He sipped his coffee and dismissed his servant. "Only one of the stable hands heard it, no one else. If Sebastian is telling the truth, then either the stable hand Thomas Adams was mistaken, or Adams was lying, and why should he?"

"Unless Adams murdered Middleton and is attempting to thrust the blame onto Sebastian," I suggested. "Adams could have killed him, I suppose. The stable hands were fast asleep. Not one of them can confirm when Sebastian returned to the stables. Thomas Adams could easily have slipped out."

Sir Montague looked thoughtful. He leaned back in a chair whose wooden arms had spread to fit his bulk, and whose seat sagged in a perfect U. "Or perhaps Sebastian and his people did not like that Middleton was in on a scheme to expand the canal. So they killed him." He looked at me, waiting to see what I made of that.

I shook my head. "An expanded canal system means the Roma could travel farther, though they'd have more tolls to pay. No, I can see no reason for Sebastian to hate Middleton, unless it was personal—for instance, if Middleton were impertinent to Miss Rutledge. But I have heard no evidence to this end. From all I gather, Middleton and those in the house rarely interacted."

"Ah, but Miss Rutledge came to the stables to ride. She managed to steal moments with Sebastian, did she not? Perhaps Middleton knew this, threatened to tell her father."

I sat back comfortably, thought this over. I liked talking to Sir Montague. He could steeple his fingers, put forth every argument, logical and illogical, and force me to counter them. He approached things without emotion, with only academic interest in a problem. I, who tended to approach everything with emotion, appreciated that he tried to make me think clearly.

"Sebastian seemed more bewildered by the man's death than satisfied," I said. "I never sensed that he had any anger toward Middleton; in fact, he was grateful to the man for letting him work in the stables."

"But you discovered that Sebastian was a liar."

"True. I am not happy with him for keeping the truth from me. I do not believe that he clearly understood what not being open right from the start would do to him, but I believe it is dawning on him now."

"The case against young Sebastian, then," Sir Montague said, "is that he and Middleton supposedly quarreled, perhaps about Miss Rutledge, Sebastian followed Middleton and killed him. He is young, he is fiery, he is Romany, and therefore, likely to be violent." He paused, studying the ceiling a moment. "However, if Miss Rutledge and Sebastian's family are both telling the truth, the timing is all wrong. Sebastian would not have had time to meet with Miss Rutledge, lure Middleton down the canal to the spot where you found the knife, kill him, get his corpse into a boat, row up the canal, deposit the corpse in the lock, row back down, get rid of the boat, wash himself and change his bloody clothes, and then meet with his family. Time would have had to stand still, or half a dozen people would have to be in on the lie. Possibly, yes; probably, no."

"You see that," I said. "The task is to get the country magistrate to see that. I did not want to involve Miss Rutledge, but it may be unavoidable."

"Unless you and I can decide what truly happened," Sir Montague said smoothly. "Which is why you are here, is it not?"

I admitted that it was. Sir Montague grinned at me. "Who else, then, would want to see Middleton dead?" he asked. "He worked for James Denis, then retired and became a groom at a boys' school in the country. A man like that could have murderous enemies from his past, of course, one of whom trailed him to the school."

"But surely a stranger would be noticed in a small place like Sudbury," I argued, remembering what Grenville had said about gossip in small towns. "Someone would mention a mysterious stranger who arrived, and then disappeared after the murder."

"Yes, mysterious strangers are always convenient. But alas, we do not have one in this case." He made a motion of dusting off his hands. "Therefore, we must look among the people of the nearby towns and the school. You describe them well, you know," he remarked, eyes merry. "Not in a way they'd find flattering, I'd imagine. Take Mr. Rutledge himself. Driven to run the school on the tightest discipline, a violent man in his own right."

I absently ran my thumb along the handle of my cup. "I have not ruled out Rutledge. If I can imagine anyone grabbing a large man like Middleton and slicing his throat, it is Rutledge. But as far as Rutledge's servants contend, Rutledge did not leave his bed that night."

"But you say that Rutledge grew angry and worried when you told him of the connection between Middleton and James Denis. Perhaps he knew of it already. Perhaps Rutledge feared Middleton for some reason—Middleton blackmailed him, Middleton was watching him for Denis—and Rutledge, in a panic, decided to do away with him."

"I will be asking James Denis if there is any connection," I said. "Denis professes that he is unhappy about Middleton's death."

Sir Montague eyed me shrewdly. "There is not many a man in England who can simply decide to question Mr. Denis. You are unique, Captain. I do hope you will tell me what he says."

I gave him a nod. "Of course."

Sir Montague tapped his forefinger. "So . . . there is Rutledge. Next is, who? Mr. Sutcliff is seen by Mr. Ramsay, who swears he ran after Middleton. What about Mr. Sutcliff? Why would he want Middleton dead?"

I shrugged. "I have no idea. He's a nasty bit of goods, though. None of other boys can stick him. Ramsay is so terrified that the lads will think he's cut from the same cloth that he is willing to put snakes in my bed and smoke cheroots behind the wall with the others." I thought a moment. "I have no idea why Sutcliff would kill Middleton, but he is a large enough lad. He could do it if he took Middleton by surprise. However, I have it that Sutcliff spent that night in bed with his mistress in Hungerford. The timing is wrong for him, as well. My actress friend tells me he was with Jeanne Lanier all night."

"Did she see him?" Sir Montague asked. "Or only hear him?"

"That is a point," I conceded. "Marianne is shrewd enough to realize the difference, but I will ask her."

Sir Montague nodded, then continued. "There are plenty of others. The lockkeeper himself, who never heard a body being pushed into his lock. The stable hand, Thomas Adams, who manufactures a quarrel to point to the Romany."

"The lockkeeper lives alone," I pointed out, "so he has no one to vouch for him. And again, the stable hands noticed nothing all night. So either he or Adams *could* have done it."

"And the tutors? Fletcher, the Classics tutor?"

"Fletcher is not very big. Middleton could easily have fought him off, even if he took Middleton by surprise. And I cannot imagine him being brave enough to lure Middleton to that remote place by the canal. The same with Tunbridge, the mathematics tutor."

"Tunbridge, you say, often went riding."

"Yes. A tenuous connection, if any. As far as I can see, Tunbridge spends his time schooling his favorite pupil, a sixteen-year-old boy who is apparently quite brilliant. He gives the lad private lessons." I'd heard a few of the other boys sniggering about those private lessons, but I'd not yet formed my own opinion.

"Well, it looks as though you need to find out much more about Middleton," Sir Montague said. "The canal maps are interesting. Why should a man like Middleton keep false maps of the Kennet and Avon Canal? You found no other papers?"

"No. Anything that could explain the maps had either never existed or been taken away."

"Indeed. I have come to respect your opinions, Captain. There is definitely more going on at the Sudbury School than meets the eye." His eyes twinkled. "I might fancy a holiday in the country."

My heart lightened. I'd hoped he'd be interested. Sir Montague was a busy man; I could not think how he would escape his duties to come to Berkshire, but I was happy that he would make the attempt.

"Now then," he said, "I suppose you're off to do what every uncorrupt magistrate in London wishes to do—question James Denis."

My good humor dimmed. "He allows me to question him only because he knows I can do nothing against him."

Sir Montague's look turned wise. "Can you not?"

"I do not see what," I said irritably. "He tells me he finds me a threat, but I believe he exaggerates."

"Do you?" Sir Montague asked. He smiled. "Well, I do not. I believe that Mr. Denis is a very intelligent man. Very intelligent, indeed."

•   •   •   •   •

I left Whitechapel and took a hackney to Mayfair, arriving at James Denis' Curzon Street house as darkness fell.

I did not have an appointment, but Denis seemed to expect me. The correct and cold butler who opened the door took me upstairs to Denis' study without asking for my card or telling me to wait.

As I entered Denis' elegant but rather austere private study, James Denis put aside whatever letter he was writing and rose from his desk.

James Denis was a fairly young man, not much more than thirty. His face was long and thin, but handsome, or would have been were it not so cold. His hair was brown, and he was tall, almost my height. His blue eyes were flinty hard, as though he'd viewed the world for a long time and found it wanting. If an old, jaded man had been reborn and decided to take the world by its heels the second time around, that man would be James Denis.

He did not offer to shake my hand. The butler brought a wing chair across the room to the desk, and I sat, grateful, in truth, to ease my leg. The ride in the hackney had been chilly, long, and jostling.

The butler then brought a tray with a decanter of brandy and two crystal glasses, poured us each a measure, and silently departed.

We were not left alone, however. As usual, two large, burly men had taken up stations, one at each window, to watch over Denis and his guest. Once upon a time, Middleton had shared this task. What must it be, I thought suddenly, to have so many enemies that one could not sit alone in a room in one's own house?

I let the brandy sit untasted, although Denis took up his glass and sipped delicately.

"Oliver Middleton left my employ voluntarily," he said, as though we were already in the middle of a conversation. "He'd tired of the city and wanted the simple life of the country."

"So might many a man," I agreed.

Denis opened a drawer of his desk and pulled out a folded paper. "Middleton spied you the moment you arrived, you know. He wrote me of it."

He handed me the paper. It was a letter, addressed in a painfully neat hand, the creases soiled. I unfolded it. The note was short and to the point. "That captain's come. Should I do anything?"

I raised my brows, slid the paper back to him. "How did you respond?"

Denis dropped the letter back inside the desk. "I wrote him with instructions to leave you strictly alone. He agreed. He said he would avoid you in case his temper got the better of him."

"That explains why I never saw the man in the stables."

Denis did not change expression. "Did you know that Middleton had received threatening letters?"

"No," I said, surprised. The school's prankster had sent letters in blood to a few students, so Rutledge had told me, but I had not heard that Middleton had received any.

Again, Denis dipped into his desk and pulled out a stack of letters. I wondered whether he had kept all Middleton's correspondence near at hand in anticipation of my visit.

"The letters implied that the writer knew who Middleton was and that he had once worked for me," he said. "Middleton sent me the bundle, asked me what to do about it."

He let me leaf through the letters. Each were printed in careful capitals, and each held a similar message. "You cannot hide your past misdeeds. Retribution is at hand," one said. Another: "You came to find peace. Hell has followed you."

"A touch gruesome," I said. "I would not have liked to receive them."

"They did not worry Middleton, particularly," Denis said, gathering the letters and refolding them. "He was a very practical man. He did not fear words. At first, he reasoned that the letters were from one of my enemies, a threat to me in general." He dropped his gaze. "He assumed I would take care of it. It bothers me that I failed him." He folded the last letter with unnecessary firmness, the first time I had ever seen anything but coolness from James Denis.

"A moment," I said. "You said that he thought the threat a general one, *at first.* Did he change his mind?"

Denis pushed the letters aside with long fingers. "He did. He sent me another message, saying that he'd discovered who had written the threats. The tone was one of irritation. He informed me that he would take care of the matter."

"And he did not say who?"

"No." He looked up at me, eyes quiet with anger. "If he did take care of the matter, I never heard. He was killed first."

Denis was bothered. I had never seen him so bothered. Uncharitably, I wondered whether his concern came from fellow feeling or the fear that he'd be perceived as weak if one in his employ was harmed. Both, possibly.

Denis lifted the last of Middleton's correspondence and handed it to me. I read the letter, which was brief and terse and said exactly what Denis had told me it did.

"From his tone," I said, "he seems to have decided the culprit weak and easy to dispatch."

"Yes, he is contemptuous."

I considered. "He could not mean Rutledge. Rutledge would rather bellow threats than write them in letters, and I cannot think of Rutledge as weak and easy to dispatch. Nor would Sebastian, the Romany arrested for his murder, be. Also, Sebastian cannot read, or so he claims."

"A tutor," Denis suggested.

"Or a pupil." I thought of Sutcliff. Was he the sort of young man who would threaten people from afar? Or would he, like Rutledge, prefer to bellow at them face-to-face? "But what on earth would anyone gain by threatening Middleton? He had no real power at the school. He had a connection to you, but you tell me he'd retired."

I studied the letter again. It also included a line that Middleton had something of interest to speak to Denis about, and hoped he could do so when he next visited London. "What had he intended to tell you? Was he involved in something for you?"

Denis twined his fingers before him. "I must assure

you, Captain, that I am as in the dark as you in this matter. Middleton was no longer working for me. He was not young any more, he was tired, he wanted to work with horses again. I found him employment in the stables at the Sudbury School."

I raised my brows. "You found him employment? That might explain why Rutledge grew nervous when I revealed I knew you. Did Rutledge owe you a favor?"

Denis gave me a wintry smile. "Let us focus on the problem at hand, Captain."

I had not really thought he'd give me an answer. I told him then of the canal maps that Grenville and I had found in Middleton's room. Denis' brow knit. "Middleton never mentioned canals to me. At Hungerford, you say? I have heard nothing of any such scheme."

Though his expression remained unchanged, I sensed his annoyance. Denis did not like to be uninformed of or surprised by anything.

I also sensed that one of his tame pugilists was watching us. The man's hands were twitching, and he kept taking a step forward, then a step back, as though unable to decide whether to cross to the desk. I caught his eye. Denis, noticing my interest, looked that way as well.

Caught, the man cleared his throat. "Begging your pardon, sir."

Unlike Rutledge, who hated when his servants interrupted, Denis merely focused a calm gaze on his lackey, waited for him to speak.

The man's voice was gravelly, his working-class accent thick. "I saw Ollie Middleton, sir, in London a month or so back. We had a pint. He said how he remembered why he hated the country, all mud and sheep shit up to his knees, but he would be all right soon. He was going to make his fortune, he said, and eat off gold plates."

"Did he?" Denis asked, arching one thin brow.

"That he did, sir. He did say something about canals. It sounded daft. I thought it was just him going on."

Denis gave him a severe look. "I could wish you had told me this before."

The man, as hard-bitten as he was, looked slightly apprehensive. "Sorry, sir. I didn't think it meant nothing."

"No matter." He kept his unwavering gaze on his lackey for a moment before finally turning away. The man moved back to his position, nervously fingering his collar.

"Perhaps he'd invested in these false canals, then," Denis said to me, "believing he'd grow rich. Though I would be surprised to learn he was that gullible. It would be likely that he was fooling others into investing with him."

I did not answer. I was thinking rapidly, remembering one other man who had rambled on over a pint that he would soon make his fortune and leave the drudgery of the Sudbury School behind. Bloody hell.

"Is something amiss, Captain?" Denis asked, his sharp gaze on me.

I met his appraising glance but did not answer. I was not certain of my speculation, and the last thing I wanted was for Denis to send his minions to fetch Simon Fletcher. Fletcher's pondering might mean nothing and might not be connected to Middleton's at all. I would prefer to question him myself, rather than let Denis get his clutches on the poor man.

"I'd rather you shared your information, Captain," Denis said, a warning note in his voice.

"I have no information. Not yet. Only ideas."

"I want this murderer found and punished, Captain—quickly. I do not have time for your scruples."

"And I am not looking for the murderer in order to please you," I returned. "I wish to clear a young man who I believe is not responsible. Whether you are pleased by it does not concern me."

Denis looked annoyed, but he was used to my temper by now. "Very well, Captain, I know you enjoy pursuing things in your own fashion. But I want the identity of this murderer. Surely we both want that."

"Yes," I admitted. "I will give it to you when I know it for certain."

He gave me a cool look but nodded. He did not trust me entirely, but he did trust my thoroughness.

He folded his hands on his desk, the interview apparently over. With Denis, one did not make pleasant small talk to end one's visit. The visit simply ended.

But I had one more question, one more reason I had decided to visit James Denis today. It was a question I was reluctant to ask, because the knowledge would pain me, but I had finally screwed up my courage to ask it.

"Last year," I began slowly, "you told me you knew the whereabouts of a lady who once called herself Carlotta Lacey."

A flicker of surprise darted through his blue eyes. He must have been wondering when I'd return to that.

"Yes. If you want her direction, you know that you have but to ask."

I sat in silence for a moment. The room was quiet, ironically, almost pleasantly so. The fire warmed the air despite the rain that beat at the windows. The other men watched me carefully, the only sound the faint whisper of clothing as they shifted their stances.

I wanted to ask, but I knew what would happen if I did. During the affair of Hanover Square and again during the affair of the regimental colonel, Denis had helped me solve the crimes by handing me facts I had lacked. He had let it be known that by doing me those favors, he expected me to be ready when he called in favors of his own. In addition, not a month ago, he had paid a note of hand I had owed, ensuring that I would be still more obligated to him. In this way, he had warned me, he planned to prevent me from crusading against him, since having had me beaten had not had much effect.

He had offered the information about my wife last summer with the same understanding—his knowledge for my obligation. And obligation to James Denis was not to be taken lightly. He used people from all walks of life and all over Europe to help him in his crimes, to procure things, to find things out for him, to let him wield quiet power. The men he hired stole for him, murdered for him, spied for him. I wondered very much what he would expect me to do, and exactly what he would do when I refused.

When I could trust myself to speak again, I asked, "Is she well?"

"Yes," he answered, studying me.

I believed him. Denis' networks could discover details about any person or any thing. He would doubtless know not only where my estranged wife lived, but with whom and where she walked and what she ate for breakfast.

He went on. "My sources tell me that your wife and daughter are well cared for."

I started to nod, then I went still as my mind registered his entire answer. "My daughter," I said.

Denis had told me of Carlotta last summer, but he had omitted, whether deliberately or because he did not think it important, that he also had knowledge of my daughter, Gabriella.

"Yes," Denis said. "She is a very pretty young woman, from what is reported to me."

I closed my eyes. I remembered Gabriella as a tiny mite with hair as golden as the Spanish sunshine. Carlotta had taken her away from me. I'd tried to go after them both, tried to find them, ready to drag my wife home so that I would not lose my daughter.

But I had not been able to find them. I'd heard no trace of them, though I'd tried, until Denis had presented me with his information last summer.

Now I learned that Denis knew where to find them both.

Gabriella would be seventeen now, a young lady, and she would not remember me.

Denis said something to one of the lackeys in the room. I could not hear the words. I opened my eyes to find the pugilist who'd told us about Middleton lifting me to my feet.

The man helped me down the stairs, more or less pressed me out of the front door, and closed it behind me. The interview was finished.

I found myself in greatcoat and hat with my walking stick in my hand, standing in the dark pouring rain in Curzon Street.

HOW long I stood there, I do not know, but at last, I blindly crossed the road and began trudging up South Audley Street in the direction of Grosvenor Square.

My hands were cold as ice, but my heart pounded. I could think nothing, feel nothing. I could only walk, and shiver, and be stone-cold inside.

Gabriella was alive. She lived with her mother in France. I could barely register the fact.

Grenville's house lay on Grosvenor Street, beyond Grosvenor Square with its elegant garden in the center. I should have turned onto Grosvenor Street on the east side of the square, but I somehow walked past it and found myself on Brook Street. I continued straight to the doorstep of Colonel and Mrs. Brandon before I stopped.

I had come here instinctively, seeking comfort, but now I hesitated. I eyed the polished door knocker, which gave me a distorted view of my nose, but made no move to knock.

I knew that Louisa would readily lend me comfort, but I'd get none from her husband, were he in the house. In fact, Brandon would likely say something acerbic, and in my mood, I would strike him. Louisa was angry enough with me as it was; I could imagine what she'd say if I bloodied her husband's nose.

While I pondered what to do, the door opened, and the Brandons' footman peered out at me.

"Good evening, sir," he said. "Mrs. Brandon has requested that I admit you."

CHAPTER 13

⁂

I was shown into the upstairs sitting room, which was homey, low-ceilinged, and warm, unlike the grand rooms in Grenville's house or the cold rooms in Denis'.

Louisa was there. She rose and came to greet me, her lemon-scented perfume soothing me as she kissed my cheek.

"Gabriel, how delightful to see you. I looked out of the window and spied you gazing at the door as though you'd bore a hole in it with your eyes. Why did you not knock?"

"I thought—" I had to stop. I had been clenching my jaw so tightly that I could barely speak.

She quickly gestured me to an armchair and set an ottoman before it. I sat senselessly, letting my arms go limp.

"What is it, Gabriel? Let me send for some coffee, or would you prefer port?"

Coffee. Coffee at least was warm, and I was so cold inside.

I must have indicated such, because she rang for the footman and sent him off for some.

"You are very white," she said. "Please tell me what has happened."

I just looked at her. Emotions spun inside me so quickly that I could not put them into words.

Gabriella had been two years old when her mother had taken her away. She had been walking sturdily for some months, and she had learned to say my name. Her favorite game was to stand on my boot and hold fast to my leg while I strode about the camp. She would laugh and squeal while Carlotta fussed and worried. I had been a fond, proud papa, taking the teasing of my men with a smile and a shrug.

When I learned that Carlotta had left me, I had at some level not been very surprised. But when I discovered she had taken Gabriella with her, I had gone nearly mad with rage. Gabriella was my child. By law, she belonged to me, not her mother. I could have gone after Carlotta, wrested the little girl away and taken her back, and Carlotta could have done nothing to stop me.

I had tried to find them, but I believed in my heart that they were better off without me. I followed the drum, and life was harsh.

But I had not known, from that day to this, whether my daughter had lived or died.

The footman carried in the coffee, set it down, and quietly withdrew. Louisa made no move to serve it.

I managed to say, "Gabriella." My eyes burned, and my throat ached.

Louisa's eyes widened. "Gabriella? What about Gabriella?"

I said nothing. Tears spilled silently to my cheeks.

Louisa sat on the ottoman in a rustle of silk. She took my hands. "Gabriel, please tell me."

I swallowed, wet my lips. "She is in France."

Then I broke down completely. I must have been a horrible sight, a large man, hunched into the chair, weeping. Louisa gathered me to her, stroked my hair, let me cry.

When my sobs wound down, she bade me tell her everything. I explained as coherently as I could what Denis had said.

"He knows where they are," I said, trying to clear my throat. "I could ask him. I could find them again." If I paid Denis' price for the information, he could send for them or send me to them. I could have it all back.

As though she knew my thoughts, Louisa took my hands again. "What will you do, Gabriel?" she asked.

"I do not know. How can I know what to do?"

She did not want me to sell myself to Denis. I saw that in her eyes, felt it in the pressure of her hands.

"What would you do, Louisa?" I countered. "Suppose it were your husband, what would you do?"

A grim light entered her eyes. "Mr. Denis has no right to do this to you. I will speak to him, tell him what I think of him."

I grew alarmed. "No, Louisa. He already knows how dear you are to me. I do not want him threatening you."

"I do not fear his threats."

"But you ought to. You—all of my friends—are right. I do not take him seriously enough. I have been a bloody fool concerning him."

She went silent. We watched each other; she troubled, me quiet, my face still wet. The coffee was growing cold, and neither of us moved to drink it.

Our vigil was broken by the noisy arrival of Colonel Brandon.

Louisa released my hands and rose as her husband entered the room. I got to my feet as well, mopping my face with my handkerchief.

Brandon had once been my greatest friend and my mentor. He was tall and broad-shouldered, with a handsome face and chill blue eyes. He'd once had fire and drive, and I'd admired him more than any other man I'd ever met.

That admiration had soured along the way, and now we regarded one another with tight suspicion. As usual, Louisa tried to diffuse the tension.

"Gabriel has come to visit," she said.

Brandon gave me a cold once-over. "That is obvious. Did you lose your employment already, Gabriel?"

I held onto my temper. "I had business in London. It is nearly concluded."

He gave me a bellicose stare. "Good."

I briefly reflected that Brandon and Rutledge would get along famously. No, I thought the next moment. Brandon is a man of feeling who hides behind sharp words. Rutledge has no feeling at all.

"You will stay for supper of course, Gabriel." Louisa gave me one of her stern looks, willing me to obey.

The last thing I wanted was to sit through a supper with Colonel Brandon, listening to his barely veiled insults and questions that were intended to put my back up. He was annoyed to have found me in his private sitting room alone with his wife, and he did not bother to hide it.

"Forgive me, Louisa," I said, never taking my eyes from Brandon. "I would like to rest in order to start early tomorrow for Berkshire. If you need me, I will be staying the night at Grenville's house."

Brandon gave me a look that told me he did not think much of a man who took advantage of his friends. I resisted telling him to kiss the devil's hindquarters and politely took my leave of Louisa.

I walked home. No, not strictly home, Grenville's home. I did not have one.

For an Englishman to not have a home was a terrible thing. Everyone needed connection to a place, however loathsome it might be. I was adrift, rather like Sebastian's family who roamed up and down the canals with no clear goal in sight.

I reached Grenville's house to learn that Anton had prepared supper for me. I distressed him by merely pushing it about the plate and dragging myself to bed.

I woke in the night with a raging fever.

I do not know whether the fever was brought on by my distress over my daughter, my walking about in the pouring rain, or my exhaustion from the business at Sudbury and my journey to London. Probably all combined to make my throat raw, my skin burning, and my limbs weak.

Bartholomew the dutiful arrived with a tonic and cool water, then he pulled the covers over me and made to douse the light.

Fevered sleep claimed me quickly. I thought that I managed to tell Bartholomew to send a message to

Grenville—"Tell him to ask Fletcher about canals," I said, or thought I said.

I drifted in and out of sleep, my dreams strange and horrible. Sometimes I lay staring at the canopy above me, my body wracked with fever, skin wet with sweat. From time to time I'd hear Grenville's servants enter the room, clean the grate and stoke the fire, and hear whispered conversations at the door.

Bartholomew would loom over me every once in a while with a worried expression, but I could not break myself out of my stupor to reassure him.

When I finally awoke, the fever was broken and I lay weak and limp and watched the sunshine at the window.

Bartholomew came to look in on me. I asked him the time.

"Four o'clock in the afternoon, sir."

I rubbed my face, a stiff growth of stubble on my skin. "Too late to start for Sudbury, then. I do not mind a night's journey, but Grenville's coachman might object."

He gave me an odd look. "You all right, sir?"

"Just tired. And powerfully hungry. Did Anton not say he would make something for my supper?"

Bartholomew's brow wrinkled. "That was two days ago, sir."

"What?" I tried to sit up. My head spun, and I held it.

"Two days you've been in bed, sir. Sick as a blind cow, sir."

I fingered the linen nightshirt I did not remember putting on. "Hell," I said feelingly. "I need a bath. And a shave." My stomach growled. "Food first, I think."

"I'll bring you a tray, sir, and hot water. And, oh—" He dipped his fingers inside his waistcoat. "A letter, sir."

"From Grenville?" I reached for it.

"No, sir. I wrote him your note, about the canals and Mr. Fletcher, like you said, and I added that you were sick and wouldn't return until you felt better. He answered saying he'd look into the matter and to give you a tonic, but nothing since yesterday."

I had half-expected Grenville to come rushing back to London to find out what was wrong with me, or ask me what the devil I meant about canals and Fletcher, but perhaps he'd realized it was best to stay and wait for my return.

I rubbed my face again. "Then who sent the letter?"

"A lady, sir."

"Mrs. Brandon?" I asked at once.

He read from the direction on the folded page. "Viscountess Breckenridge." He tossed it into my lap, then went into the hall and shouted for someone to fetch me hot water and coffee.

I opened the letter. It was a formal invitation, addressed to me, informing me that Lady Breckenridge was hosting a musicale at eleven o'clock on the evening of March 16th, and would I attend?

"What day is it, Bartholomew?" I asked as he began to fill the shaving basin with steaming water from a kettle.

"Sunday, the sixteenth of March, sir. The year of our lord, eighteen-seventeen."

I studied the invitation again. "Can you make me presentable? And get me to South Audley Street by eleven o'clock?"

"You sure you're feeling all right, sir?"

"Perfectly fine," I said. The fever had left me and now I was only restless and very hungry.

"I will endeavor, sir," Bartholomew said as he stropped my razor. "I'll shave you now, sir, while Anton fixes your dinner."

DONATA Anne Catherine St. John, née Pembroke, was known better to me by her title, the viscountess Breckenridge. She lived in South Audley Street, enjoyed the comforts of a vast fortune given to her by both her father and her late husband, and moved among the most fashionable people. Tonight it pleased her to host a musicale in order to introduce a young Italian tenor to the London *ton*.

I was still tired from my illness, but curiosity made me answer her invitation. I walked to the house, ignoring Bartholomew's bleats of protest about traveling there on foot. I was tired of the stuffy indoors and wanted to clear my head, the night was clear, and South Audley Street was not far from Grosvenor Street. Besides all that, my daily rides in the country had strengthened my muscles, and I wanted the joy of using them.

The door of Lady Breckenridge's house was opened by a liveried footman. Her butler, Barnstable, stood beyond him and gave me a smile of pleasure when he saw me. "Captain Lacey, welcome. How is your leg?"

"Much better," I said.

I'd hurt my weak leg badly earlier this spring, and Barnstable had given me his cure—scalding hot towels and a concoction of mint and other oils that had done my muscles well. Barnstable was proud of it.

"Excellent, sir," he beamed.

He led me upstairs through Lady Breckenridge's very exquisite, very modern, very white house.

The musicale was being held in a drawing room on the first floor. Double doors had been opened between front and back rooms, rendering them one large, high-ceilinged rectangle. A harp stood before rows of chairs, and a plump woman was plucking the harp's strings, sending tiny strains of music over the crowd.

Lady Aline Carrington, a spinster of fifty, and like Lady Breckenridge, a believer in women speaking their minds, presented the tenor to me. Lady Breckenridge stood next to them, dressed in a white silk high-waisted gown and holding an ostrich feather fan. Her only adornment was a necklace of diamonds, and her dark hair was pinned into innumerable coils.

The tenor's name was Enzio Vecchio, and he had only recently reached England from Milan. I bowed to him politely. He gave me a bored glance and mouthed a greeting.

"Mr. Vecchio will take London by storm, Captain," Lady Breckenridge said, her shrewd gaze on me. "You will shortly comprehend why."

Mr. Vecchio cast a fond glance upon Lady Breckenridge. "Only because you, dear lady, will make it so."

Lady Aline, behind him, looked at the ceiling. Lady Breckenridge took his fawning without changing expression. "Captain Lacey has shaken the country dirt from his boots to join us," she told him.

I made a brief show of studying my boots, then I replied, "For a short time only, my lady. I believe the boots will be thick with mud again in a day's time."

She deigned to smile at this feeble witticism. Lady Aline snorted. Vecchio only stared at me. Lady Breckenridge slipped her hand under Vecchio's arm and guided him off to other eagerly waiting guests.

As I watched the white-gowned Lady Breckenridge walk away on the arm of the black-garbed gentleman, I experienced a dart of annoyance. The annoyance bothered me. Why should it matter if Lady Breckenridge paraded about with a very young, black-haired Italian? It should not matter to me in the slightest.

But it did matter, and that bothered at me.

Lady Aline broke my thoughts. "Let us find chairs, Lacey, before we're forced to stand like rubes in the back of the room." She took my arm with strong fingers and more or less shoved me toward two empty chairs. Politely, I settled her, and asked if I could bring her lemonade.

"I am not thirsty," she said. "I've drunk tea with Lady Breckenridge and her callers all afternoon." She patted the chair beside her. "Sit down, dear boy. I always welcome a chance to speak to you. Your conversation is intelligent. You do not say what you are expected to say."

I smiled and took my seat. "A high compliment, one I am happy to accept from you."

"Never mind the Spanish coin," she said sternly, though she looked pleased. "Donata is no fool; Vecchio's voice is quite fine. Have you heard it?"

I shook my head. "I have been buried in the country

since the Season began. I have heard nothing but the bleating of sheep and the shouting of schoolboys."

"How idyllic."

"Not really. Early, noisy mornings, cold draughts at breakfast."

"And murder." She tapped my arm with her fan. "I will not forgive you for not mentioning it in your letters. I had to hear the news from Louisa."

"It is rather sordid. Nothing a lady need hear."

"Do not be ridiculous. I enjoy sordid things. But are you not in danger? Louisa says you do not believe the Romany did it. You never do."

I suppose she meant that I never liked the easiest solution. "Things are not as straightforward as they seem."

In fact, they were a muddle in my brain. The fever had not helped.

"I want to hear the entire story from you, you know," Lady Aline said. "I wanted to tell you that Hungerford, and canals, reminded me of something. There is someone I believe you should speak to."

I turned to her, alert. But just then, the crowd quieted as Vecchio walked past the chairs to the front of the room.

"I will tell you later," Lady Aline hissed.

I curbed my impatience and turned to watch Vecchio take his position near the harp. Lady Breckenridge had seated herself in the first row of chairs. Ostrich feathers drifted back and forth as she slowly fanned herself.

The woman at the harp, whom I did not know, introduced Mr. Vecchio as a new prodigy with the voice of an angel.

The prodigy was little above twenty years old. His black-eyed stare as it roved the room told me he did not think much of his audience—middle-aged women in finery, overdressed gentlemen, bored debutantes, all waiting to be entertained. Vecchio needed their approval if he would make a career, but he seemed to hold them in contempt.

The harpist played a few strains. The tenor opened his mouth, and then all contempt vanished.

So did the audience's boredom. From Vecchio's lips came sounds as sweet as any I had ever heard. His voice soared, filling the room with music, shaking the very beams of the ceiling, then it dipped to sounds soft and true as a lover's whisper.

As he sang, the music swept away the remaining mists of my fever. The sadness in my heart, the painful indecision about my wife and daughter, did not leave me, but the sounds touched my soul in a way nothing else had in a long while.

I sat as one entranced. I was sorry Grenville could not be here—he who loved all things beautiful would have been enraptured by Vecchio's voice.

I was not the only one moved. Next to me, Lady Aline blew her nose into a large handkerchief. The lady seated before me wiped her cheeks, and a tear trickled from the corner of her husband's eye.

The beauty of his voice was incredible. He wound to the height of the aria, holding one note high and clear that had us all trembling on the edges of our seats. Then he brought the note down, gave a rousing crescendo, and ended the piece with a flourish of his hand.

For a moment, the crowd sat in stunned silence.

Then as one, we burst into applause that shook the room.

The young man closed his mouth, and the magic vanished. He became a petulant youth again, despising the crowd who cheered him.

He entranced us with two more pieces, each still more beautiful than the last, then he made his final bow, and the entertainment was over.

Thunderous applause surrounded him as he stood quietly after his last aria. The harpist, too, clapped her hands, eyes glowing, cheeks pink. The crowd then surged to surround him, each guest vying to get near him.

I did not join the throng. I helped Lady Aline to her feet and reminded her of our conversation before the music started. "You mentioned Hungerford," I said. "Said you were reminded of something."

"Your keenness of mind amazes me, Lacey," Lady Aline said with a smile. "You never forget anything. A friend of mine was complaining of canals to me earlier this week. He is here tonight; let me find him."

I followed Lady Aline while she craned her head to look over the sea of people surrounding Vecchio. She used her bulk and a few loud-voiced "I beg your pardons" to move us through the crowd toward the door.

A tall, thin man stood near the open doorway, conversing with a few ladies who had either already greeted Vecchio or did not want to fight the throng to do so. The man had a long face that matched his long body, and a self-deprecating smile. No one, that smile said, can be as great a fool as I can be.

Lady Aline greeted the gentleman fondly, then

turned to me. "Captain Lacey, I would like to introduce an old and dear friend, Mr. Lewis. He is a writer."

Lewis held out a long-fingered hand to me. "Not the famous 'Monk' Lewis, alas," he said. "I am Jonathan Lewis, writer of books for youths. Have you read my *Boy in the Yorkshire Dales* by any chance?"

I shook my head. "I am afraid I have not."

He regarded me sadly. "The story is poignant, quite poignant, or so my publisher tells me. But young men, Captain, do not want poignancy. They want daring adventure and harrowing escapes, and a bit of skirt does not hurt, either. Oh, I do beg your pardon, dear Aline."

Aline looked amused, not offended. "Captain Lacey is staying in Sudbury, near Hungerford."

Lewis' expression changed from sadness to vast irritation. "Oh, my dear, do not speak to me of Hungerford. Hungerford, heart of my sorrow, font of my madness. Speak to me not of Hungerford."

I hid a smile. "I found it an atmospheric little town."

"Oh, yes, atmosphere. Old England and all that. I've never been there, myself."

I was mystified.

"Explain yourself, for heaven's sake, Lewis," Lady Aline prompted.

Mr. Lewis shook his head, sighed theatrically. "An evil man did me an evil turn. 'Give me your money, Mr. Lewis,' he said. 'I will make you rich.' Such a declaration was too much for a writer of stories to resist. Alas, I should have remembered Swindler Tom in *A Boy's Days on the Cornwall Coast*. Tom came to a bad end, as well he should. But this time, it was I who came to the bad end."

My pulse quickened. "How is this related to Hungerford?"

"Canals, my dear Captain. 'Invest in canals,' he told me. 'It is the future of England.' 'It is England's past,' I said. Canals are everywhere. 'But these canals will connect other canals, and we shall prosper.' And so I gave him the money." He shook his head mournfully. "I lost all of it, Captain. Every last farthing."

"An offshoot canal that would stretch from Hungerford north," I said excitedly. "An offshoot that never happened, or never was intended to happen."

"Alas, no. I was a fool. Good God, do not tell me you invested, too? We are fools together, then."

"Who was this man?" I asked. "The one who asked for your money?"

"A friend." Lewis' long face grew longer still. "Or I'd thought him a friend. We had fellow feeling, I thought ... struggling to live by the thing we loved most."

He looked across the room, as though thinking deeply on the follies of following one's heart.

"His name?" I prompted.

Lewis sighed. "A Latin scholar. A dear friend. By name of Fletcher."

"Simon Fletcher," I responded, staring.

"Yes," said Lewis. "That's the chap."

Thoughts whirled in my brain. "Ask Fletcher about canals," was the message I'd told Bartholomew to send to Grenville.

Bartholomew had obeyed. My breathing grew sharp. What had I done?

"Lady Aline," I said abruptly. "Mr. Lewis. Good night, I must away."

"What, now?" Lady Aline's brows climbed.

"At once. Please thank Lady Breckenridge for the invitation. It was most enjoyable."

I babbled a few more phrases and got myself out of the room. As I hurried away, I heard Lewis' lugubrious voice behind me. "Goodness. Who was that rude chap?"

IT occurred to me as I hastened down the stairs and sent the footman scurrying for my coat that Grenville probably had not come to any harm as a result of my slowness—if he had, I would likely have heard of it by now. Grenville was famous enough so that all newspapers in England would report anything untoward happening to him.

Even so, I worried about him staying alone at Sudbury. I needed to get myself back there and seek out Simon Fletcher. At once.

I heard a step behind me, but it was not the footman with my coat. I turned to see Lady Breckenridge glide downstairs and across the cool black-and-white hall toward me.

I was in a hurry, but I was not displeased that she'd come after me.

"You are leaving?" she asked as she reached me. "I know it cannot be disapproval of the entertainment that drives you away. You have enough sensibility that Vecchio's music could not help but touch you."

I nodded. "He is astonishing, yes. You are right. He will take London by storm."

She smiled, but with a tightness about her eyes. "Why flee, then?"

"I have business in Sudbury. I must go there at once."

Her brows arched. "In the middle of the night?"

"That cannot be helped. I will reach Sudbury by dawn."

Lady Breckenridge placed a gloved hand on my arm. "Several of my guests are commenting on your abrupt departure."

"Please give my apologies to any I annoyed." I glanced up the stairs. "You do not have to see me off. Your tenor must be waiting for you." If I put a touch more acid in my voice than usual, I hoped she did not notice.

She made a face. "He is wallowing in adulation. Vecchio is brilliant, but he was spoiled and petted in Milan. Londoners will take a certain amount of rudeness, but if he is rude to the Prince Regent, he will be out, no matter how lovely his voice. He must learn this."

I tried to make a joke. "It will be as well, then, if *I* never meet the Prince Regent."

She did not smile. "No, I do not believe he would like you."

The footman was taking a dashed long time looking for my coat. Lady Breckenridge made no move either to summon him or to return to her guests.

"I enjoy receiving your letters," I remarked, for lack of anything else to say.

Her brows lifted. "Really? I thought you'd find them a bit pointed for your taste. Yours, as I observed, are quite dull. You even made the murder sound dull."

"I know," I said. "I have not the wit for writing. Not like Mr. Lewis."

She gave me an odd look then burst into laughter. I'd never heard her laugh before, not truly. It had a warm sound. "You do have wit," she said. "You simply show it to very few people."

"There are very few who care to hear it."

"Perhaps," she said, her fingers tightening on my arm, "you will include me in those few."

Our gazes met. From upstairs came the noise of many people talking and laughing, but the downstairs hall was nearly silent.

"I wonder," I asked eventually, "what has become of my coat?"

Lady Breckenridge gave me a half-smile. "Barnstable is tactfully letting me say my farewells in private. Perhaps when you return to London, Captain, we may meet for another evening of music?"

I lifted her hand and twined my fingers through it. I expected her to pull away, but she allowed the liberty. "I enjoy music. Mr. Vecchio has a fine voice."

The contact between our hands was fine, too, even if we both wore gloves.

"He can be made into something," she said, "if he stops behaving like a boor." She withdrew her hand, and flicked an invisible speck of dust from my lapel. "Go back to Berkshire and write more letters. But make them interesting this time."

"I will," I said. I traced her cheekbone with my fingertips.

Barnstable chose that moment to come bustling

from the rear of the house, saying, "Your coat, sir," as though he'd searched for it long and hard.

I let my hand drop and bowed to Lady Breckenridge. By the time Barnstable had helped me into my coat and seen me to the door, Lady Breckenridge was halfway up the stairs. She did not turn back and tell me good-bye.

I made my way as quickly as I could back to Grenville's, my walking stick a rapid staccato on the stones.

Bartholomew was still awake when I reached the house. I told that him I wanted to set out for Sudbury at once, and, unsurprised, he rushed away to fetch the coachman and pack my few things.

We rattled out of town through dark, empty streets. The wealthy were still enjoying their revelries, and the respectable middle class and poor were asleep in their beds. Only beggars, game girls, thieves, and other night wanderers moved through the darkness. They gave our rapidly moving coach and Grenville's snarling coach-man a wide berth.

We arrived at the Sudbury School just before dawn. I thanked the coachman and told him to take a much-deserved rest. He growled that the horses needed to be tended to first and went off to do it.

Bartholomew and I entered the quad through the gate. The clouded sky was black, forcing us to pick our way across the rain-slicked cobbles with great care.

As I stepped beneath the arches near the door of the Head Master's house, I tripped over a large object lying across the stones and fell, my stick clattering to the pavement. I climbed to my knees, the breath struck out of me.

"Are you all right, sir?" Bartholomew whispered hoarsely. "What is it?"

My groping hands found a man stretched across the stones, lying there unmoving. The man's coat was soaked with liquid, and my fingers closed around the unmistakable form of a knife's hilt protruding from his chest.

CHAPTER 14

L IGHTS!" I cried. "Bring a light."

"What is it, sir?" Bartholomew repeated.

"Get a light, for God's sake. Someone's here and hurt."

Bartholomew brushed past me and thumped away into the house.

I had no idea who lay at my feet. Grenville? I stripped off my gloves, felt my way across the man's shoulders. He still breathed, whoever he was, labored, gasping breaths that were loud in the darkness.

"Grenville?" I whispered, hoping to God I was wrong. "Lie still. Bartholomew has gone for help."

He coughed. "Lacey?"

My heart turned over. It *was* Grenville. I felt the soft weave of his expensive coat beneath my fingers and the fine cloth of his cravat.

I loosened the cravat's knot and drew the folds from his throat. "Grenville, old friend," I whispered. "Who did this?"

He took a long time to answer. "Don't know. Too dark."

Too much blood stained his chest. My hands were sticky with it.

I cursed. I was tired, and my hands shook. He must have come down to take a breath of air, or to follow someone, or . . . I didn't know, and I couldn't think.

His face was clammy and cold. I thanked God I did not hear the deadly bubbling sound that meant the knife had pierced his lung—I had heard that horrible sound often enough on the Peninsula. But I feared to withdraw the knife until I could see, lest I hurt him further.

"What happened?" I persisted. "Why were you out here?"

Grenville drew several breaths, as though trying to speak, but he never answered.

My heart beat hard with fear. I found and grasped one of his hands. "Don't try to talk. Squeeze my hand if I am right. Did you see someone down here?"

A faint pressure on my fingers answered me.

"Did you think you'd seen the prankster?" I asked.

Another answering pressure.

"Why the devil did you come down here alone? No, no, don't answer. You can tell me all later." I peered into the darkness of the house. "Damn it, Bartholomew, where are you?"

I heard Bartholomew just then through the open door. He trotted out swinging a lantern from his large fist. His brother, white and sleepy-eyed, came after him.

Bartholomew saw Grenville and gasped. The lantern swayed, and hot wax sprayed me.

"Hold it steady," I snapped.

Grenville looked terrible. His face was paper white, his eyes half-closed. His ivory waistcoat was thick with blood. In the center of the circle of blood stood the unmoving hilt of a knife.

Bartholomew stood transfixed with shock. Matthias gave one horrified stare then bolted back into the house.

Grenville's lips quirked. "I frightened him."

I snarled, "Don't you dare talk again unless I give you leave."

He obediently fell silent. By the light of Bartholomew's swinging lantern, I saw Grenville's chest rise and fall, too rapidly, not deeply enough.

Matthias hurried out of the house again. He hadn't run away in fear, he'd gone to fetch a pile of towels.

"Good lad," I said. I snatched the topmost towel and pressed it to Grenville's chest, below the protruding hilt. "I must take out the knife. We cannot chance that his heart or lung will not be cut when we move him."

Bartholomew bit his lip. Matthias crouched next to his master. "What do I do, sir?"

"Hold his shoulders. He must not move." I willed my hands to cease trembling. "Do you hear me, Grenville? You must not move. Think of yourself as a boulder. Heavy. Strong. Immovable. Think on it."

I did not give him time to prepare himself. I knew that men often flinched from anticipated pain, and I wanted it over with before he knew it had started. I simply grasped the knife and in one swift, silent pull, drew it out.

Grenville did move. He gasped and his body almost left the ground, but Matthias, big and strong, held him down. I clapped another towel straight over the wound and pressed down hard.

More hot wax sprayed my face. "Damn it, Bartholomew."

I heard footsteps, and then Didius Ramsay burst out of the house. He was in a dressing gown and slippers, and his eyes were wide. "Good lord! Is it Mr. Grenville?"

"Ramsay, send someone for a surgeon," I said. "Quickly."

Ramsay took a few gulps of air then started back inside and ran full tilt into the bulk of Rutledge.

Rutledge shoved Ramsay aside and came out, a candle in his hand. Several boys and tutors in dressing gowns followed him. Rutledge took in the scene, my bloody hands, and the knife. He bellowed, "What the devil is going on?"

"Fetch a surgeon," I repeated while Ramsay stood there in dismay. "A good surgeon, not a quack of a doctor."

Ramsay scampered away. Rutledge lifted his candle to study Grenville. Grenville screwed up his eyes at the light.

"What happened here?" Rutledge repeated. "Lacey, what have you done?"

I ignored him. "Matthias, is there any laudanum?"

"I can look, sir."

"No," Grenville's voice came feebly. "Not laudanum."

"It will take away the pain," I said.

"There is no pain." He drew a breath. "Don't send me to sleep."

"Damn you, will you stop talking?"

"Aye, sir," he whispered.

"Matthias, can you carry him? I want him off this walk, out of the damp."

Bartholomew rose, shoved the lantern at Matthias. "I'll do it."

"Matthias, run up to his chamber and make certain it's plenty warm. Stoke the fire high. And fetch water."

Matthias pushed past Rutledge and the staring pupils, hurrying to do as I bid. Bartholomew leaned down. With gentleness I'd never seen in him before, he scooped Grenville into his arms.

I leveraged myself to a standing position, leaning heavily on my stick. My bad knee pounded with pain. I held the towel to Grenville's chest and walked with Bartholomew into the house. The crowd of curious lads and tutors opened before us.

Rutledge was still demanding to be told what had happened. The tutors and pupils pattered after us anxiously, watching, round-eyed.

Even in my worry, I noticed two absent—Sutcliff and Fletcher.

Once inside Grenville's chamber, Bartholomew laid Grenville carefully on the bed. Matthias had the fire stoked high. A basin of water already steamed before it.

Grenville's head lolled on the pillow. I saw the glimmer of his eyes, but his lids were heavy and waxen.

"Don't you die on me," I told him. "I'll not have it said that your death was my fault."

"*My* fault, sir," Bartholomew said. "I should have been here to look after him."

"No, mine," Matthias put in. "He told me not to wait up for him, and I went to bed."

I broke in. "Well, now that we have thoroughly flogged ourselves, shall we go about making certain he stays alive? Matthias, bring that basin."

While Bartholomew and Matthias hovered like worried aunts, I opened Grenville's clothes and bathed the wound. The gash was small, but it was deep and had bled much. I could have no idea what the blade had cut going in.

"Bloody fool," I said as I worked. "What were you doing rushing about in the middle of the night? Going down to confront a villain alone? You should have taken Matthias. Or waited for me."

If Grenville died, it truly would be my fault. Grenville would not have come here at all had he not taken interest in me and my adventures, as he called them. He would be safe and bored in London, busy making satirical comments about other people's clothes and manners.

"Lacey," Rutledge said behind me. "What is all this?"

"Where is the damned surgeon?" I demanded.

"How the devil should I know? And where have you been? You said you would take a day in London, and you wander back three days later in the small hours without a by-your-leave."

I lost my patience. "I was ill, and you have more things to worry about. Send someone to Fletcher's chamber and do not allow Fletcher to leave it."

I felt Rutledge's stare on the back of my neck. "You think *Simon Fletcher* did this?"

"Well, it was not Sebastian. Bartholomew, go."

"Yes, sir."

"And if you see Sutcliff on the way, kick him in the seat of his trousers."

"Yes, sir." Swift footsteps told me he'd gone.

Rutledge breathed heavily. "You are sacked, Lacey."

"Excellent. Where is the surgeon?"

The surgeon arrived shortly. Rutledge hovered in the room like a gargoyle, still demanding to be told everything. I was weary and weak from the effects of my fever, and I bluntly told him to close his mouth. If he'd truly sacked me, I saw no more reason to be polite to him.

The surgeon sewed the lips of the wound together and bathed it again. I and Matthias finished undressing Grenville, and the surgeon wrapped a bandage around him. Grenville lay in a stupor, never acknowledging what we did, his face so white that his brows stood out like black marks on parchment.

The surgeon departed, giving us strict instructions to not let him move and to change the bandage once a day. I sank onto a chair in front of the roaring fire, perspiring freely, feeling sick and weak.

I sat there, watching Matthias sponge Grenville's face, feeling the vestiges of melancholia swarm about me. If Grenville died—

No, I could not bear to think about that. I could not afford to wallow right now in guilt and grief. I needed to get him well again and find the person who did this. Then, I'd be free to retreat into melancholia and contrition as much as I liked.

Matthias finished cleaning Grenville's face and re-

turned the basin to the fireplace. He went back to the
side of the bed and just stood there, distress on his hon-
est face.

I had examined the knife that I'd pulled from
Grenville's chest. It was small and sharp, the kind a
man might keep to pare apples with, and had nothing
helpful on it like engraved initials or a name. It was a
well-made knife, but not one of obvious expense—it
was the kind anyone might possess. I would ask
Matthias and Bartholomew to quiz their network of
servants until they found out who in the school was
missing a knife.

I sighed. Even that course of action felt ineffectual
and slow. And the knife could easily have been stolen.

After a long time of silence, I became aware of
sounds in the quad. The day had dawned, and boys
were scurrying to chapel as usual, although they were
somewhat subdued.

But over that I heard different sounds, a shout of
alarm and Rutledge swearing freely.

I rose and went to the window in time to see
Bartholomew hurry out the front door of Fairleigh.
Rutledge barked a question at him, then pushed past
Bartholomew to rush into Fairleigh.

I got to the door by the time Bartholomew had entered the Head Master's house and run up the stairs. He
stood panting heavily on the threshold, his face
flushed.

"Mr. Fletcher ain't going nowhere, sir," he said.
"He's dead as a stone, sir."

●   ●   ●

I ordered Matthias to stay with Grenville and let no one near him for any reason. Matthias took up his post at the foot of the bed, arms crossed, as immovable as a statue.

Bartholomew and I hastened together across the wet quad. Bartholomew breathlessly explained as we went what had happened.

"His door was locked when I arrived, sir, and he didn't answer. I decided I'd stand guard until he came out. Then a maid wanted in to stoke the fire, and I saw no harm in letting her. She had a key. She unlocked the door and went in, and then she started screaming. I went in after her and saw him, doubled up at his desk and dead."

We entered Fairleigh. The house was smaller than the Head Master's but not much different in layout—a square hall surrounded by a staircase and doors that led into rooms and corridors.

Fletcher's room was on the second floor in a corner. Rutledge was already there, his face nearly purple with rage. The surgeon who had stitched up Grenville was leaning over Fletcher, who sat slumped against his desk as Bartholomew had described.

"No saving this one, I'm afraid," the surgeon said.

He lifted Fletcher's head. A dark bruise circled his throat, and his tongue was thrust out, probing for air he could not find.

"Oh, God," I said.

On the desk before him was a long piece of twine, coarse and utilitarian. It had several knots in it. I remembered seeing Fletcher hurrying about the school, carrying piles of books bound with such twine. It must have been lying, discarded, nearby, and the murderer had caught it up.

Rutledge, as usual, began shouting. "I want everyone in the quad in ten minutes. Everyone—from the lowest pupil to the house masters. I will discover who did this if I have to beat each and every one of them."

"Do you think that will work?" I asked.

"Nothing you have done has. A sound thrashing will solve more problems than all your so-called inquiries."

He stomped away to put his plan in motion. Because he'd sacked me, I saw no reason to follow or to help. His blustering had not prevented the tragedies and would probably have no effect now.

I began looking about the room. Fletcher had led a Spartan existence, from all evidence. The room was mostly bare, the bed-hangings and furnishings plain. The bookcase that had housed his beloved books was empty, with a line of dust remaining where the books had not reached to the backs of the shelves. I ran my hands into the corners and under the lips of the shelves to see if anything important lingered there. I found nothing but more dust.

"Something here, sir," Bartholomew said.

He was squatting before the fireplace hearth. I looked over his shoulder and saw a small knife with a blade about an inch long lying on the stones. The hilt was plain metal, with no decoration. A practical, workaday knife. Bartholomew lifted it. The tip was broken off, leaving a blunt end.

"That didn't kill anyone," Bartholomew said.

"No," I answered. "But I wonder why it was dropped here."

"Could be someone was trying to shave some kindling, and broke the tip."

"Could be." I took the knife from him and put it into my pocket.

I swept my gaze over the room again. Poor Fletcher sat in his chair, his right hand on his throat, as though he'd tried to clutch at the strand that choked him. His robe lay in a black puddle on a chair near him. Remembering something Fletcher had said before I'd gone to London, I lifted the robe and probed its lining.

I found what I hoped I'd find, a small book.

Bartholomew's brow wrinkled. "I thought all his books were burned, sir."

"Apparently, one escaped. Let us see, shall we?"

The book was nothing more than a Latin grammar, or so I thought. I laid it on the desk, turned over the leaves. At first I saw only pages and pages of noun declensions and verb conjugations. In the middle of the book, however, I began to find folded pieces of paper shoved between the pages, one or two pieces every four or five pages. I extracted a few, laid them on the desk.

My pulse quickened. "The damned canals again," I said, unsurprised.

"What was that, sir?"

"These are lists, Bartholomew. Lists of people who gave money to Mr. Fletcher to invest in a canal that would never exist. This is why Fletcher sometimes talked about leaving this existence behind and living like a king. He was swindling people, planning to retire well on the money of the gullible." I touched the name *Jonathan Lewis*, the gentleman I'd met at the musicale. "Including those he considered his friends."

"Ought to be ashamed," Bartholomew said.

I regarded Fletcher in half-sorrow, half-anger. "Poor, stupid fool. Was he killed by someone he swindled? Or a fellow swindler?" I gathered the papers, slid them back into the book.

"And why did they cut Mr. Grenville?"

Bartholomew was angry. He and Matthias doted on Grenville, were proud to work for him, rather rubbed other footmen's noses in it that the pair had such a good place. They regarded Grenville as though they owned him.

"It's likely the murderer did not even know who he stabbed as he ran by," I said. "The killer heard Grenville come out of the Head Master's house and simply lashed out."

Bartholomew's brow clouded. "Mr. Grenville ought not to have been there. He should have called Matthias."

"I know. But likely he thought that the person would get away if he took the trouble. I'd have done the same, simply gone down to catch the culprit myself."

"But you know how to defend yourself, sir. He doesn't. He's too trusting by half, too sure of his own good luck."

"I know," I said glumly.

Bartholomew balled his fists. "When I find out who did this, I will murder him myself."

"You will have to queue up behind me."

Bartholomew simply stood there, looking morose.

I found nothing more interesting in the room than the book and its contents and the broken knife. I found little personal at all in the room, and no other letters or papers.

I finished and led Bartholomew out, Fletcher's book under my arm. I hated to leave Fletcher alone, but perhaps that was best for him. Let him sit in peace.

I removed the key from the inside of the door, closed the door, and locked it from the outside. I left the key in the keyhole, and then Bartholomew and I departed.

RUTLEDGE had the entire school assembled in the quad under the gentle March rain. Bartholomew and I skirted the crowd and made for the Head Master's house. Sutcliff stood at Rutledge's side, looking sullen and half-asleep. Several of the boys craned to watch us, rather spoiling the effect of Rutledge's diatribe.

Back in Grenville's room, I sat down to look over the papers I'd taken from Fletcher. Grenville had not woken from his stupor, and his pallid face bore a sheen of perspiration.

I knew I needed to sleep. My head buzzed and my vision was fuzzy, and I was still weak from the fever. But I could not bring myself to leave the room again.

I was as angry as Bartholomew. Whoever had hurt Grenville would not be safe from me.

I found much of interest in Fletcher's book and its secrets. The swindling scheme was much bigger than I'd thought. Fletcher had tapped his old school friends, which included many prominent men of London. Some were fathers or other relations of the boys of Sudbury.

I found contracts and letters of agreement and particulars on what percentage return the investors could expect to see. Middleton was named on the documents as a "surveyor," which explained the maps. One other person, not named, was referred to as a "banker."

Fletcher had received letters from investors asking eagerly when the canal would be started, finished, opened—when would the money come rolling in? There were letters from the more canny souls who began claiming that they'd found no evidence that a canal was even proposed, and what was Fletcher up to?

Fletcher must have been planning to disappear very soon.

I had another thought—what if Fletcher's books were burned not because of a malicious prank, but because the killer had been looking for this particular book with all its damning evidence?

The maps in Middleton's room were just that, maps. They meant nothing by themselves. But Fletcher's documents could not be ignored. He'd fraudulently taken money from gullible people and promised them rainbows.

Bartholomew brought me coffee and told me to go to bed, but I still would not leave. I knew Bartholomew and Matthias would stand over Grenville like faithful watchdogs, but I could not bear the thought that something might happen to him while I slept. I feared the killer would not chance that Grenville had not seen who'd struck the blow. The murderer had made certain that Fletcher and Middleton had not told tales; he might make certain Grenville did not, either.

The coffee cup crashing to the floor woke me. Paper slithered to the carpet to soak up the black liquid.

"Sir?" Bartholomew hung over me.

"I'm all right." I passed my hand through my hair. My eyes were aching and sandy. "I'll take a walk around the quad, clear my head."

Bartholomew helped me to my feet. Matthias dozed in a chair near Grenville's bed. Grenville lay unmoving and wan.

"Watch over him," I said in a low voice. "Do not let anyone into this room for any reason, not Rutledge, not a maid. You and your brother take care of him yourselves, do you understand?"

Bartholomew gave me a grim nod. He understood quite well.

The noon hour struck as I left the house. Outside it had warmed somewhat, and the rain had thickened. The air braced me. Despite all the tragedy, the spring day still smelled clean and refreshing.

I walked heavily across the quad, my stick tapping the stones. Boys drifted into and out of the houses, wandering to lessons, to their rooms, to whatever task they'd been set on. They were rather subdued—a murder and a near-murder so close to home was exciting but frightening.

I heard a commotion by the gate and headed that way. The porter was arguing with a person outside who did not want to listen.

"Madam," I heard the porter say in a pained voice

Timson came sauntering toward me from the gate, a grin on his face. "I say, Captain, your bit of muslin is asking to see you."

I started. "My what?"

Timson just smirked and winked, so I hurried on.

"Lacey!" a woman cried.

Marianne Simmons held onto the bars of the gate, her white skirts rain-soaked and blotched with mud.

"What are you doing here?" I asked her.

"I need to speak to you. Tell this lummox to let me in."

"Now look here, you—" the porter began.

"Never mind," I said quietly. "Let her in."

The porter gave me an exasperated look. "Women are not allowed, sir. Particularly not women like *her.*"

"Oh, that is nice," Marianne sneered.

"Baiting him will not help you, Marianne. Let her in," I told the porter. "I will let Rutledge berate me later."

The porter's face darkened, but he opened the gate. Marianne stuck her tongue out at him as she sailed inside.

Timson and a few other boys stared at Marianne's thin dress in great enjoyment. Timson let out a wolf-whistle.

"Mind your manners," I told them. In the relative privacy of the middle of the quad, I turned Marianne to face me.

"What is it?"

She pulled her silk shawl closer about her shoulders and shivered. From the worry in Marianne's eyes, I knew she'd already heard that Grenville had been hurt. The news must have spread quickly through the village and thence to Hungerford.

What she told me, however, I was not expecting.

"Jeanne Lanier's run away," she said.

CHAPTER 15

I looked at Marianne in surprise. "Oh, she has, has she?"

"Indeed, she has." Her gaze slid from mine to the windows surrounding us. "Tell me the truth, Lacey. Is he all right?"

"He is alive," I said.

When she looked back at me, her eyes were wet. "For how long?"

I could only shake my head. Grenville could heal or die. The blade could have torn him up inside in ways we could not know. I could only hope that the cut was clean, and that his body would heal itself.

"Will you let me see him?" she asked.

I started to answer, then I spied Sutcliff coming out of Fairleigh. He saw Marianne, recognized her, and froze.

"Mr. Sutcliff," I called.

He hesitated then at last came toward us, his expression wary.

"Hello, Mr. Sutcliff," Marianne said, with forced cheerfulness. "I came to tell you that your ladybird's done a bunk."

Sutcliff's face went white. "What?"

"I said your ladybird's done a bunk. Cleared out this morning without a word to Mrs. Albright."

Sutcliff stared at her in pure anger. Marianne smiled. No woman could give a man a more scornful smile than could Marianne Simmons. "Gave you a start, did it?" she asked. "I take it this news is unexpected?"

Sutcliff's face reddened, and he raised his hand to strike her. "Impertinent whore."

I caught his arm. "Keep a civil tongue," I said, "or I'll thrash you worse than Fletcher ever did."

His lip curled. "Unhand me. You do not know your place."

Marianne gave a sharp laugh. "He knows better than you. *He* is a gentleman. Your father is a trumped-up clerk."

Sutcliff tried to hit her again. Marianne hid behind me.

"Marianne, be quiet," I said sternly. "Mr. Sutcliff, go away."

I pushed him off. He glared at me, then he turned on his heel and marched back into Fairleigh.

I faced Marianne. "I'll take you to see Grenville, but you must keep quiet. Provoking the students will not help."

She made a face at the door Sutcliff had just slammed. "He puts my back up. He swaggers around like he's something, while Grenville is worth fifty of him." Her voice faltered.

"I agree. But keep your thoughts to yourself, or I will not be able to stop Rutledge having you bodily removed. Do not speak again until we reach Grenville's chamber, agreed?"

She started to answer, then closed her lips and nodded.

Good. For now.

I took her by the arm and led her into the Head Master's house. Boys stared. Tunbridge tried to stop me. I gave the mathematics tutor a look that sent him scuttling away and took Marianne up the stairs.

Bartholomew and Matthias had locked the door. When I knocked, Bartholomew opened the door a crack and peered out with one blue eye. He saw me, opened the door wider. He eyed Marianne askance, but I pulled her inside and shut the door.

Marianne approached the bed, her boots whispering on the carpet. She removed her bonnet and dropped it absently, her face white. She looked down at Grenville for a long time. His face was still starkly pale, the flesh of his bare shoulders nearly as white as the bandage that wrapped him.

Marianne took his hand. His fingers lay limply in her grasp.

"Is he going to die, Lacey?" she asked in a low voice.

"No," I said, trying to sound certain. "We will not let him."

"Such a comfort you are. You are not a doctor. How the devil should you know?"

"I have seen men with wounds far worse recover and live as though nothing had happened," I answered. I did not add that I'd seen men with smaller wounds die for no reason I could discern. Grenville could so easily sicken, take fever. He could die while we sat helplessly and watched him.

Marianne said nothing. She gently stroked the hand in hers. Grenville did not respond.

Matthias heaped more coal on the fire. Bartholomew leaned against the bedpost, at a loss for what to do.

I was tired, and my short nap had not helped. I settled back into my chair, stretched my bad leg toward the fire that Matthias had stirred to roaring. "Marianne, tell me about Jeanne," I said.

She did not look at me. "She's gone. What is there to tell?"

I thought about Jeanne's charming smile and winsome conversation. She had been very practiced. "When did she go? Did she pay up and depart or simply disappear?"

Marianne kept her gaze on Grenville's pale face. "She went out the window. Or so it looks like. Never a word to anyone. Mrs. Albright didn't think anything of it when Jeanne didn't come down for breakfast, because she always likes to lie abed in the mornings. But later, when Mrs. Albright went up, she found the window open and Jeanne and her things gone."

"Did Mrs. Albright send for the constable?"

Marianne shook her head. "Mrs. Albright cursed something fearsome, but let it be. Mr. Sutcliff paid to the end of the month, so if Jeanne wants to run off, Mrs. Albright does not much care. She has her money."

"Money," I said, thinking hard. "Yes, that would explain it."

"You are babbling, Lacey. Explain what?"

I should be talking this over with Grenville. My anger stirred. I would get the man who'd done this to him, and I'd pot him.

I snatched up Fletcher's papers and spread them out. "Three people: Middleton, who drew the false maps; Fletcher, who had the connections; and the banker, who kept the money. The contracts are here, the maps are here, but where is the money? I believe it flew out the window of a seedy boarding house this morning."

Marianne finally looked at me. She cocked her head. "What are you talking about?"

"A grand swindle. Fletcher came up with the scheme—he was clever enough yet innocent-looking enough to trick men into investing in a canal that would never be built. Canals make money. Boats move whether it's raining or snowing or sunny. One does not have to worry about bad roads. No matter what, the boats *keep going*. Investing in canals is sure money."

"But not in canals that don't exist," Bartholomew added.

"Yes, but unless you have access to all the proposed canal routes in England, how would you know whether one was truly planned? A canny man would check, of course, but most men want to make an easy fortune— to give the money to a trusted friend and he will take care of the complicated details. That is why so very many people are swindled, Bartholomew—they want things to be easy."

He watched me, eyes round, as though I were dispensing great wisdom.

I stood and began to pace, trying to think. "The average gentleman like Jonathan Lewis, who earns little from his writing, would be eager to put money into something with so sure a return. So Fletcher persuades him to invest. Fletcher is a likable man, easy to trust. Good old Fletcher, his friends say, let's throw our lot in with him."

"To their misfortune," Bartholomew said gravely.

"Very much so. But Fletcher couldn't do it all himself—he didn't have the time or the resources. So he recruited others. Perhaps Fletcher chose Middleton because he knew Middleton had worked for Denis. Middleton would know how to shut people up if they began to squawk, in any case. So, Middleton drew the maps, perhaps even took gentlemen out to show them where the survey stakes would be."

All three had turned to listen to me now. I continued, "They have a third person to collect the money, a person with connections in the City who can assure Fletcher and Middleton that their portion would be taken care of. But—in the end, the 'banker' gets greedy, perhaps frightened that Middleton will tell James Denis everything, murders Middleton and Fletcher, and flees with the money."

They looked at me like I'd run mad. I was breathing heavily, my blood pounding with excitement. Marianne raised the first protest. "You are never saying that Jeanne killed them. And stabbed *him*. You're wrong, Lacey. She'd never be able to get into the school. You saw how the porter nearly posted me off to jail when he spied me at the gate."

I shook my head. "She murdered no one. She never could have killed Middleton; he'd not have let her. Nor do I think she sneaked into the school in the middle of the night to kill Fletcher. No, she is working with someone, and that someone sent her away with the money."

And I knew who.

"I must go to Sudbury," I said crisply. "Jeanne Lanier must be found. I wish Mrs. Albright had called in the constable, but it can't be helped."

"Shall I go with you, sir?" Bartholomew said, coming alert.

"No. Stay here, protect Grenville. He was stabbed because he saw Fletcher's murderer leaving Fairleigh. The murderer cannot be certain that Grenville did not see him, and he will try again. Marianne, you must remain here, as well. You will not be safe at the boarding house."

"What about you?" she countered. "Waltzing off to Sudbury all alone? For all the killer knows, Grenville has already told you his name, and he'll be waiting along a lonely stretch of road to gut you."

"I have my walking stick," I said. I hefted it in my hand. "And I trust no one in this school, pupil or tutor, no matter how innocuous they seem."

Marianne came to face me, hands on hips. "Don't be a bloody fool, Lacey, you are not invulnerable. Take Bartholomew. To get to Grenville, the murderer will have to come through me. I'll fight them just as hard as anyone."

She cared for him. I saw in her eyes that today she had realized what she might lose.

I gave in. "Very well. Come along, Bartholomew. And bring that book."

I borrowed a horse to ride to Sudbury. Bartholomew chose to walk. He carried Fletcher's book under his arm, wrapped in a bit of canvas to keep it out of the rain.

As we rode, I mulled over ideas for catching the murderer. I had one excellent resource I could tap, though I cringed from it. Also, Rutledge would be an obstacle—a very loud, very stubborn obstacle.

When we arrived in Sudbury we discovered that the magistrate had gone to Hungerford to visit an important official who'd just arrived from London. The constable was a bit harried, having to deal with both Fletcher's murder and a farmer whose sheep had wandered onto a large landlord's holding and who complained that the landlord would not return them.

Bartholomew and I went on to Hungerford. Impatient, I let the horse trot ahead, while Bartholomew came behind, hunkering into the rain.

I found the magistrate at the inn on the High Street. The important official he visited was Sir Montague Harris.

I exhaled with relief when I saw Sir Montague. He beamed at me when I greeted him as though we were meeting to renew acquaintance over a pint of bitter. But he was shrewd man and had already drawn conclusions from the Sudbury magistrate's description of matters today.

Bartholomew lumbered in, shaking rain from his hair. I bade him sit down and unwrap the book.

I showed both magistrates Fletcher's papers and explained the canal scheme and Middleton's part in it. I recalled the letter Middleton had sent Denis, implying he'd discovered who'd been sending him threatening letters and stating that he wanted to tell Denis something interesting. I speculated that Middleton might have been killed because he'd been about to tell James Denis about the canal swindle. Perhaps he'd wanted Denis to take over the scheme; perhaps he'd only wanted to win Denis' praise.

I finished my tale with Jeanne Lanier's departure and my belief that she needed to be found.

The two men, sitting side-by-side on the bench and looking much alike—rotund bodies and red faces—could not have had more dissimilar reactions.

Sir Montague's eyes glowed with interest, and he smiled, intrigued. The Sudbury magistrate frowned at me, white brows knitting over a bulbous nose.

"This Frenchwoman was ladybird to an upper-form student?" he growled. "Likely she tired of him and fled. Received a better offer."

"I see something a bit more sinister in it," Sir Montague countered. "I will put the word out about her."

I thought of Jeanne Lanier's pleasant smile, her shrewd eyes. I doubted she would debunk out a window and run to another lover. She'd finish her contract with Sutcliff and then calmly enter into a contract with another. She was a businesswoman.

It would be a pity if Jeanne Lanier were involved in

the murders. She'd be arrested, no matter how pretty and charming she was. I had a brief, pleasant fantasy of myself convincing the magistrates that she was an innocent dupe, and her, in gratitude, taking up with me.

I smiled inwardly and let the fantasy go.

"What about the Romany?" Sir Montague asked.

The Sudbury magistrate looked annoyed. "What about him?"

I said quickly, "You certainly cannot pin the death of Fletcher on him, nor the assault on Grenville. Sebastian is young, and he is passionate, but these murders were not the work of passion. They were planned, from fear and greed."

"Greed can destroy so much," Sir Montague nodded.

"In this case, two men's lives," I said.

The Sudbury magistrate frowned at the both of us. "If I release the Romany, what do I tell the chief constable? That I have no one to pay for the murder of the groom? The Romany is likely guilty of something, anyway, even if not the murder."

"Would the chief constable rather hang the wrong man?" I asked.

Sir Montague nodded gravely. "He might, Captain, he just might."

"That is ludicrous."

Sir Montague agreed. I hated this.

"If you let him go," I repeated, "I will bring you the true culprit."

"You will mind your own business," the Sudbury magistrate snapped. "My constables are investigating this crime, and they will bring me the true culprit. I agree that the Romany cannot have killed Mr. Fletcher or stabbed your friend, but he could very well have killed Middleton, and that is final."

"He could not have," I said. "Middleton had been dead two hours before Sebastian returned to the stables at Sudbury. And he was gone all night before that. He has witnesses, about ten of them, to prove this."

"Romany witnesses," the magistrate growled. "Which are no witnesses at all."

I snatched up my hat. "I will bring you one. Not a Romany."

Sir Montague had sat through this exchange with a characteristic half-smile on his face. Now he looked at me in slight surprise.

I coldly wished them both good day. Bartholomew, who had remained silent, followed me. I left the book in Sir Montague's hands.

"What witness?" Bartholomew asked while he gave me a leg up to my horse.

"A very young one," I said.

DIDIUS Ramsay was eating his dinner in the hall along with his fellow students when I returned. Rutledge was also prominently in his place at the head table, glaring fiercely at the boys eating below him. The atmosphere was subdued. The students focused on their plates, and the tutors pushed their food about in silence. None wanted Rutledge's growls directed at him.

I waited in the quad for dinner to finish, not in the mood to eat with Rutledge. Bartholomew brought me a bit of mutton, which I ate readily. My last meal seemed long ago and far away.

The boys filed out of the hall, drifted toward their houses. The tutors followed, then Rutledge, who first glared at me then pretended to ignore me.

Of Ramsay, there was no sign.

"The little bugger, where is he?" I asked.

"There's a servants' door in the back of the hall. He might have ducked out there," Bartholomew volunteered. "Won't be a tick."

He jogged away, leaving me shivering. I wanted to go up to Grenville's chamber and look in on him, but I did not wish to lose Ramsay.

The porter sat on his bench by the gate, his chin on his chest. He came awake with a gasp as Bartholomew suddenly appeared on the other side of the gate and rattled the bars. Bartholomew's livery was soaked with rain and mud.

"He's scarpered, sir," Bartholomew called to me. "Cook says he ran through the kitchens and out the scullery."

I started for the gate. "Get after him. I will catch you up."

Bartholomew nodded and ran off. I had every faith that if anyone could catch one small boy, it would be Bartholomew.

Ignoring the gaping porter, I let myself out of the gate and walked as fast as I could after Bartholomew's retreating back. He was running, bounding over brush and clumps of grass in his path. I came along more slowly, my walking stick sinking into the mud.

Not surprisingly, Ramsay ran to the canal.

Bartholomew sprinted after him. I saw Ramsay's small form dart off the towpath, and for a moment, I thought he would plunge into the canal. But he leapt to the top of the stone lock, balanced on the narrow parapet across the canal toward the pond and the lockkeeper's house.

Bartholomew climbed after him. I stifled a shout. Bartholomew was sure-footed, and I didn't want to startle him and have him topple into the lock. I would never traverse that path, so I waited on the near side, watching.

Ramsay ran for the lockkeeper's house. The lock-keeper came out, stared at him and Bartholomew and said, "What the devil?"

Ramsay ran past him into his house, slamming the door. Bartholomew skidded to a halt before it. He rattled the door handle, then banged on the door.

I walked on down the towpath. The next bridge was about a hundred yards along. My leg hurting, I made the bridge, climbed it, and crossed to the other side. The stretch of canal and the greenery around it was shrouded in mist, a lovely scene. I ignored the beauty and climbed down the other side of the bridge, making my way to the lockkeeper's house as quickly as I could.

By the time I arrived, Bartholomew and the lock-keeper had succeeded in breaking open the door. Didius Ramsay tried to run out past them. Bartholomew snatched him.

Ramsay wriggled and kicked, and Bartholomew lost his hold. Ramsay ran out of the house and straight at me. I spread my arms, trying to stop him. Ramsay dodged to the right. I sprang after him and grabbed. I came down on my bad leg and sent myself and Ramsay slithering down the wet grass to the canal.

A pair of powerful hands grabbed my legs just before I would have slid into the water. I seized Ramsay under the arms and hauled him back from the muddy bank.

CHAPTER 16

I T was a muddy, dripping, red-faced Didius Ramsay that I faced in the lockkeeper's house not long later.

The lockkeeper lived simply, in a flagstone kitchen with a stair leading to a loft. Ramsay sat on the settle near the fire, holding onto the seat, knuckles white. I took a stool opposite him. My clothes dripped water onto the stone floor, and a light steam began to rise from both of us.

"Ramsay," I began.

The word galvanized him into speech. "I did not kill him, sir, I swear I did not."

"I know," I said.

He stared at me, mouth open. The fire sparked and sent a tendril of smoke into the room.

"Freddy Sutcliff said . . . he said you'd blame me," Ramsay stammered. "He said I'd pay for it, that no one would believe me."

I said calmly, "You could not have killed Middleton. You are not tall enough."

Ramsay gaped anew. The lockkeeper, who had fetched a kettle from the fire, now returned with mugs of coffee. He handed them to us, looking interested.

I sipped the coffee. It was bitter and thick and hot, and I was cold and exhausted. "Middleton was a big man, used to fighting," I said. "He could have agreed to meet you by the canal, but if you'd tried to hurt him, he would have tossed you into the water and had done. The only way you could have cut his throat were if he was kneeling. And he was not." I indicated the muddy patches on my own trousers. "When I saw him in the lock, he had no mud on his knees. Depend upon it, he was standing, and a man cut him from behind."

Ramsay's teeth chattered. "Sutcliff said you'd blame me for Mr. Grenville. And that you'd kill me."

"I know you did not hurt Grenville," I said, keeping my voice steady. "For the same reason. He was stabbed with a downward thrust. If you had stabbed with a downward thrust, the knife would have gone in much lower than it did." I leaned forward, looked him in the eye. "So you should rejoice, Mr. Ramsay, that you have not grown as much this year as you could have wished."

He stared at me, as though still believing I'd snatch him up and drag him to the magistrate. He swallowed, and his face regained some color.

"How much have you been paying Sutcliff, Ramsay?" I asked.

Ramsay took a gulp of coffee, wiped his mouth. "Oh, a good bit, sir. My allowance is high, and he knows it. He gouges me more than he does the other boys."

I sat back, cradled the cup in my hands. "So he has a nice blackmailing scheme here to supplement the tiny allowance his father gives him. I wondered how he managed to pay for his mistress; she did not seem to be a woman who came cheap. I imagine Sutcliff receives money from Timson about his cheroots, from some of the other boys about their various little vices."

"The tutors, too, sir," Ramsay said in a small, shamed voice.

"I do not doubt that. In a small place like this, I imagine that both pupils and tutors have secrets, great and small, that they wish to stay secret. Everyone knows that Rutledge is not a man to look the other way at vices, no matter how trivial."

Ramsay looked relieved that I understood. "Just as you say, sir."

My anger rose to new heights. Doubtless a student who filched an extra slice of bread at dinner lived in as much fear of the sneering Sutcliff as did Tunbridge, the mathematics tutor, whom I suspected was having it off with his star pupil. If Sutcliff told Rutledge, both pupil or tutor would be banished, which meant that Tunbridge would never get another place, and the student would be sent home in disgrace.

Poor Ramsay had paid over as well, I thought, though I could have told him that Rutledge would never banish him. His family was too wealthy. Likewise, Sutcliff was safe because of the vast amount of money his father donated to the Sudbury School.

I found it mildly ironic that the only straightforward person in the entire school, the only one immune to blackmail, was Rutledge himself. He was a tyrant, but he had no hidden vices. He was a man who lived his

life in the open and be damned to anyone who did not
like it.

"You all ought to have formed a league against Sutcliff," I remarked. "He was going over the wall to see a
lover. I am certain Rutledge would have disapproved of
that."

Ramsay nodded. "I thought of that. But there's no
way around him, sir."

"Especially as Sutcliff knew that you played all the
pranks."

Silence fell. Bartholomew stared in surprise, his coffee halfway to his lips. Ramsay sank further into the
bench. "How did you know, sir?"

"Because no one peached on you," I said. "If Sutcliff, or even Timson, had played the pranks, someone
would have spoken up by now. But the boys like you,
don't they? So they kept silent so you would not be
punished."

Ramsay stared at me. Bartholomew was still not
happy. "Are you saying, sir, that this lad here poisoned
those other lads and set the fires? He needs a good
strapping."

"I agree with you," I said, giving Ramsay a severe
look.

"I would not have hurt anyone, not really," Ramsay
protested. "I added purge to the port, only to make
them sick. They'd never have died from it."

"Bloody hell, Ramsay," I said.

"I made sure the maids' chamber was empty before
I set the rubbish alight. It only smoldered."

I eyed him evenly. He looked ashamed, but I saw in
his eyes a tiny bit of pride at his cleverness.

"My man is right," I said, "someone should take a strap to you. You seem a sound lad in other respects, Ramsay. Why on earth should you set rooms alight and write letters in blood? It is bizarre."

"So the others wouldn't think I was like Sutcliff, sir."

"Ah, I thought so. You told me before. You and Sutcliff come from the richest families of the school. You did not want anyone to think you and he were cut from the same cloth."

He shook his head fervently. "No, sir."

"A perfectly understandable wish. Sutcliff is a nasty bit of goods. He puts himself above the other lads. You wanted to show that you did not. I comprehend your motives, but it was a rather dangerous way to go about it."

"Yes, sir."

"It stops, Ramsay," I said, giving him a stern look. "Reptiles in beds are one thing. Settings fires is dangerous. Not meaning to hurt someone and not hurting them are two different things. Never forget it."

"Yes, sir."

I could not know whether my words had impact, or whether he thought me just another adult giving a lecture. I had not come here to reform him, in any case. I'd come to wring information from him.

"Let us speak of the night of Middleton's murder, Ramsay. Or, rather, the morning when he was discovered. I believe you rose very early that day."

Ramsay probably thought I knew everything there was to know about him. He nodded without denial.

I went on, "At daybreak, it was quite misty and gray. You were near the lockkeeper's house. You saw a barge come up the lock, and you hid. Am I close?"

Ramsay nodded, eyes round.

"I must ask you, Ramsay, what were you doing out here? Going to start another fire?"

Again, Ramsay nodded. He swallowed, his face paling. "I was going to light some rubbish near the lock. Make lots of smoke."

"So people would come panicking to put out the fire. I will tell you, Ramsay, that if I catch you doing such a thing, or even believe you have done such a thing, again, I will certainly thrash you. It will be worse than anything Rutledge can give you. I know quite well how to do it so that you will never forget." I'd learned from my father, who'd been a master at beating his son.

Ramsay's gaze fell on my sword stick with a flicker of fear. "Yes, sir."

"I will take you at your word," I said. "While you were skulking by the lockkeeper's house, you saw the boat. Tell me about it."

"It was the Roma, sir. No mistaking it. There were three men on the deck, all smoking pipes. And two dogs and a goat."

"Where did they stop?" I asked him.

"Right in front of the lock. I thought they'd come and rouse the lockkeeper, but they just stopped the horse and backed up the boat until they could turn it around."

I watched him intently. "Anything else?"

Ramsay nodded. "Sebastian got off. He came out on deck with a woman and kissed her. One of the men said something to him I couldn't understand. Sebastian ignored him. Just walked away without a word."

"Where did he go?"

Ramsay shrugged. "Down the path, toward the stables. The woman went back inside, and the barge floated back the way it had come."

"Did Sebastian stop at the lock, look in it, or anything?"

"No. Just walked toward the stables. He walked fast, like he wanted to get as far from the canal as quick as he could."

I exhaled slowly. Megan was an observant woman. Only she had seen the shadow skulking about the lock-keeper's house. And with that slender thread, I'd concluded that she'd seen the prankster, not the murderer. The murderer had no reason to stay near the lock; indeed, he'd want to be elsewhere as quickly as possible. That left the prankster, up to no good, fearing to be caught. Timson I'd dismissed as being too cocky. Ramsay, on the other hand, as Fletcher had once told me, walked about with an air of innocence. Ramsay, who had friends in both houses. Ramsay, who'd easily climbed a tree, snake in hand, unseen and unnoticed.

"You might have told the magistrate all this," I said. "And saved Sebastian much trouble."

Ramsay frowned. "Didn't Sebastian tell him?"

"No. Sebastian was foolishly trying to save another from scandal. Besides, a magistrate is not quick to believe a Romany, no matter what he says."

Ramsay conceded this. "But could Sebastian not have killed the groom, anyway? Earlier?"

"Perhaps. Indeed, several people could have killed the groom that night—Sutcliff, Sebastian, the stable man, Thomas Adams, who probably invented that argument, and you." I turned to the lockkeeper.

The big man blinked in astonishment. "Me, sir?"

"You are the correct height and build. You could have overpowered Middleton and cut his throat. We have only your word that you heard no one come to the lock that night. And who would be better placed to dispose of a body in the canal?"

The lockkeeper's rather florid face slowly drained of color. "Why should I kill 'im? Never knew 'im."

I made a placating gesture. "Do not worry, I do not believe that you did. I said only that you could have." I turned back to Ramsay. "Would you be willing to tell a magistrate what you just told me?"

"The magistrate would not listen to me. Not in Sudbury. He pays Sutcliff, too."

I closed my eyes briefly. Damn Sutcliff. "Another magistrate has arrived, a friend of mine, from London. He would be most interested in what you have to say."

Ramsay eyed me doubtfully but nodded.

Bartholomew regarded Ramsay in curiosity. "What does the magistrate pay Sutcliff for?"

"He has two wives," Ramsay said promptly. "One here and one in London."

"Good Lord," I said. "Well, Sutcliff did not exactly keep that secret, did he? The magistrate should demand his money back."

Ramsay shrugged. "Sutcliff didn't tell me. I found out the same as he did. I was with Sutcliff in London when we met the magistrate's London wife."

MUCH later that afternoon, Bartholomew and I walked home from Sudbury on the towpath. The rain had ceased and a bit of blue sky shone between the clouds. Spring flowers poked yellow heads from the clumps of grass beside the path.

Ramsay had told his tale to Sir Montague. The Sudbury magistrate, the one calmly practicing bigamy, had remained doubtful. I let Ramsay go after that and left it to Sir Montague to argue with the other man. I even whispered the magistrate's secret into Sir Montague's ear. Sadly, I was not above a little blackmail myself.

"Little bleeders," Bartholomew muttered. "Poisoning each other, blackmailing each other. Goes to show what happens when you try to get above yourself, doesn't it?"

"Greed, fear, and ambition can be a terrible combination," I remarked.

Bartholomew scowled. "They think people will regard them as gentlemen because they've got buckets of money."

"And many will, Bartholomew."

"That ain't right, sir. Mr. Grenville, now, he's a gentleman through and through and always will be, even were all his money to go away. You too, sir."

"You flatter me."

He shook his head, his blue eyes sincere. "No, sir, it's the truth. You're more a gentleman living in your two rooms above a bake shop than Mr. Sutcliff ever will be in a gilded palace. Don't matter how many gold plates he has, he'll never have what you have. He'll always be the son of a banker's clerk."

Marianne had said much the same thing. The Rothschilds had copious amounts of money and power, but they would never be received in many houses of the *ton*. And yet, banker's clerks were beginning to rule the world.

"Me mam has the right of it," Bartholomew continued. "If you keep to your place and be your very best in it, you'll know happiness. You try to move outside, you'll never fit in, no matter how much money you have. You try, you'll just get misery."

The philosophy of a nineteen-year-old, I thought cynically. Bartholomew's place at present was footman to one of the wealthiest and most generous men in England. He might not be talking about keeping to one's place so complacently if he worked for a miserly gentleman who enjoyed beating his servants.

I understood Sutcliff's need to blackmail, however. I thought of his rather shabby suits and his willingness to take handouts. His father, as wealthy as he was, kept Sutcliff in straits, for whatever his reasons. Sutcliff, the scheming little devil, had to find some way to supply himself with the missed money.

Sutcliff had gone so far as to convince Ramsay that he would be accused of the murder and forced him to pay for silence. It was Sutcliff who needed the strapping.

We reached Grenville's chamber, and Matthias let us in, looking tense and drawn. Grenville was unchanged. Marianne sat by the bed, watching him.

I suggested both brothers take a nap, but they refused. "One of us stays," Bartholomew said. "In case they try again, like you said."

I could not argue. Having one of the footmen close by in a fight would be a good idea. Bartholomew suggested I be the one for the nap, but I could not bring myself to leave the chamber again. Bartholomew brought me soup and ale from the kitchen, and I settled myself in a wing chair with a blanket over my legs. I ate without much tasting the food, then made myself lay back and close my eyes.

Exhaustion coupled with overtiring my leg sent me to sleep. I barely heard Bartholomew take away the tray.

I slept hard, drifting in and out of dreams. I dreamed of Jonathan Lewis standing in Lady Breckenridge's parlor, drawling about his novels. I dreamed that Grenville stood by my side, his satirical smile on his face, listening to him. The dream changed, and I thought Louisa stroked my hair, her lemon perfume touching me as she soothed me in her sitting room.

I dreamed of Lady Breckenridge, wreathed in cigarillo smoke, as she said acidly, "Good God, Lacey, can you not stand on your own?"

I dreamed of my boyhood, and my father thrashing me so hard that I'd had to crawl away to my bed. Lady Breckenridge's voice sounded again. "He's dead and gone, Lacey. He cannot hurt you any longer."

But he could still hurt me. Things could crawl at you out of the dark and hurt you again and again. The past did not always stay dead.

I opened my eyes with a start. Darkness had fallen. Someone had lit candles on the mantel, and they flickered feebly in the greater light from the fire. Matthias slumped in a chair across the room, snoring loudly.

Marianne was holding Grenville's hand again. His eyes were open, and he looked calmly back at her.

CHAPTER 17

I wanted to leap from my chair, but my aching limbs would not let me move.

Grenville's dark eyes were half-closed, his lashes black points against his white skin. He did not see that I was awake; he saw only Marianne. "Good Lord," he whispered to her. "It's you."

"So you are alive, then," she returned.

"I seem to be." His voice was too weak. He tried to turn his head, grunted with the effort. "Am I in London?"

"Berkshire," Marianne said.

"Why are you here?"

"Heard you'd gotten yourself stabbed," she answered lightly. "I came to make sure you'd live to give me more coins."

The corners of his mouth twitched. "I should have known." He faltered. "Is there any water?"

I shoved away the blanket and got to my feet. The

other two did not seem to notice me. I poured water from a porcelain pitcher into a glass and brought it to the bed.

Marianne took it from me. "I'll do it."

As gently as I'd seen her handle her son, she slid her arm beneath Grenville's neck and lifted his head. She poured the water between his lips. The liquid dribbled from the side of his mouth, but he managed to swallow.

Marianne lowered him back to the pillow, dabbed his lips with her handkerchief.

Grenville looked up at me. "Hello, Lacey. You look terrible."

"You look worse," I said. "Lie as still as you can. The knife went deep."

He grimaced. "Do not remind me." He touched the bandage. "Hurts a bit."

"Do you want laudanum?"

"No," he said quickly. "No."

"You might do better to take it. You should not move too much, and it will help you sleep."

"I do not want it, Lacey," he said, his frown increasing. "I will not move."

I wondered at his aversion, but I did not pursue it. I had learned to appreciate the benefits of laudanum on the nights when my leg pained me so that I could not sleep. I knew people grew addicted to it, so I tried to resist as much as I could, but some nights, there was nothing for it.

Our conversation had awakened Matthias, who sat up and rubbed his eyes. Grenville seemed slightly amazed to find us all in the room with him.

"I do not wish to tire you," I said. "But will you please tell me what the devil happened?"

Grenville studied Matthias' watchful face, then moved his gaze back to Marianne. Their hands were still clasped.

"You must have guessed most of it," Grenville murmured. "I saw someone moving about the quad, or thought I did. So naturally, I tried to investigate." He paused, resting for a moment until he could speak again. "I am not certain what happened. Someone brushed past me, and I never felt the knife go in. But all of the sudden it was there, and I was falling."

"A tall man?" I asked.

He nodded. "Tall. I thought it was you at first."

I leaned against his bedpost. "Tell me, Grenville, why were you dressed and wandering about the school in the middle of the night?"

"Yes," Marianne said, "that's a bit unusual, don't you think?"

He looked from me to Marianne, his look ironic. "When you are both finished scolding, I will tell you. I had been to Hungerford. I met Sutcliff's lady in the public house there."

"Met her?" I asked. "Why?"

"To question her, of course. I know you had spoken to her before you went to London, but you were a bit vague about the details."

He sounded put out. I had so enjoyed my visit with Jeanne Lanier and hadn't wanted to share our conversation with anyone, other than to reveal relevant information about Sutcliff.

"What did you discuss with her?" I asked him.

"Canals, of course. She is a very charming woman."

"Yes, I found her so," I agreed.

"Indeed," Marianne said scornfully, "she has measures of charm. She must, otherwise she could not earn a living."

"It is a studied charm, I do admit," Grenville said. "She wished me to invest a good fortune in a canal scheme proposed by one of her friends. Quite convincing, she was."

"I imagine so," I said. "Her friend was Fletcher, and he is now dead."

Grenville's eyes widened. "Good Lord."

"And the lady herself has vanished. Likely with all the money. Sir Montague Harris will put the hue and cry out for her."

"Is it over then?" Grenville asked. "The murders?"

"No. The culprit has not been arrested, but I have a few ideas about that. Marianne," I said abruptly. "I would like you to go to London."

Marianne gave me an astonished look. "What the devil for? I do not wish to, if it's all the same to you."

"I need you to," I countered. "You must deliver some messages for me. They are most important."

"Go yourself," she answered.

"I do not want to leave Grenville alone, but we need to put an end to this business."

Her expression turned belligerent. "Only this morning, you told me it would be dangerous for me to leave."

"I will send Matthias with you, and you will ride in Grenville's carriage. You will be much safer in London, in any case."

Her mouth formed a bitter line. "Back to the cage."

"Marianne," I said warningly.

Grenville had listened to this exchange with a weary expression. He released Marianne's hand. "Stay there to be safe for now. When it is over, go where you want. I no longer care."

Marianne stilled. Grenville closed his eyes. Marianne stared at him, looking stricken.

I thought them fools, both of them.

MARIANNE at last acquiesced to my request. I saw her and Matthias to the stables where Grenville's coachman had bunked. I knew the coachman would let absolutely no one near Grenville's horses and coach, so I did not fear too much that the vehicle would have been sabotaged.

Indeed, the coachman checked the axles and braces and the harness carefully before he even let Marianne into the carriage. I handed her in and told Matthias to not let her out of his sight. The coach rolled away toward the Hungerford road and the highway to London, leaving Grenville and Bartholomew and I stranded at the Sudbury School.

I did little for the next two days. Marianne sent me a message that she had arrived in London and was carrying out my instructions. She also added, very like her, that she expected large compensation for approaching the people I'd asked her to contact.

After Marianne's departure, Grenville relapsed into a stupor, and then a fever took him. Bartholomew and I took turns bathing his face, changing his bandage, trying to force broth into his mouth. But he could not eat and could barely drink. Bartholomew and I watched him worriedly.

At last I put a few drops of laudanum in his water and made him drink it. When he tasted the bitter sweetness of laudanum, even in his languor, he tried to spit it out. I forced him to swallow. Let him curse me when he got better.

The school went on as usual but remained quiet. No more pranks or murders marred the routine. Ramsay, it seemed, had taken my words to heart, at least for now.

I knew Ramsay had not burned Fletcher's books, however. He denied that with the sincerity of a thief who is certain of the one thing he had not stolen. I suspected the murderer had done it, trying to destroy the evidence of the fraud. But Fletcher, even in death, had thwarted him.

Bartholomew had at last discovered who'd owned the knife that had stabbed Grenville. The maid who cleaned the tutor's rooms said that Simon Fletcher had complained of missing his knife a day or so before he died. Most helpful, I thought. The knife that I found in the room had no doubt been used by the murderer to cut the twine that strangled Fletcher.

Sir Montague Harris at last succeeded in getting Sebastian released. He sent a message to me, and I left Grenville in Bartholomew's care and traveled to the village.

Sebastian was much subdued. When the constable let him out of his cell, his bravado had left him, and his eyes were haunted.

"Thank you, Captain," he said as we walked toward the school together. "I was afraid I would die inside that place."

"Thank Sir Montague," I said. "His persuasion far outweighed mine."

I rather believed that Sir Montague's knowledge of the magistrate's guilty secret had much to do with Sebastian's release, but I kept such thoughts to myself.

Sebastian shook his head. "You did this for me." He looked about again at the rolling land and the common where sheep wandered freely. "I never want to be inside again, I think."

"A visit to your family might be in order."

He stopped. We'd reached the canal bridge. Below it, the water rippled serenely, stretching to the horizon in either direction. Beyond the canal, the peaked roofs of the Sudbury School showed through the trees.

"I want to see Miss Rutledge," he said.

I gave him a severe look. "It might be better, might it not, to simply go?"

"I want to speak with her. I want to tell her good-bye."

"Then you are returning to your family?"

His dark eyes showed resignation. "Yes. My uncle is right. I do not belong among your people. I will never be one of you. When things go wrong, their eyes turn first to me, the Romany." He paused, let his gaze rise to the horizon. "Megan . . . she is a good wife."

He pronounced it like a sentence of doom.

"A wife who can share your heart," I suggested.

He did not believe me. He had decided he must do his duty, nothing more. I hoped that Megan would make him realize that his duty could also be his greatest pleasure.

"I will see what I can arrange," I promised.

IN the end I had to recruit Bartholomew's help. He met clandestinely with the maid, Bridgett, who communicated with her mistress. I felt vaguely like a character in a Sheridan farce, in which servants handed round love notes and lovers hid behind screens.

I planned to accompany Belinda Rutledge to her meeting with Sebastian. Sebastian had grown much subdued during his imprisonment, but I did not trust him to not turn romantic again and make a dramatic gesture, such as running off with her.

In the meantime, Grenville grew no better. He sweated and threw off his covers, and not even the laudanum could keep him quiet. I feared him tearing the wound further and bleeding inside. I also feared that he'd die of the fever, which increased. The wound, when we took off the bandage, was yellow and oozed pus and blood. I kept washing it, not knowing if it did any good, but wanting to see it clean.

Sir Montague Harris returned to London. He had business there, he told me. I explained to him what I meant to do. He did not like it, but he agreed that the killer might get away with his crimes otherwise.

When I met with Belinda a day later to arrange her meeting with Sebastian, Rutledge caught me talking to her in his study.

Rutledge was supposed to have been visiting with Timson's father all afternoon. Timson's cache of cheroots and business selling them to his fellow students had been found out, and Timson's father sent for. I wondered if Sutcliff's blackmail network had begun to break down or whether it had simply been bad luck on Timson's part.

Rutledge was not in the best of moods when he stormed in and encountered us. He stared, mouth open, for a full minute, then the shouting commenced.

"Lacey, good God! What do you mean by this?"

He halted under the portrait of his handsome, smiling wife. Before I could answer, he plowed on, "The only reason I have not packed you off is because of Grenville. That does not give you leave to wander about as you will and have private conversations with my daughter."

I planned to extemporize that Belinda had been asking me about Grenville, but I did not get the chance. Belinda, who was already distraught about the meeting with Sebastian, burst into tears and fled the room.

I faced Rutledge, deciding not to explain. A simple silent stare was more effective with him than explanations, in any case.

"I never wanted you here," Rutledge said. "I took you on Grenville's recommendation, but I regretted it from the first. You are rude, arrogant, and insufferable. I am surprised you had a career in the army at all."

I was too tired of Rutledge to be stung by his remarks. "As I said, my commander agrees with you. But I managed to lead men for nearly twenty years and lose very few of them. A man does that by being arrogant and insufferable and rude enough to tell a general that his plan is stupid and deadly."

Rutledge did not care. "Be that as it may, you do not know your place, sir."

"On the contrary. My place is by the side of my friend, who lies hurt because of my own stupidity. You, sir, allowed two men to die, because you could not see what was happening under your very nose."

I had said too much, as usual. Rutledge, though he annoyed me in every way possible, was not wrong about me.

"Perhaps you, Lacey, simply do not understand the reality of being headmaster of a school. To keep fifty boys disciplined, to make them actually learn something, for God's sake, to placate their boorish fathers so that they will continue to send their money, is a continuous and mountainous struggle. Forgive me for not foreseeing the death of a criminally minded groom and a Latin tutor equally as criminally minded. Their greed brought about their own ends."

"That is essentially true. But there is unhappiness here, and fear, and you have chosen to bluster your way over it. Your prefect, Frederick Sutcliff, is an exploitative little monster, but of course, his father provides much money."

"What I decide about Sutcliff is my business," he growled, "and the school's. Other boys fall into his power only because they have something of which to be ashamed."

I stared at him, amazed. "So you let him be your substitute bully to keep order?"

"His methods work."

"You're a bloody tyrant, Rutledge."

"It no longer matters. Fletcher was a weak fool, and

Middleton was tied to unsavory characters. I will simply find a better Classics tutor and a groom. I am amazed at you for letting the Romany go. I still believe he killed Middleton, and the woman must have killed Fletcher."

I smiled an angry, almost feral smile. "No, it was not that easy. If I tell you who I suspect, you will stop me, and I will not allow that. But I warn you to lock your door at night."

He glared. "I do not believe you. You can have no evidence, or the magistrate would have arrested him already."

"The magistrate is no more intelligent than you are, nor any safer." I made a bow. "Good day to you."

"Where are you going?"

"Back to my place," I said coldly, and left him.

RUTLEDGE, after that, left me to my own devices. He said not one word about finding me with Belinda. In the *haut ton*, a man found in private with an unmarried young woman could unleash great scandal, often hushed up by a hasty marriage. Rutledge, on the other hand, decided to pretend it never happened, much to my relief.

Rutledge would have been apoplectic with fury if he'd seen me meet Belinda the next afternoon on the path to the stables and lead her to the canal and Sebastian.

I had arranged the meeting for the dinner hour, because I knew that Rutledge would be in the hall scowling at his students. Belinda, on the other hand, always took her meals in their private rooms, so her absence would likely not be noted. She had wanted to go in the dead of night, but I had talked her out of so foolish a course.

I had chosen a place halfway between Lower Sudbury Lock and the next bridge. Sebastian stepped out from behind a tree as we approached, and Belinda, like a heroine in a novel, ran to him.

I, the chaperone, stood back out of earshot and let them have their little romance.

Sebastian took Belinda's hands in his and began to talk. I saw Belinda falter, saw her shake her head. To all appearances, he was keeping his word and telling her they could not be together.

They made a pretty tableau, Sebastian with his dark hair and tall body, Belinda with her fair skin and sundappled hair. I envied them the intensity of their infatuation, but at the same time, I was relieved that I had left such things behind me.

Or had I? I thought of Lady Breckenridge and her smile and the feeling of her hand in mine. A man could still be a great fool at forty.

After a time, I spied a shadow moving near the lock. I knew it was not the lockkeeper going about his duties, because I'd seen him enter his house as we approached. Stifling a sigh, I turned and strolled back down the path, leaving Belinda and Sebastian alone.

Sutcliff rose from his hiding place next to the lock's gate as I passed it. He stayed in the shadow there, arms folded, and waited for me.

I exaggerated my limp as I moved to him, but when I reached him, I took a step back, unsheathed the sword from my walking stick, and put it to his throat.

"Put it down."

He looked startled, then he gave an I-do-not-care shrug and dropped the pistol he'd hidden in his hands into the tall grass.

"This is interesting," he sneered, looking in the direction of Sebastian and Belinda. "Are you a procurer now? Selling Rutledge's daughter to the Romany?"

"Miss Rutledge will return to the school with me," I said. "And you will say nothing."

"Why not? Because you will run me through if I do? I think not, Captain. You are not a murderer."

"Others have thought so," I said, my tone suggestive.

The light of fear that entered his eyes pleased me. In all of Sutcliff's plans, I was the one unexpected puzzlement. He had never known what to make of me.

"I know what you have done, you little tick," I said evenly. "I know all of it."

He smiled, as I'd expected he would. "What you know does not matter. You have no evidence. No magistrate will charge me."

I moved the tip of the sword closer to his throat. My walking stick was new, and this was the first time I'd used the sword within it. I found it well-balanced and quite suited to my purpose. "I have something better than evidence," I began. I did not want to give myself away, so I damped down my rush of temper. "You sent Jeanne Lanier away, did you not? You sent her to the Continent, to smooth the way for you."

He faced me down the length of the sword. "Then you know nothing. I am not flying to the Continent in shame and fear. I gave her enough money to settle down and enjoy herself. I will visit her from time to time." He snorted at my look of surprise. "Why should I leave England? Everything I have is here. When my father dies, I will be a rich and powerful man, one who will be able to crush you underfoot in a trice. I look forward to it."

I gazed at the uncaring coldness in his eyes. I had seen that coldness before, in the eyes of James Denis. "There are men out there more powerful than you," I said. "I have met them."

"If you like to think so."

I ignored that. "I believe I understand you now. It is not simply the money you enjoy from blackmailing others. You like their fear that you will tell their dirty little secrets. You like gentlemen handing you money while you quietly swindle them. You must have enjoyed sniggering behind your hand the entire time."

He smiled again. "You are a fool, Captain. No, it is not the power. Only you, with your swagger because you were born to a gentleman's family and your pride that you have the most popular man in England to back you, could think it was power. You are a pauper, you can have no idea. My father believes I am not clever enough to handle money. But I am clever. I can turn anything into money—an idea, a secret, anything. I play the game so well that soon I will own the game. My father will come to understand that I am as ruthless as any aristocrat ever was. He will know that I can run his business better than he ever could. You will never know what that is like."

He was no doubt correct. "Greed is all-consuming," I remarked.

He laughed. "You poor idiot. The day of the gentleman is over. Only those with money will matter, only those who can pay will command respect and attention. You are puffed with pride because of your so-called honor, but your honor will disappear. Wealth will become honor, and I will have all of it." His smile widened. "You are not answering, Captain? What is the matter?"

My voice went cold and hard. "I have no wish to waste time lecturing you. You are a fool, and soon you will learn how much of a fool."

I eased the sword from his throat but held it ready. "Go back to the school. You will say nothing to Rutledge, or to Miss Rutledge."

He took a step back, making no move to try to retrieve the pistol. "I will say nothing because it suits me. For now."

My temper fragmented. The point of the sword went to his throat again, dug in a little. "I know what you've done, you little swine. And you will pay for that with every breath you draw, from now until the day you die."

His lips parted as he observed me and my sword. He did not know quite what to do, and I liked that. My sergeant, Pomeroy, had used to claim that I was mad. "You get that look, sir, like you'd do anything," he used to say. "The lads would rather ride out and face the Frenchies and their muskets than you when you look like that."

Sutcliff seemed to agree with him. I knew this young man did not give a fig about honor, did not even know what it was. All I had to do was stick the sword into his throat, and the blight would leave the earth. I would hang for it, but what did that matter?

It was not honor that stayed my hand, but knowledge. I knew that Sutcliff would soon be doomed. I did not have all the pieces put together yet, but soon, very soon.

I withdrew my sword, stepped back. "Get out of my sight," I said.

He gave me another uncertain look, then he turned on his heel and scurried away, rather swiftly. I retrieved the pistol, which hadn't even been primed correctly, and sheathed my sword.

CHAPTER 18

❧

BELINDA wept as I led her home. I had little comfort to give her. Inwardly, I decided that I'd rather see her weep than have her walk in cold silence. When a woman, or man, wept, they released their humors, which allowed healing to begin. Holding it inside, I well knew, led to melancholia and other dangerous maladies.

Belinda would weep, and then her heart would mend. I did not tell her that this heartache would likely be easy compared to others she'd face in her life. Let her believe that this was as difficult as things would ever be.

That night, Grenville's fever reached its peak. I did not sleep at all, but sat at his bedside while his skin burned and his pulse beat so fast that I feared his heart would burst. Bartholomew and Matthias continuously bathed his face and body in cold water, but nothing brought down the fever.

Sometimes he swam to consciousness and looked about him with glazed eyes. He would not know us, or he would call the names of people we had never heard of. His hair was matted with sweat, and black stubble marred his face. The room stank of his fever. Grenville, the man so fastidious about his appearance, lay helpless and sweating, and soiled his own bedding.

We washed him and changed the linen and held him down when he thrashed. He'd groan and cry out, then fall into another stupor.

The morning dawned gray and rainswept. I opened the window, no longer able to stand the stuffy sick-room. The air was a bit warmer, April fast approaching. Soon meadows would be filled with flowers and the arch of sky would be a soft blue.

Bartholomew lay stretched out on the carpet, ex-hausted and snoring. His brother slept in a chair, his blond head lolling. And Grenville . . .

His chest rose and fell evenly, his hands resting qui-etly on the coverlet. His dark eyes were open, and he was looking at me in cool appraisal.

I stepped over Bartholomew, who never moved, and hastened to the bedside. I touched Grenville's forehead. His skin was clammy and cool, the fever broken.

"Where is Marianne?" he asked.

I sank into a nearby chair, my legs suddenly weak. "Good Lord, is that all you can say?"

He gave me the ghost of his usual sardonic one. "I prefer to see her when waking. She's much prettier than you are."

"You must be feeling better."

"No, I feel like absolute hell." He turned his head on the pillow, gazed at Matthias who snored on. "Good Lord, do they always make that racket?"

"I am afraid so." I rested my elbows on my knees. I did not like to hope at this point. I'd seen men awaken from fevers then relapse so very soon.

"A wonder I could sleep at all." His gaze roved the room again, turned puzzled. "How long have I been ill?"

"Four days," I said. "You were stabbed early Monday morning, and it is now Friday."

"Good Lord." He was silent a moment, then he drew on his usual bravado. "Never say you have played nursemaid to me all this time."

"I have. And Bartholomew and Matthias. One of us at least has always been here."

His famous brows rose. "What remarkable dedication. Surely you could have asked a servant."

"There are none that I trust here. Besides, neither of the lads would leave. They guarded you like lions."

"Good Lord," he said again. Color stole over his pallid face. "A bit embarrassing."

"Why?" I smiled, the first time I'd felt like smiling in days. "Have you never been ill before?"

"Never like this. I was always healthy enough, except for my motion sickness." He moved his tongue over his lips, made a face. "You gave me laudanum, damn you. I can taste it still. I told you not to."

"You were in no condition to protest. In any case, it let you sleep."

"I told you I did not like it."

I frowned. "Why not? It cut the pain. Surely that was good."

He continued to look put out. Then he sighed. "I've always had a horror of the stuff, Lacey. When I was a lad, an uncle of mine took laudanum in water when he retired one night. He never woke again. Whether he misjudged the dose, or he did it on purpose, we were never certain. After that, I always refused it."

"Ah. I understand."

He looked at me. "If you had known that, would you have given it to me anyway?"

"Yes," I said.

His expression became perplexed, then offended. At last he smiled. "What a bastard you are, Lacey." He sobered. "Where is Marianne? Is she resting?"

"I sent her to London. Do you not remember? You were awake when I asked her to go."

"No." He lifted a weary hand to his eyes. "If you are carrying out your promise to return her to the Clarges Street house, there is no use in that. She will not stay. I realize this now. It is foolish of me to make her try."

I sat down by his bedside, happy to be able to talk things out with him again. "I needed her to do things for me in London. I sent her with messages." And I told him what the messages were and to whom I'd sent them.

Grenville smiled, but his eyes drooped. "I was right about you," he murmured. "You are a bastard."

"So others have said." I hesitated. "Marianne left only reluctantly. She wanted to stay with you."

"But she went," Grenville pointed out.

"Cursing me. Depend upon it. If not for me, you would have awoken to see her by your side."

"Damn you, then." His voice drifted to a thin whisper, and then stopped.

His body relaxed, and he slept again. But it was a

natural sleep, a healing sleep. The fever was gone. The murderer had not won, not yet.

GRENVILLE and I stayed in Sudbury three more days before I decided to risk moving him back to London. I did not feel easy about Grenville staying at the school. The murderer could never be certain that Grenville did not see him in the darkness that night, and Grenville would be much safer far from Sudbury. I still did not have the evidence needed to have the murderer arrested, but I hoped, if Marianne's errand was successful, that I'd have it soon.

Grenville's traveling coach contained a seat that eased into a flat platform, which could be made up into a bed. Grenville, shaved and dressed and insisting on walking alone, allowed Matthias to help him into the carriage and settle him on the makeshift bed.

Rutledge came to say a grudging good-bye. He did not bid me good journey but hoped that Grenville would soon recover. I tipped my hat and thanked him for my brief employment, but he merely grunted and turned away.

I saw Belinda at the gate of the school, with her maid, watching us go. Didius Ramsay, too, ran after the coach to wave farewell. That was all. I saw nothing of Sutcliff or Timson or any of the others, nor did I see evidence of the Roma on the canal.

Then the school dropped behind us and was gone.

Grenville slept most of the way to London, which allowed him respite from his motion sickness and lingering pain.

Even so, by the time we reached London, he was exhausted, and Bartholomew and Matthias and his man, Gautier, carried him immediately upstairs and to bed.

Grenville invited me to stay with him, but I told him that I'd return to my rooms in Covent Garden.

"Whatever for?" Grenville asked from his bed. His sumptuous chamber was well warmed with a fire and glowing with candlelight. He lay back on a mound of pillows in his deep bed, thick coverlets laying over him.

"I want to think," I explained.

I had nearly come to a decision about asking Denis of my wife's and daughter's whereabouts, but I did not want to discuss any of this with Grenville. The matter was too tender to share, and Grenville would try to dissuade me from personal dealings with Denis.

"I am afraid I cannot think well in these surroundings," I added lightly. "Your house is so elegant that I would feel guilty for brooding in such a place."

Grenville looked pensive. "I had thought you'd like to remain here permanently. I suggested it once, remember? You can pay me a rent to satisfy your pride."

"You are generous, and I will not dismiss the offer outright. But for now, I want to be alone. I need to be alone. When I stayed here last week, a servant popped in every five minutes to ask if I wanted anything."

He smiled ruefully. "My fault. I told them they were to treat you as royalty. I can tell them to cease."

"No. Let me be cold and miserable for a while. I need to distance myself from this. To think," I repeated.

He looked resigned. "If that is your pleasure."

"I do thank you for your generosity," I said, a bit awkwardly.

He sighed. "I do wish you would all cease being so kind and grateful. Matthias and Bartholomew tiptoe around me as though I am fragile porcelain. You worry me. Am I that close to death's door?"

"No, but you were. And we realized what we might lose."

He flushed. "Please stop. It's becoming embarrassing. Go if you must, Lacey. But do not think you must be alone always." He fell silent a moment. "I believe I will be up to visiting Marianne in a few days. If we have a nice, quiet cup of tea, that is. And if she is there at all."

Grenville had told me on the journey that he'd decided to take my advice and allow Marianne to come and go as she pleased from the Clarges Street house with no questions asked. I knew she had not told him of her son in Berkshire, but I believe he had realized she had been in Berkshire for some time. He had spoken to Jeanne Lanier before her flight; perhaps Jeanne had told him.

"Talk to her," I said. "Have a conversation."

He snorted. "I do not believe I am strong enough for Marianne's conversation. I will simply . . . ease away, as you suggested. She has proved she will not be held, so I will cease trying to hold her." He shielded his eyes by studying his hands on the coverlet. "I will try, in any case."

I left for my rooms above the bake shop in Grimpen Lane, rooms I had called home for two years. Mrs. Beltan, my landlady, greeted me effusively. Yes, she still had my rooms open. She'd let the rooms above

mine to another gentleman, but he was away on business. She put the key in my hand, promised a bucket of
coal right away, and gave me a loaf of bread.

Bartholomew stoked the fire and helped me put
things to rights. Mrs. Beltan had kept the rooms aired,
and so they smelled clean and not musty. The rooms
had once been a grand salon and bedchamber when this
entire house had been home to gentry one hundred
years ago. Now the paint had faded and the grandeur
was tarnished, but I was used to it.

If Bartholomew was disappointed that he'd had to
exchange his comfortable rooms in Grenville's lavish
mansion to the cold attics of Grimpen Lane, he made
no complaint. He went about his duties cheerfully,
whistling a tune as usual.

I wrote my friends that I had returned to Grimpen
Lane, and the next day, letters began arriving. Lady
Aline wrote of her delight at my return, then made it
clear that she meant for me to grace her gatherings the
remainder of the season. Her letter ended with a veritable schedule of card parties, soirees, at homes, and garden parties certain to send fear into the heart of the
sturdiest male. I sincerely hoped that Grenville would
counteract it by taking me along to the more masculine
pursuits of boxing and horseracing.

Lady Breckenridge also sent me an invitation, in the
form of a personal letter, to listen to a new poet, a shy
young man who needed introduction to society. She would
have a gathering at her house to ease him and his wife into
the right circles. She would be pleased if I would attend,
and she assured me I would enjoy his poetry. "It is exquisite," she had written, "rather like Lord Byron, so intelli-

gent and rich, without the bitterness or the airiness of the frivolous Mr. Shelley."

I had begun to realize that Lady Breckenridge, for all her enjoyment of flirting with scandal, had fine taste and the ability to locate it in obscure places. She almost had a nose for it, like a hound who could find the choicest grouse lost in the reeds.

I responded, telling her I would be most pleased to accept.

I also received a packet from Rutledge. To his credit, Rutledge had paid me in full for the three weeks I'd been in his employ. My heart lifted slightly. I could certainly use the funds.

His letter, brief and gruff as usual, said he'd found another secretary, thank you very much. "The new fellow has said that he found everything in order. Despite your shortcomings, he tells me you were somewhat efficient. Rutledge."

I tossed Rutledge's letter aside, not surprised at his tone.

More significantly, I also received, later that day, a hand-delivered message from James Denis.

My pulse quickened as I broke the seal and opened it, and still more when I read the words.

"I found Jeanne Lanier and had her brought back to London. She is more than willing to speak to you and your magistrate. Please attend us this evening at six o'clock."

I folded the letter, grimly cheerful, and ordered a hackney to Curzon Street.

CHAPTER 19

✦

JEANNE Lanier looked fresh and neat when I greeted her in the front drawing room of Denis' house. Her dark hair was sleek, her dress clean, in no way betraying that she'd fled to Dover and been dragged all the way back by Denis' men. Her face, however, was lined with worry.

Like the rest of his house, Denis' drawing room was elegant, austere, and cold. Jeanne Lanier rose from a silk covered settee as I entered. She looked quite surprised, then relieved, to see me.

"Captain," she breathed.

I bowed to her. "Madam. Are you well?"

She nodded, though her eyes flickered nervously. "Quite well. Mr. Denis has been courteous."

"Indeed, Mr. Denis can be very courteous," I agreed.

The corners of her mouth trembled. "I do not quite understand why I have been brought here. Am I being arrested?"

"Not at all. I asked Mr. Denis to find you. I wagered that he could more quickly than the Runners, and I was right."

She looked confused. "You asked him?"

I gave her a nod. "You see, I believe Frederick Sutcliff murdered the groom Middleton, as well as the tutor, Simon Fletcher, and attempted to murder Lucius Grenville. But I have no evidence of this to present to the magistrate. Sutcliff's father is a rich and powerful man. If I have no proof, how difficult would it be for him to convince the magistrates that I am either a madman or persecuting Sutcliff for my own ends? However, you can provide me with just the evidence I need to bring about his conviction."

Her face had gone white during my speech. "I see."

I stepped closer to her. "If you help me, I can help you. I have a friend, Sir Montague Harris, who is a magistrate. He is here. If you tell him the truth, he has promised to believe that Sutcliff coerced you and concede that you are not at fault in this matter."

Jeanne sat down abruptly. Her pretty face was strained. "Captain Lacey, I am French, I am a woman, I am alone in the world. I am not a fool. A magistrate will have no sympathy for me."

"He will," I assured her. "He has promised this, as a favor to me."

She gaped. "Why? Why should you ask him to spare me?"

"Because," I responded, my voice hard, "Frederick Sutcliff stabbed Grenville, and I want him arrested. And I believe that you helped him because you were dependent on him and had no choice."

Her gaze fell, her dark lashes brushing her cheeks. "I had a choice," she said softly. "I could have left him, or betrayed him."

"Then where would you have gone?"

She would not look at me. "I do not know. I do not know where I will go now. You have narrowed the choices for me."

"He is a murderer," I said.

She lifted her head. I saw a hardness in her eyes that matched the hardness in Marianne's. Both women had to grasp for their survival; Jeanne Lanier simply did it with more grace. "If I will not speak, then I face possible arrest for helping him. But if I betray him, then I betray myself. What man will hurry to protect me if he knows I will not remain loyal?"

I allowed myself a smile. "Gentlemen, madam, can be amazingly obtuse."

I remembered sitting in the shabby parlor in Hungerford while she conversed with me. In that hour, she had made me feel as though I were the only person in the world who interested her, the only person with whom she wished to be. She had a gift for making any man she faced believe that. I was willing to wager that she could make a man believe that however much she'd betrayed Sutcliff, she'd never betray *him*.

She met my gaze but did not return the smile. "Well, Captain, I will see your magistrate. I do not love Frederick Sutcliff, and what he has done is abhorrent to me. I will speak my peace."

"Thank you," I answered with sincerity. "I will see to it that you do not regret it."

She smiled at me then. I was struck again by her gift,

and I found myself wishing that I could personally ensure that she never regretted anything in life again.

Instead of saying anything so foolish, I bowed to her, then left the room to summon Sir Montague.

SIR Montague Harris seemed to be enjoying the novelty of an invitation to the house of James Denis.

He limped into the drawing room and seated his bulk in the chair a footman brought forward for him. The footman arranged a footstool for his gouty leg, then poured out a glass of port to place at his elbow. The footman poured port for me as well, and offered Jeanne a glass of lemonade, which she declined.

The same footman also assisted Matthias and Bartholomew in settling Grenville. I'd known Grenville would be furious if I did not let him attend the interview with Jeanne Lanier, and so I'd sent for him. I also believed that he deserved to hear the truth. Sutcliff would have killed him if he'd been able.

Grenville sat back in his chair, I supposed calling upon his sangfroid to hide the fact that he was in pain. Dark patches like bruises stained the skin under his eyes.

Denis himself arrived last. He nodded coolly to me, took the port his footman handed him, and sat in a straight-backed, armless chair, the least comfortable-looking seat in the room.

"Mr. Denis," Sir Montague beamed. "I compliment you on your lovely home."

Denis gave him a nod, irony glinting in his eyes. Sir Montague turned his gaze to the paintings and other objects of artwork in the room, clearly speculating on whether they had been procured by not-so-legal means. Denis ignored him.

He sent a cold nod in the direction of Jeanne Lanier, who watched him, apprehensive. "Captain, please ask your questions."

I moved uncomfortably. I had hoped that Sir Montague would interview Jeanne Lanier, but the magistrate merely drank port, a smile on his face, and motioned for me to carry on.

"You told me," I began, addressing her, "that Frederick Sutcliff came to you the night of Middleton's death at a little after ten o'clock. I do not believe that is true. What time did he actually arrive?"

Jeanne plucked once at her skirt, then she raised her head and looked at me with clear eyes. "He arrived at a little before midnight. I let him in through my bedroom window. He climbed the tree outside."

I remembered the thick tree growing near that window; Jeanne had waved at me through its branches one afternoon.

She went on. "He was laughing and shaking, nearly half-crazed. He had blood on his hands and quite a lot on his coat. Blood was splattered over his face."

"What did he say to you?" I asked.

"He said, 'I've done it. Now the money need be shared only two ways.'"

Sir Montague nodded thoughtfully. Denis remained cold and still.

"What did he do then?" I prompted.

"He removed his clothes and washed himself. He asked me to hide the clothes for him. He kept a second suit in my room. I do not know whether he'd put it there for this purpose or simply to have it on hand."

"Did he tell you he'd killed Middleton?"

"Not then." Jeanne flushed. "He was in quite a buoyant mood, laughing and talking feverishly. He did not quiet until very early morning, and then he rose and left me. But the next day when I saw him, he was calmly triumphant. 'None know who killed the groom,' he told me. 'And none will know. The magistrate is a fool.' Since that day, he often boasted to me how cleverly he'd done it."

"He was not ashamed at all, then?" I asked softly.

"No, Captain. He was proud."

Denis gazed at her, his face unmoving, but I saw the anger in his eyes.

"What happened was this," I said for Sir Montague's and Denis' benefit. "Sutcliff runs after Middleton the night of the murder. He might have seen Sebastian leaving the school as well, and had the idea to push the blame for the crime onto the Romany. He probably paid Thomas Adams to pretend to overhear a quarrel between Sebastian and Middleton."

Grenville broke in. "Middleton must not have seen Sutcliff as a threat, if he agreed to go with him to the place where you found the knife."

"No," I said. "It was foolish of him, but he'd been a man feared for his strength for so long, he likely did not think a nineteen-year-old boy could best him. Or perhaps he'd had the thought to thrash Sutcliff himself. But Sutcliff takes him by surprise and cuts his throat. Sutcliff drops the knife in the dark and bundles Middleton into the rowboat he's secured there for the purpose. It is late and dark, the bargemen would have moored for the night or gone to find a pint in the nearest tavern. Sutcliff dumps Middleton's body into the lock, hides or abandons the boat somewhere down the canal, and races to Hungerford to meet with his mistress."

"A moment," Grenville said. "If Sutcliff did not arrive until twelve, what about the landlady, who claimed she heard the bed frame squeaking and all that, well before midnight?"

"It was Marianne who'd told me that," I said. Grenville flushed, although he did not look very surprised. "But, she could not swear she heard *both* of them. How difficult would it be for Jeanne to shake the bed and make the expected noises? One does not like to listen to such things; one is embarrassed and tries to ignore it. You were alone in that bed," I said to Jeanne, "until Sutcliff arrived near to midnight."

"Yes," she said simply.

"Did he ask you to destroy his clothes?" I went on. "Either by burning them or tossing them over the railing of a ship heading for France?"

"He did not specify. He only told me to get rid of them."

"And did you?"

She pressed her lips together a moment, then answered. "No. They are still hidden under a board in the Hungerford house."

Sir Montague Harris took a long gulp of port. "Ah, excellent. You are a clever young woman."

Jeanne shook her head and sent Sir Montague her winsome half-smile. "Not clever. I could not decide how to destroy them without calling attention to my-self. Cloth burning in a fireplace smells foul, and I did not want to risk being arrested in Dover carrying a man's suit with blood on it."

"Most excellent," Sir Montague repeated. "I will dispatch a Runner to find them. Do you believe, Cap-tain, that your former sergeant Pomeroy would be in-terested in such a commission?" His eyes twinkled.

"I believe it would interest him greatly," I answered. Pomeroy, a tall, solid, bluff man, once my sergeant and now one of the famed Bow Street Runners, liked noth-ing better than an obvious piece of evidence. He would arrest Sutcliff with glee.

Denis' face was as hard as marble. I could feel his anger at Sutcliff, and I reasoned that Sutcliff would be lucky to be arrested by Pomeroy. Pomeroy would make sure that Sutcliff was punished by the full force of the law, but Denis' retribution would be far more frightening. I re-membered the coachman who had displeased Denis in the affair of Hanover Square. He'd dispatched that man with-out turning a hair, and he had not been as angry as I saw him now.

Grenville fingered the stem of his glass. As though understanding the tension in the room, he went on with his questions. "What I do not understand is why? Sut-cliff and the others were making a nice little fortune on their canal scheme. Why kill Middleton and Fletcher and end all that?"

"Because," I said, "Middleton was preparing to re-port everything to James Denis."

"Indeed," Denis answered, the word tight.

Grenville nodded. "I believe I see."

"Denis' servant told us that Middleton was growing weary of living in the country," I said. "He was a city man, for all his love of horses. And working for Rutledge is trying, as I came to know. Perhaps Middleton wanted out, perhaps he was ready to tell Denis about it, perhaps preparing to turn over the scheme to him."

"And so Sutcliff killed Middleton," Grenville said slowly.

"And Fletcher knew he did," I went on. "He must have known, perhaps threatened to reveal all. So, Sutcliff was forced to kill Fletcher, as well."

"Poor man," Grenville said feelingly.

"Fletcher must have been excellent at drawing people into the swindle. Who could resist hardworking, friendly Fletcher? If Fletcher had thought I had money, he likely would have tried to persuade me to invest. If he had not been distressed by Middleton's murder by the time you appeared, I imagine he would have begun persuading you, as well. I liked poor Fletcher, but he certainly fleeced quite a few people."

Grenville frowned. "But why on earth did Sutcliff burn Fletcher's books? To frighten him? It seems to have made Fletcher terribly angry instead. Remember how he thrashed Sutcliff that day?"

Sir Montague leaned forward, listening avidly. Jeanne listened, but she kept her eyes on the carpet, her posture neutral, as though she had no interest in the rest of the story.

"Sutcliff burned the books because he knew that Fletcher kept the contracts hidden in them. He went to Fletcher's rooms, stole the books, set them alight, and chucked them into the quad. Rutledge assumed it was just another prank—Sutcliff knew he would. But Sutcliff's motive was twofold, to destroy the incriminating papers, and to warn Fletcher to keep quiet about Middleton."

"But he missed a book."

"Yes, the one Fletcher kept hidden in his robe. Sutcliff must have been looking for that on the night he killed Fletcher. Perhaps Fletcher surprised him, or perhaps they quarreled, or perhaps he'd intercepted my note to you telling you to ask Fletcher about canals and knew the game was up. Sutcliff told Jeanne to get ready to depart with the money for France, then he returned to the school and went to Fletcher. After he killed Fletcher, he looked for the book, could not find it, knew the household would be stirring soon, and fled back to the Head Master's house. But he ran into you in the quad returning from Hungerford. Panicked, he stabbed you as he ran past you and into the house."

Grenville scowled. "The little bugger. He ruined my suit."

"Hang your suit," I said evenly. "You are lucky you aren't dead. Sutcliff is a murderer, and I do not intend to let him get away with it."

"Nor do I," Denis said coolly.

"He'll be arrested," Sir Montague said. "We'll pin it to him, a murderer and a blackmailer, too." He turned to Jeanne. "You may have to give evidence in court, but if we find the blood-covered suit, it will help a great deal."

"I will show you where it is," Jeanne said, raising her head. "But Captain Lacey told me—"

"I know what the good captain told you," Sir Montague said. "Yes, madam, if you help us, I will help you. I have given my word."

He clicked his glass to the table and heaved himself to his feet. "Thank you, Mr. Denis, for your hospitality. I will send for Pomeroy, and we will depart for Berkshire. Madam, if you will remain here until I return from Bow Street?"

Sir Montague, for all his bulk, could move swiftly and decisively. I also believed that he wanted his hands on Sutcliff and the evidence in case Denis, in his anger, decided to act on his own.

Denis, too, rose and bowed coldly. "I will provide your transportation, Sir Montague. Captain, will you remain behind? I wish to speak with you."

As if responding to a cue, his servants came forward, removed the port glasses, and opened the doors. Our gathering was at an end.

Sir Montague stumped out of the room, a smile on his face. The servants helped Grenville from his chair. He moved slowly to the door, his form upright, his face white with pain. Matthias and Bartholomew hovered near him, but he walked out of the room without assistance.

Only Jeanne Lanier remained, fixed on the settee. Denis said nothing to her. I wanted to linger and thank her, but Denis ushered me out and closed the doors before I could so much as say good-bye.

ONCE upstairs in his study, Denis seated himself behind his desk and motioned for me to sit down. A refreshment of brandy was offered, and I declined it.

"I wanted to speak to you privately," he said without preliminary, "to thank you for clearing up this matter for me."

He might have been speaking of my having thwarted a minor piece of gossip at a garden party. I inclined my head. "I wanted Sutcliff found out."

"I imagined," he said, "that you would discover the murderer's identity and a manner in which to gather the proof sooner than the magistrates, and you did not fail me. I am pleased at the outcome."

"Grenville nearly died," I said, tight-lipped. "I want Sutcliff to pay for that."

"He will. Captain, you can understand my anger about Middleton, because it matches yours about Grenville. Sutcliff had no right to do what he did."

He sat back, palms flat on the desk. "Sir Montague will arrest him and bring him to trial. That will be an end to it. Though you may not like my gratitude; in this case, you have it."

I nodded. I did not like Denis, but I decided to unbend and at least accept his thanks.

"In return," he said, his voice still cool. "I will give you this."

He removed a folded, sealed piece of paper from his desk and pushed it across the bare wooden surface to me.

I went still. No writing appeared on the outside of the paper, but I knew what it was.

He had offered me this information before, the whereabouts of my wife and daughter, in return for steadfast loyalty to him. He wanted to own me utterly, he'd said, and had pulled whatever strings would draw me into his web. He had found the right strings with my wife and daughter.

Now he gave this to me freely, as a reward. I did not

need to take it. Taking it would indicate that I accepted payment for a task he had bid me to do. Thus he would win a round of the endless game that he and I played against each other.

I stared at the paper for a long time, my thoughts stilling. Then, my hands unsteady, I reached for it. Under Denis' scrutiny, I broke the seal and unfolded the paper.

Written in a clear hand was a direction, the name of a house in a village. "Near Lyons," it continued. "In France."

I stared at the words for a long time. Carlotta and Gabriella were there. Alive, in the French countryside near Lyons. Years of wondering, of doubt, of fear fell away, and my eyes grew moist.

"Thank you," I said.

I folded the paper, put it into in my pocket, rose from my chair, and walked out of the room.

I accompanied Sir Montague, Jeanne Lanier, and Pomeroy back to Berkshire to the boarding house in Hungerford. Under the scrutiny of an avidly curious Mrs. Albright, Jeanne pulled up the board in her room and removed the suit of clothing that Sutcliff had worn when he murdered Middleton.

Leaving Jeanne at the boarding house, Pomeroy, Sir Montague and I went to the Sudbury School, found Sutcliff, and, to Rutledge's great fury, arrested him.

Sutcliff fought, but Pomeroy, tall and muscular, was practiced at bringing down culprits. "Now then," he said, locking his great arms around Sutcliff to the delight of the boys looking on. "It's a wicked murderer you are. A nice reward I'll get for this conviction."

The other boys, led by Timson, shouted with glee that their tormenting prefect had been taken, until Rutledge bellowed them all to silence.

I left them with the magistrate and went back to Hungerford to fetch Jeanne Lanier. She waited for me in the tawdry parlor with its shabby furniture, where I had spoken to her before.

The day had darkened, and the room was lit with a sconces that flickered in the gloom.

Jeanne's face had lost its animation. Her lips were white, her eyelids dark. "It is done?" She spoke the words tiredly.

"Yes," I said.

She let out her breath. "Good."

We stood in the center of the room, facing each other. I still carried the paper Denis had given me inside my pocket. It felt heavy to me, knowledge that burned.

Jeanne stepped close to me. "I want to thank you, Captain, for your promise to not have me arrested. It was good of you."

I was not certain I wanted any more thanks. Rutledge bellowing at me at the school had actually seemed refreshing. "You had the best evidence," I said. "You might have made it to France had I not told Denis to stop you. Do not thank me."

She made a small shrug. "If I had reached France, what then? I believe you would have found the means to arrest Frederick sooner or later. But what would have become of me?"

"I believe you will endure very nicely," I said.

I had great belief in this woman's resilience. She felt frightened and alone at present, but I knew she would soon wrap another gentleman around her finger.

Her worried look left her, and she flashed me a smile. "Touché, Captain. You have seen my true colors, peeked beyond my façade. Can you forgive me that?"

I hadn't forgotten the afternoon I'd spent here in her company, and how she'd made me feel—amusing, intelligent, wanted.

"I believe I can forgive you," I said.

Humor glinted in her eyes. "You are too kind." She hesitated. "You may think me a fool, but I wonder whether, when all this is over, you might condescend to receive me as a friend." Her voice softened, and she sounded almost shy. "Indeed, I believe we might have many interesting conversations together."

My lips parted as I gazed at her in astonishment. Her smile was hopeful, her eyes warm. She was asking, if I was not mistaken, whether I'd be willing to be the next gentleman whom she wrapped around her finger.

I certainly did not mind such a wish coming from a lady as pretty as she, but I had to wonder why.

"Madam, you know I am not a wealthy man," I began.

"No," she admitted. "But I have met your friends, Mr. Grenville and Mr. Denis. They are powerful gentlemen."

I raised my brows. "You are saying you wish me to ask Grenville or Denis to pay for the keeping of you on my behalf?"

"Yes," she said. She flushed. "I know it is most irregular, but that is what I wish, Captain Lacey."

"You amaze me," I said softly. "Though I understand that you must survive. Like Marianne."

"It is not only that. I have seen enough of men, Captain, to know when one is worth much. And so I make
bold to propose such a thing to you."

My heart beat hard. I hardly knew what to say. She
flattered me, but at the same time, I knew she made her
living by flattering. She was lovely, she could soothe
me, and I would be ten times a fool to accept her.

I wished that I had the wherewithal to be so foolish.

I touched her cheek. "I am sorry," I said. "I would
that circumstances were different."

She looked at me a moment longer, then gave her
head a shake, conceding defeat. "As am I."

"You are resilient," I stated again. "You will fare
well."

She gave me a rueful smile, the practiced courtesan
vanishing for a moment. "You have much faith in me,
Captain." She touched the lapel of my coat. "Thank
you."

"Thank you," I told her. I raised her hand to my lips,
and then the carriage that would return us to London
rattled to a halt at the end of the lane, and we made to
depart.

CHAPTER 20

A few days later, Grenville felt well enough to join me and Pomeroy in the tavern in Pall Mall that we often frequented.

"We'll get a conviction," Pomeroy said, his blond hair slick with the evening's rain. "Sutcliff's papa is rich enough to buy them off, but Sir Montague is a stickler. He'll push it through."

"We can hope so," Grenville said dubiously. He was much stronger, but he moved slowly and flinched simply lifting his tankard of ale. He had visited Marianne earlier that day, and from the pinched lines about his mouth, I understood that the encounter had not gone well.

Pomeroy, oblivious to such things, rambled on. "Why should a rich cove's son like that swindle and blackmail and murder, eh Captain? He's got everything handed to him on gold plates."

I sipped my ale, which was rich and warm against

the March rain outside. "Because his father wouldn't give him the gold plates," I answered. "Kept him on a meager allowance and refused to let him come into the business until he grew up a little. Sutcliff told me himself he'd wanted to prove to his father that he could make money on his own and be as ruthless as any nobleman."

"Rich gents," Pomeroy said derisively. "Me own dad never had nothing, so I took the king's shilling. I didn't need to prove nothing."

I had run away from home to the army, as well, though I'd gone with Brandon to receive an officer's commission. In my heart, I'd wanted to prove myself better than my father. I hated to think that I understood Frederick Sutcliff all too well.

Grenville lifted his brows. "My father kept me on a strict allowance as a lad. He was generous with gifts, but not such a fool as to give me enough money with which to make an idiot of myself. Funnily enough, I never resorted to blackmail and other crimes to supplement my income."

"Yes, sir, but you're not wrong in the head." Pomeroy tapped his forehead. "That Sutcliff chap is a bit crazed."

"I'd feel sorry for him," Grenville said. He put his hand to his torso and winced. "Except for this bit of a hole in my middle. Perhaps I'll make it a fashion, a knife slit in coat and waistcoat, a hairsbreadth shy of the heart and lungs."

Pomeroy guffawed, but I knew Grenville's anger. It had been too close.

Pomeroy drained his glass and wiped his mouth.

"Well, young Sutcliff is for it. The father will probably get him transported instead of hanged, but that's the rich for you. Now, it's back to Bow Street for me, though I'll walk slowly and see how many criminals I can catch in the act."

He chuckled, touched his forelock to us, and left the tavern. I had no doubt that he'd arrest several unlucky pickpockets and prostitutes along the way.

"To think," Grenville said, absently turning his tankard. "That I thought a post at a boys' school would be restful and unexciting." He shook his head. "More fool I."

"I have come to appreciate the quiet of Grimpen Lane," I said, smiling a little.

He did not return the smile. "Marianne," he began in a low voice, "will not tell me why she traveled to Hungerford. She made it plain that she did not want to tell me. I know, however, that you know." He lifted his tankard and drank. "And that you, too, will not tell me."

I felt a twinge of remorse, but I shook my head. "I am sorry. The secret is hers, and I gave her my word."

He lifted his gaze to mine. The pain in his dark eyes did not come from his wound. "You are a singular man, Lacey. You will keep your word to an actress who is little better than a courtesan, but you will not answer to a man with the power to break many a gentleman in his path."

"I know," I said.

He held my gaze for a moment, then looked away. "So be it," he said.

He turned the conversation, as only he could, to

other, inconsequential things, but I knew it would be a long time before he would bring himself to forgive me.

POMEROY'S prediction that Frederick Sutcliff would never hang for murder proved to be true. He did appear at trial and was condemned, but Sutcliff's father was wealthy enough and powerful enough to have the sentence commuted to transportation. I watched from the gallery as Sutcliff stammered his way through the trial. Jeanne Lanier appeared and behaved very prettily, easily charming the judge into believing her an naïve Frenchwoman easily duped.

It sealed Sutcliff's fate. Rutledge also attended the trial. When I saw him in the street afterward, he growled at me and blamed me for the entire affair. I tipped my hat to him and walked on.

LOUISA Brandon visited me the next day. I had at last written her that James Denis had given me the information about Carlotta and my daughter. She had not written back, but when I saw her carriage in the street outside Grimpen Lane, my heart lightened.

Once I had sent Bartholomew and Louisa's footman away, I could not keep from her. I kissed her cheek, then I held her hands and simply looked at her.

"I missed you," I said.

"I missed you, as well." She frowned at me. "Now I want to hear the entire awful tale of everything that happened at Sudbury. To think I imagined you'd gone to enjoy green meadows and rides along quiet lanes."

"The country is a brutal place," I said, hoping to make her smile. I sat her down and began to tell her all that happened.

She asked questions, and I answered, and the tension between us fell away. We talked long and easily, as we'd done in the army when she and I and Brandon had spent the end of every day together. Louisa and I had gabbed like old gossips, making light of our fears for the morrow.

After our conversation had wound to its close, I pulled out the paper Denis had given me and handed it to her.

She scanned it in silence, her eyes a mystery. "What will you do?"

"That is why I asked you here. To tell me what to do."

"Gabriel . . ."

I rose and paced, unable to keep still. "I cannot trust my own heart, Louisa. It has been too long. Shall I rush to France and wrest her from a life where she has been happy? Demand my rights as a husband and father? How will that make anything better?"

She watched me with troubled eyes. "You do not know she has been happy."

"Of course she has. Carlotta was not the sort to live in silent misery. If her French officer made her unhappy, she would have flown elsewhere, again and again, until she felt safe. Or she'd have flown back to England, to you, not me. She was a woman who ever needed comfort and protection."

"That is so," Louisa agreed, though she sounded skeptical.

"If I go . . . If I see her . . ."

How would I feel? Angry? Petulant? Happy that she was happy? Was I ready to release her? I had lectured Grenville to let Marianne be, but could I do the same with Carlotta? I had let her go, when she first fled me, but had I ever let go in my heart?

"Perhaps you ought to see her," Louisa said, "if only to say good-bye."

I ceased pacing. "It is still like a knife in my heart, Louisa."

"Why? Because she had the gall to leave you? Or because you loved her?"

I opened my mouth for a sharp retort, then closed it. Louisa's words were harsh, but they were also shrewd.

"If it were only Carlotta, I would not even consider," I said. "But I long to see my daughter. I want to see how she has grown and whether she is happy. Damn it, Louisa, she is mine."

"And what if she does not know you?"

"I will tell her who I am."

Louisa held my gaze. "And what if she does not know that Gabriel Lacey, and not the French officer, is her father?"

I stopped. "Do you think Carlotta would have kept that from her? Would she have been that cruel?"

Louisa nodded. "Yes, I think she would have been."

I studied her a moment. "Do you know, I believe that when she left, you were as angry as I was. But you had never much liked Carlotta."

"I believed her a fool," she answered crisply. "She never understood your true worth."

"She understood well enough. I was worth nothing

beyond my pay packet and my overblown sense of honor."

"No," Louisa said in a hard voice. "She never did understand. Never appreciated what you were, and what she had."

Our gazes met. Louisa's eyes were a steely gray, her cheeks flushed. I held her gaze for a long moment, while thoughts flew by that went unsaid.

At last I turned away. "Well, she is gone now," I said softly.

"If you go to France, Gabriel, I will go with you."

She sat very primly on my armchair, her tone matter-of-fact. For one heady moment I pictured us traveling side by side, chattering away as we liked, her golden head on my shoulder as she rested in our traveling coach.

The vision shattered at once as I realized that if she came with me, her husband would accompany us. Colonel Brandon would never allow his wife to travel alone with me to the Continent as long as he was alive. I thought of his stiff-necked silence on the days and days of the journey through France and shuddered.

"I will think on it," I said. "Thank you."

We spoke further, trying to turn to neutral topics, but nothing interested us much.

At last Louisa rose to take her leave. I kissed her good-bye, let my hands linger in her cool ones just a moment too long, then I let her go.

THAT night I sat in Lady Breckenridge's drawing room with Lady Aline Carrington and Lucius Grenville and others of the *ton* and listened to a rather young poet read beautiful and moving words. My heart was still heavy, but I allowed myself to be soothed by his verses.

When we broke for refreshment, I found myself with Lady Breckenridge in an unoccupied corner.

"Your eyes are tired, Captain," she said. "Did you not enjoy the poetry?"

"I did like it," I answered with sincerity. "The young gentleman shows great promise. I admit, however, to liking the company still more. An evening spent with friends is refreshing."

One corner of her mouth turned up in a half-smile. "Dare I be flattered? Or did you refer to Mr. Grenville and Lady Aline, your dear friends?"

I smiled. "I referred to Mr. Grenville and Lady Aline and Lady Breckenridge."

She took this attempt at a compliment with a cool nod, but looked pleased. "I am happy that we have drawn you back from the country, then."

"The city also has its joys," I said. "I meant to once again thank you for the gift of the walking stick. It became most useful."

Her smile deepened. "I was certain it would be."

We shared a look, her dark blue eyes holding something warm and intriguing.

I decided then and there that I preferred her conversation to that of Jeanne Lanier. Jeanne knew how to flatter, how to draw a man out, how to put him at his ease. She could smile and laugh as expected and make a gentleman feel that he was exceptional.

Lady Breckenridge spoke her mind and did not always soften her barbs. But she would always be sincere. A flattering word from her was well earned and well meant.

She slid her hand beneath my arm. "Shall we return? Mr. Tibbet will recite lines he composed while staying in an ancient castle in Scotland. Very atmospheric."

I smiled down at her as she led me away. I found the warmth of her slender fingers in the crook of my arm quite satisfactory.

Author Biography

Ashley Gardner has lived and traveled all over the world, and is currently settled in the southwestern United States. Learn more about the Regency mystery series through its Web site, www.gardnermysteries.com, or contact Ashley Gardner directly at ashleygardner@gardnermysteries.com.

ROBIN PAIGE

The Victorian Mystery Series

❖ ❖ ❖

*Read all the adventures of Lord Charles Sheridan
and his clever American wife, Kate.*

❖ **DEATH AT BISHOP'S KEEP** 0-425-16435-7

❖ **DEATH AT GALLOWS GREEN** 0-425-16399-7

❖ **DEATH AT DAISY'S FOLLY** 0-425-15671-0

❖ **DEATH AT DEVIL'S BRIDGE**.............................0-425-16195-1

❖ **DEATH AT ROTTINGDEAN** 0-425-16782-8

❖ **DEATH AT WHITECHAPEL**................................0-425-17341-0

❖ **DEATH AT EPSOM DOWNS** 0-425-18384-X

❖ **DEATH AT DARTMOOR** 0-425-18909-0

❖ **DEATH AT GLAMIS CASTLE** 0-425-19264-4

❖ **DEATH IN HYDE PARK**...0-425-20113-9

❖ ❖ ❖

AND NOW IN HARDCOVER:

❖ **DEATH AT BLENHEIM PALACE** 0-425-20035-3

"AN ORIGINAL AND INTELLIGENT SLEUTH...A VIVID
RECREATION OF VICTORIAN ENGLAND."
—JEAN HAGAR

**Available wherever books are sold or at
www.penguin.com**